Chatelaine of the Guild

by

James Odell

Table of Contents

Novels in The
'Queen Victoria's Magicians' Series

Chatelaine of the Guild
The Chatelaine and the Storm
The Chatelaine and the Enigma

The Accidental War
The Black Regiment

Introduction, 6 April

The maid walked into the Senior Common Room of the Bloomsbury School for Young Ladies. Samantha looked up from the book she was trying to study. She was due to attend a lecture on the principles of electricity and she wanted to complete her pre-course reading. All of the girls hushed, surprised at this interruption.

The maid bobbed a curtsey. "Excuse me, Miss Hampden, but Mrs. Beale would like to see you in her office as soon as is convenient."

Samantha jumped up. "Yes, of course." When the headmistress said 'as soon as is convenient' she meant 'come at once'.

When she walked into the office and made her curtsey, the man sitting in the guest chair courteously stood up. She guessed him to be twice her seventeen years. Despite his age, he could be called handsome. His eyebrows slanted upwards towards his temples. He was just under six feet tall, well proportioned, with good shoulders and neatly trimmed black hair. His movements were graceful and dignified.

He was wearing a fashionable frock coat. It was an eye-catching blue and green plaid, tailored so as to fit tightly at the waist and so emphasise his shoulders. Samantha judged that his shoulders really did not need emphasising, so the overall effect was rather silly.

His glance, while appraising, was in no way flattering. She considered herself to be plain and rather too short. She saw no virtue in her curling brown hair.

"I'm sorry I took so long, Mrs. Beale."

The headmistress showed no hint of impatience. "Miss Hampden, may I present to you Lord Radley, your cousin."

She was surprised. Edward Radley was a second or third cousin. He was also the Earl of Culham, head of the family. They shook hands. "Good morning, my lord."

"Miss Hampden, it is my sad duty to inform you that your aunt Lady Constance died two days ago. Her daughter died last month. So you are her nearest female relative."

"I'm sorry to hear that. But I never saw much of my aunt. She disapproved of my father. She was always busy at the College. Although ... she had promised to present me at court and bring me out."

Mrs. Beale spoke kindly. "Won't you sit down, my dear?"

Samantha realised this was a hint and seated herself.

Mrs. Beale nodded and Lord Edward sat down too, his fashionable walking stick between his knees.

Samantha could not avoid eyeing his garish coat. She detested it on sight.

He misunderstood her expression. "Yes, it is the height of fashion, but I shall have to put this away until my mourning is over."

"Yes, my lord."

"What do you know about the Guild of Magicians, Miss Hampden?"

"Well, it's very powerful. And, er, secretive. And they don't admit female students." She tried to think of something else to say. "A lot of people think it's a sham. They take the government's money for nothing ..."

Mrs. Beale tutted at this, but Lord Edward merely nodded.

"My aunt seemed to devote all of her time to the College. My mother said her duties were very onerous."

"Yes. The most important person in the Guild is the Master of the College. To support him there are two hereditary posts. One is the patron of the Guild, which by tradition is held by the Earl of Culham. The other is Chatelaine of the College, who does our book-keeping."

"Is that what kept aunt Constance so busy – wait, did you say the task is hereditary?"

His smile had no humour in it. "Yes, through the female line. Your aunt had several peculiar duties at the college which now pass to you. It's a very old tradition. You may think it foolish, but unless there's a very good reason we can't break it."

"Oh. My."

"You have the right to refuse. It might be best for the college if you did, but it would cause a scandal. I would have to report to the Prime Minister, questions would be asked in the House of Commons ... it would be very noisy for a while."

"And England is already in a crisis," Mrs. Beale said.

"I don't want that, my lord." Would a scandal harm her father's career in the diplomatic service? Another idea distracted her. "Would I have to study magic?"

"You wouldn't have to, no. Your aunt hated it. She always said she preferred the magic of numbers."

She felt that he had evaded her question. "But would my studies be forbidden?"

"Not at all. You have some magical skills, I suppose?"

Mrs. Beale tutted at this.

Samantha decided to lie about this. "My mother taught me just enough to prevent me from doing harm."

"You have received instruction in household accounts and book-keeping?"

Mrs. Beale answered. "Oh, yes, Lord Edward, we received instruction that dear Miss Hampden was to receive extra tuition in that. We brought in a specialist ..."

"Good. I must take you to the college tomorrow. You

will have a set of rooms there."

"Lord Edward ..." Mrs. Beale was upset about something.

"Oh ... I shall, of course, bring a suitable chaperone."

Chapter 1 The College of Magicians

London, 7 April

Lord Edward led the way down the school steps, followed by
Lady Mary and Samantha. Lord Edward had introduced
Mary as Lady Clifton. She was a third cousin of the Earl, the
daughter of a duke. He had explained that she was the widow
of a college fellow and had her own set of rooms at the
college.

Samantha's initial impression was that Lady Mary was
not very bright. She was of middle height, slim, elegant, with
long blond hair pinned up and covered by a straw bonnet.
Her dress was frivolous, with too many flounces and
furbelows. It contained too much pink. Samantha realised
that she disapproved. Was this woman to be responsible for
her conduct?

Samantha, in mourning for her mother, was wearing
her best black dress, with no flounces at all. Her bonnet, dark
blue with black trim, was tied firmly in place. She clutched
her shawl of dark blue wool around her shoulders.

Lord Edward was wearing a dark green frock coat this
morning. Samantha noted that it was less tailored at the
waist than the blue one and therefore less ridiculous. On the
other hand, his collar points did seem rather high. As he
walked across the pavement to his carriage, a young man in
grey stepped forward to open the door for them.

Lady Mary automatically took her place on the
superior, forward-facing seat. Samantha hesitated. "You go
next," Lord Edward said. "Take the seat next to Lady Mary."

Samantha felt awkward because she had to use her left
hand to hold her shawl in place. Lord Edward climbed in

after her and took the inferior, rearward-facing seat. If he thought her clumsy, at least he did not say so.

Samantha could count on one hand the number of times she had ridden in a gentleman's carriage such as this.

She smiled. "My father's too poor to afford a carriage. He said that he could afford the carriage but not the horses. So he put the money in his rainy day fund. Mother called it my coming-out fund."

"I see," Lady Mary said. She eyed Samantha's dull dress. "We shall have to buy you some more dresses, my dear. You are in mourning, of course."

"Yes, for my mother, and now my aunt. I had hoped to be presented at court. My aunt had promised to do so and to provide the dress." That had been postponed upon the death of her cousin. "But now ..." Her mother died three months ago. Her female cousin died one month ago.

Lord Edward nodded. "Your presentation? We shall have to do something about that."

She tried to think of something else to say. "I have been attending a course of lectures at the University of London, studying electricity. I wanted to find out how it interfered with magic."

He smiled. "Indeed? It seems you'll fit in better than I thought. The college is full of experimenters."

"Can I continue my studies, my lord?"

"I have no particular objection. If you can find the time."

The carriage slowed and turned a corner.

"What do you know about the Guild of Magicians, Miss Hampden?"

"It was created by the first Earl Culham. It's restricted to men who studied at the college, here in London."

"Yes. Back in 1715, he wanted to compare the rival theories of Dee and Newton."

"I've read about both men, but I never thought they'd

be compared."

He smiled. "Yes, the very thought of it gives me a headache. He hoped the two theories were compatible, the two sides of the same coin. Instead, he realised that both theories were full of gaps. A better image was two faces of a dice."

Lady Mary was looking bored. Perhaps she had heard it before. But Samantha was interested. "Did that help?"

"Oh, yes. Knowing there were gaps, and knowing where they were, allowed him to move forward. He came up with a general theory. It explained what he knew, and pointed the way to further research. Everybody at the college has studied that theory ever since."

He smiled. "Perhaps, your hope of comparing that with electricity might add a third face."

The carriage stopped outside an elegant Georgian town house, halfway up the western side of Berkeley Square. It was four storeys high, built of dark red brick. Its only distinguishing feature was the stone archway around the inset front door.

The door opened and a man in black hurried down the steps to open the carriage door and let down the steps. Lord Edward led the way up the college's granite steps. "Come on, Miss Hampden. The servants will see to your luggage."

A woman in a plain grey servant's dress was waiting for them in the lobby. "Oh, there you are," Lady Mary said. "Miss Samantha, this is the College housekeeper, Mrs. Hudson. She will take care of your needs."

The housekeeper bobbed a curtsey. She was of middling height, with careworn face. "Let me show you to your room, my lady."

"Thank you." Samantha followed Mrs Hudson through a door into a rectangular atrium that dominated the building. Above them were two rows of balconies. The building was larger than front entrance suggested.

Mrs Hudson pointed to the doors on the left side of the atrium. "Through there is the big dining room. You'll dine there most evenings, I daresay. And there's the lounge and the smoking room, but you won't be going in there. And through the other doors are the general library and the lecture hall."

"How many people live here?" Samantha asked. It looked more like a club, or a college, than a family residence.

"There's fifty apprentices in residence. Then there's graduates who are visiting for one reason or another. Then there's the Fellows of the College who do the teaching. Most evenings we have upward of a hundred people sitting down to dinner ...

"Married guild members, you see, are allocated married quarters. All over the West End. Most days they dine at home."

Mrs. Hudson led the way up the northern staircase, past the colonnaded balcony, to a second-storey hallway lined with heavy wooden doors

"If your room was lower down, miss, you'd have apprentices traipsing past your door day and night."

"I'm glad I'm not carrying my bags," Samantha said.

Mrs. Hudson led the way into a set of rooms. One of them was dominated by empty bookshelves and a writing desk, the second by a four-poster bed; the third by a large bathtub. A maid, busy laying the fire in the study, bobbed a curtsey. Mrs. Hudson told her to wait outside.

"These are your rooms, Lady Samantha. I suggest you spend some time resting and preparing yourself, then you can join the fellows at dinner. We dine at six."

Samantha was too worked up to rest. She wanted to learn. "Mrs. Hudson, I'm sure you are fully competent to run the household. Do you prepare the household accounts?"

"Thank you, my lady. But the household accounts are kept separate from the College accounts. And I'm afraid of presenting the accounts to 'the authorities'. We need a lady to do that. That's your task."

"I'm not the head of the household, as well, am I?"

"Well, the nominal head of the household is Lady Mary. She's a widow, you know. But Lady Mary is always going off to balls and grand dinners and such." Samantha interpreted this as a hint that Lady Mary was too lazy to administer the college.

"Who pays for the College? The upkeep, I mean."

"Well, there's the rents from the Culham Estate, to pay for research, and a donation from the government, to pay salaries. But I'll send in that maid, to help you change for dinner."

Samantha felt that Mrs. Hudson knew all about the College administration. She really was wasting her talents as a housekeeper.

*

Samantha dressed for dinner in her best navy-blue woollen dress and accompanied Lady Mary down the stairs to the dining hall. Lady Mary had changed into an off-white silk dress with lots of flounces and rather too much silk trim.

Samantha tried to squeeze some information out of the older woman. She had already decided that Lady Mary was lazy.

"Yes, my dear, I do have some magic potential, but I'm just too busy to study. And a lady cannot *practice* magic." Lady Mary turned down a side corridor. "The senior staff have their own entrance to the dining hall. And that includes the ladies, of course. Follow me, my dear."

Samantha's first glance told her that the hall was a large oak panelled room, hung with portraits. Were they of previous masters of the College? A long wooden table ran the length of the room, taking up most of the space. Fifty or sixty young men were standing by their chairs. The 'high table' was placed at right angles to this at the near end of the hall. Several ladies and gentlemen were already at their places. The gentlemen at the high table stood as Lady Mary walked in. The students at the long table turned to face the newcomer. Samantha, unnerved, almost turned and fled. Lady Mary ignored the men at the long table and walked towards the high table's central chair. Samantha summoned her courage and followed the widow.

Lord Edward was waiting for her, standing behind his chair. As she approached, he smiled and held out his hand. Why did he want to shake hands now? Obediently, she held out her own hand and was taken completely by surprise when he lifted it to his lips. All of the ladies cooed and Samantha blushed.

"Welcome to the College, my lady."

"Thank you, sir."

"Firstly, may I introduce Archibald Knight. He is the Master of the College. You will be working with him."

Archibald bowed over her hand. "Charmed, young lady." He was tall and thin, dressed in a dark blue suit. He looked jaundiced, and was accompanied by his plump wife.

The Earl went on to introduce her to some of the lecturers. She thought of them as the fellows of the College. The oldest fellow, Humphrey Ives, was broad-shouldered, a sprightly widower with white hair.

The other person she remembered was Oswald, who was in a wheelchair and did not get up with the other gentlemen. He had scanty white hair and a gentle smile.

"In theory, each of the seniors runs his own team and his own budget, so there will be no need for him to bother you," Lord Edward said.

"I see, my lord."

"We have a strong sense of tradition here," Mr. Knight

said. "Most of the time, the College runs itself. You can only intervene if you feel that the tradition is no longer sufficient."

"So I'm just a figurehead, sir?"

"Except at budget time," Humphrey said.

Lady Mary took a step closer. "You've been given the place of honour at Lord Edward's right hand," she whispered. "All the married men have turned up, and brought their wives to meet you, which is why there are so many other ladies present."

The ladies took their seats, followed by the gentlemen. Finally, the students resumed their places. Some of them looked at her, curious. She could not possibly look these men in the face. Then she remembered that a lady was not supposed to look directly at a man. Staring down at the table would be mistaken for maidenly modesty, not fear.

The small-talk at the high table avoided magic or finance. Instead they discussed the Chartists, the March riots and the Queen's withdrawal to Osborne House.

Samantha noticed that most of the young men at the lower table were wearing grey, while a few were wearing black. She was curious enough to ask Edward.

"All the first-year apprentices wear grey. There's a legend that your aunt - or perhaps your grandmother - bought a job-lot of cloth and they haven't used it up yet. The older apprentices are allowed to buy their own clothes, and most of them choose fashionable black."

When Lady Mary gave the signal for the ladies to leave the table, all of the men stood too. Mr. Knight held up his hand. "Ladies, gentlemen, one of the requirements of our chatelaine is that she has some skill with magic. I think it is time that Miss Hampden demonstrated that skill."

Lord Edward frowned. "The tradition is that she merely has to demonstrate a knowledge of magic. Enough to know what we're talking about."

"All of the previous holders of the office have been

proficient."

"What do I have to do?" Samantha asked.

Lady Mary was shocked. "In the dining hall? In front of everyone?" Samantha realised that everyone was staring at them.

Lord Edward was embarrassed. "If we do it in private, everyone will wonder what we're hiding."

"Demonstrate Light for us. That's the simplest," Mr. Knight said. He held out his right hand, palm uppermost. He curled his hand into a fist and then opened it out again. As he did so, a tulip-shaped light, the size of an orange, appeared in his palm. The petals flickered red and yellow. "A student takes years of study to bring the flame under control. Any novice can produce a burst of heat that can set a tree on fire. A lasting flame requires skill."

Samantha stared at the flickering light. "It's beautiful." She glanced at Lord Edward.

He nodded. "Do the best you can, my lady."

She held out her hand, concentrated, and mimicked Mr. Knight's gesture. "Partum a luce". An intense white light, the size of a billiard ball, appeared three inches above her palm. "I can't make it flicker, though." Several of the fellows gasped. "What's the matter?"

Lord Edward laughed. "A white light is said to be the most difficult to master. It takes years of practice."

"Well, I've been practising this for years. Mummy taught me this when I was twelve."

Mr. Knight ignored this. "Now the left hand."

She concentrated, held out her left hand, and tossed the ball of light across. This caused another gasp.

Lord Edward smiled. "You make that look very easy."

"I thought it was. Mummy didn't approve. She called it a parlour trick."

"But can you create the light with your left hand?" Mr. Knight said.

"Let it go, Archibald," Lord Edward said. "The lady's already demonstrated as much delicacy and control as anyone here."

Samantha ignored this. She obediently closed her fist to snuff out the light. "Partum a luce." She opened her palm and the light reappeared. She concentrated and to her delight achieved a gold shimmer. The ball of light expanded to the size of an orange, deepening in colour as it did so. "Beautiful," she said.

"Never mind that. Can you perform Heimlich's manoeuvre?" Mr. Knight said.

She was shocked. "No. Not here. It's too dangerous."

Lord Edward interrupted. "If Miss Hampden knows enough about Heimlich's manoeuvre to know how dangerous it is, I think we can agree she has demonstrated sufficient knowledge of magic. Besides, do we really want to provide a bad example to the students by pulling that stunt in a confined space?"

Everyone nodded. The oldest fellow, Humphrey, looked disappointed. "But could you do it? Outside, perhaps? In the morning, when you're not tired?"

"Probably, sir. But you would have to demonstrate it to me first." She bobbed a shallow curtsey and allowed Lady Mary to lead her from the room.

*

When the gentlemen joined the ladies in the withdrawing room, Samantha asked Lord Edward about her responsibilities. "Mrs. Hudson said I had to present the annual accounts to the fellows."

He raised his eyebrows. "Did she really say that? No, you have to present the accounts for the whole guild to the Prime Minister and the Chancellor."

She glared at Lord Edward. "Stop mocking me. If what

you're saying was true, I'd be the most powerful person in the guild." She had been told that whoever held the purse-strings held the power.

He smiled. "Well, it depends how you measure power. But if any of us wants anything done, we must ask you to provide it."

She realised that he was perfectly serious. "What's the catch? There must be one."

"If we gang up on you, you're doomed."

"You can't agree upon the time of day. If you said the sun rose in the east, the Master would say it rose in the west."

He smiled. "Well, there you are."

"It's a heavy burden."

"That's one reason they're eager to dump it on you."

"What's to stop you from bullying me into doing what you want, my lord?"

He grinned. "If I tried that, the Master and everyone else would combine against me. Working together, they'd crush me. And all my efforts at conciliation would be lost." He shrugged. "We've always done it that way. But the world's changing. I suppose they'll abolish the post soon. Force us to hire a salaried accountant."

"Don't I get paid, then?"

"Only an allowance. Board and lodging are free, of course. And your dress bill. You'll have to represent the guild at society events, so that cost will be huge. You'll have your own personal maid. And full use of one of the college's carriages."

"And I'm responsible for all of it?" Her cry was anguished.

"Well, not everything. Most of the research is paid for by the Edward family estate. There's a rival guild in Sheffield. They use magic in steel-making. They make lots of profits, so they're immune to your accounting. But they send

18

their brightest boys to the college to learn formal magic, so that comes under your domain."

"My lord, how did this start? The guild's hereditary chatelaine?"

"Well - It goes back to your great-grandmother. She had no brothers, so when her father died she became countess in her own right. She put all the family resources into building up the guild. She understood accounting and the male fellows didn't, so she tended to win arguments over money. Her son died before she did, so she brought up her grandson. Have you seen her portrait? She looks delicate, but I suspect she was tough as old boots -." She suppressed a giggle.

He smiled. "So, when she died, everybody agreed the master of the guild had too much power. The role was split up. The role of patron went to her grandson, while budgeting went to her daughter."

"But - wouldn't it have been better to hire a professional accountant?"

"With hindsight, yes. But it probably seemed a good idea at the time. And now we're stuck with it. Unless you make a mistake so big that forces the government to hold an enquiry."

"Don't say things like that!"

Chapter 2 Osborne House

8 April

The next morning, Samantha and Lady Mary climbed into the coach alongside Lord Edward for a short ride down the King's Road to Chelsea. They crossed the decrepit Battersea wooden bridge. Lady Mary, not a morning person, hardly spoke at all. Both ladies were wearing fashionable yet practical travelling dresses. Samantha wore a rimless hat with pompom. This was regarded as fashionable for single ladies for riding or travelling. Lord Edward had asked them to bring heavy travelling coats.

Samantha was disappointed by her view of Battersea Airship Port. She had expected a wide grass field, with rows of gleaming airships. And perhaps a fashionable hostelry to offer her some mulled wine. Instead the place consisted of riverside wharves, soot-darkened warehouses, and a pier built out over the Thames.

A single small airship was perched on the pier, moored fore and aft. Samantha had never seen an airship close up before. It was silvery-grey in colour, with a passenger gondola forward on the centreline and a smaller engine car behind it. "But it's so small," Samantha said.

"This isn't a normal airmail flight. We're not going to France," Lord Edward said. "This vessel is classified as a yacht."

"Is it yours? The college's, I mean?"

"No. How could I justify that to our stingy treasurer?" He grinned. "Usually, railway travel is sufficient for our needs. I chartered this for the occasion."

The forward part of the gondola was open to the elements, with low plywood sides. The rear section was fully enclosed, with tiny portholes.

The crewmen were wearing duffel coats, despite the heat, and knitted stocking caps that made them look piratical. The young commander greeted them on the open forward section. He was wearing a heavy duffel coat and a French-style kepi with a low crown. His white silk scarf made him look quite dashing. "Welcome on board, ladies, my lord. You have a choice. You can make the voyage on the observation deck or in one of the passenger cabins aft. The cabins have bench-seats that fold down to form bunks."

Lady Mary chose a cabin. "I have brought a prayer book with me."

The grandly named observation deck was bare, except for a brass binnacle for the compass, a steering wheel, and a bridge telegraph.

"I choose the observation deck. I want to see as much as possible," Samantha said.

Lord Edward handed her a pair of goggles. "And now's the time to put your coat on." He shrugged into his own riding-coat.

"I would be grateful if you would stand at the rear of the open deck, my lord. It keeps the craft steady and avoids obstructing the crew," the commander said. "And I would be grateful if you could assist us by keeping a lookout for other craft."

They cast off the mooring lines and ascended from Battersea. Samantha noted with disappointment that the vista over the East End and the Thames Estuary was obscured by smoke and fog. As they gained altitude, the air cooled markedly. Samantha was soon wishing that her coat was heavier. They headed south-west and crossed the North Downs at Guildford. They followed the railway line and she watched in fascination as a train slowly overtook them. The smoke from its chimney was blown gently east.

"Is this vessel really steam powered?" she asked.

"Of course," the commander said. "There'll never be anything more powerful than steam. What is unusual about us is our fuel. We use paraffin to heat the water. Coal won't do. It produces a lot less heat per ton."

Edward grinned. "I'm told that the first experiments in liquid fuel used whisky."

The commander smiled back. "I can't comment on that, my lord."

Samantha went into the cabin to see Lady Mary. The upholstery was embossed purple velvet, with miniature curtains over the porthole. Lady Mary was sitting on her bunk, reading her book.

"Are you all right, Lady Mary?"

Lady Mary looked up, quite unconcerned. "Thank you for asking, my dear. The rocking from side to side is quite soothing, don't you think?"

Samantha had not noticed the swaying before. She decided the cabin was stuffy and retreated back to her post on the observation deck.

They crossed the South Downs at Petersfield. The young commander ducked into the main cabin and had a look at his chart table. "We need to go further west. South-west by west, helmsman."

The man turned the wheel a fraction. "South-west by west, sir."

The commander walked back to where they were standing. "I intend to pass west of Portsmouth, my lord. It might be unwise to go too close to a naval base."

"Undoubtedly," Lord Edward said.

"And the lookouts need to look below us as well as to each side. The navy has some patrol vessels based here."

Half an hour later they crossed the coast. The

commander ducked into the cabin and made a note on his chart. "Alter course, helmsman. South by west."

This course took them across the Solent to the Isle of Wight. Samantha stared at the multitude of sailing ships and steam tugs far below.

Lord Edward smiled. "If we'd been on that train, we'd now be stowing our bags on a ship. This sea crossing is what makes an air journey worthwhile".

The airship reached the island, just east of the port of Cowes. "Turn into wind, helmsman," the commander said, and used the bridge telegraph to signal for reduced speed.

Samantha noticed a bright red flare on the ground. The smoke was blown eastwards.

"Osborne House. That means we don't have permission to land," the commander said.

Lord Edward turned to the commander. "I believe you are carrying signal flags. I want you to lower four flags, J, H, F, K, in that order. That's our identification code."

"Yes, my lord." The commander collected four brightly-coloured flags from the navigator's desk. He handed them to a crewman, who tied them in the correct sequence and lowered them over the side. A minute after their flags had been lowered, the red flare on the ground was replaced by a green one.

*

Samantha knew from her lessons that Osborne House was a royal residence in East Cowes. Building had commenced in 1845 for Queen Victoria and Prince Albert to use as a summer home and rural retreat.

The open carriage took them along the west side of the house. This was L-shaped, with a carriage circle in the centre. They turned onto the carriage circle. Lady Mary leaned forward. "The door on the left, with the stone columns, is for royalty. It leads direct to the royal apartments. We use the door on the right."

The carriage swept past the columns and stopped outside a modest doorway, flanked by two iron lamp-posts. Lord Edward climbed out first and courteously helped the ladies step down. The door opened. Standing there was a lady dressed in a deep blue silk dress, with a tall footman standing behind her.

The lady stepped forward. "I am Lady Spencer, lady-in-waiting to her majesty. Welcome to Osborne House. Come this way, if you please."

"This is known as the marble corridor," Lady Mary said.

Samantha could see why. There were marble statues every six feet. Most of them were classical. Some of them, she noticed, were scantily clad. Between each statue, marble slabs had been let into the wall. They came to a short windowless corridor leading off to the right.

"The receiving room is down there," Lady Spencer said. She ignored it, continued on for a few steps and turned left along a shorter corridor. This had windows on the left, enabling Samantha to catch a glimpse of the carriage drive and their carriage. The windows shed light on more statues, some of them bronze rather than marble. They reached the royal doorway and the main entrance hall, decorated in grey marble. Lady Spencer turned right and opened a door.

"This is the snooker room." She led them past the table and through a curtained doorway. "This is the drawing room."

Samantha received an impression of walls covered with oil paintings, three spectacular chandeliers, and high windows. These looked out over the terrace and gave a view of the blue of the Solent and the white sails of yachts. The heavy red curtains swayed in the breeze and Samantha realised that all of the windows were open.

Lady Spencer opened a door between two of the windows and stepped out onto the terrace. Samantha noted more statues, made of concrete this time.

Lady Spencer turned to face them. "Her Majesty is fond of fresh air. It is her invariable custom to have breakfast outside. You must remove your coats."

Lord Edward stood while the footman pulled off his coat. Samantha followed his example.

Lady Mary touched Samantha's sleeve. "You will not comment on the Queen's preferences, my dear."

"No – no, of course not." The idea that she might accidentally make a tactless comment terrified Samantha.

Lady Spencer led them across the terrace and onto the grass towards a tent. Lady Mary followed at her heels. She was now much more energetic. Samantha realised that the two people sitting in high-backed chairs beside a wrought-iron table were the Queen and Prince Albert.

Victoria was small, showing signs of plumpness. Her eyes were pale blue, slightly protruding. Prince Albert was quite as handsome as his portraits suggested. Another lady in waiting stood behind the Queen's chair. A red box, with its lid open, rested on the table. Three more boxes, lids firmly closed, lay at the Queen's foot. Samantha realised these were the famous despatch boxes, sent down each morning for the Queen to read.

Lord Edward approached the Queen and bowed. She smiled at him. "Lord Edward! How delightful to see you again." Her voice was light and musical.

"Thank you, madam." To Samantha's surprise it was Lord Edward, not Lady Mary, who introduced her. "Your Majesty, may I present to you Lady Samantha Hampden, the College's new chatelaine."

Samantha, remembering her training, sank into a curtsey. She waited for permission to rise.

The Queen leant forward, her arm stretched out.

Samantha realised that the stories were true. She was permitted to kiss the Queen's hand. She leant forward and remembered just in time that she must not touch the Queen: the gesture alone was sufficient.

"You are welcome, my dear," the Queen said. "There is no need for formality today.
The breeze this morning is refreshing is it not?"

Samantha stood, trembling. She knew that you must never contradict royalty. "Yes, bracing, your majesty." She noticed that no-one else shared the Queen's enthusiasm.

"She is so young, Lord Edward."

"Lady Samantha is qualified, madam. And she is energetic. The college needs shaking up."

The Queen turned to Samantha. "Your father is in the Diplomatic Service, we understand."

How had the Queen learned that, Samantha wondered. "Yes, madam. He was sent to Vienna in February."

"Vienna has suffered from violence too. The emperor is in fear of his life. No-where seems to be safe."

"Yes, madam. The newspaper reports are shocking. I am concerned for Papa's safety."

The Queen's expression was kindly. "Lord Edward, should we ask Lord Palmerston to recall Mr. Hampden?"

Samantha was appalled. What should she say? "Madam, I believe that my father would wish to do his duty."

Lord Edward stepped forward. "Madam, we could ask Lord Palmerston whether Mr. Hampden could easily be spared from his duties."

Samantha had thought of another danger. "And, and, in these troubled times, travelling across Europe could be dangerous."

"This is not an easy decision," the Queen said. "Your father is probably glad that he left his daughter at home."

"My mother's death made it difficult for me to accompany him."

26

"That is true, my dear girl. We have a telepath here, provided by the Guild, to keep us in contact with St. James's Palace. But he is so masculine. Would it be possible to find us a lady with the same skills?"

Lady Mary gasped. Samantha understood why. Ladies were not supposed to show the least interest in the vulgar art of magic. But this was a royal command. "I shall see what I can do, madam."

"Thank you. We are worried about the Chartists. Those riots in March were terrible."

Before Samantha could think of a reply, Lord Edward intervened. "Strictly speaking, madam, the riot in March was nothing to do with the Chartists. It had no leaders at all. We must hope that the Chartist leaders keep their meeting under control."

Prince Albert leaned forward. "We have heard a story that the gathering in Trafalgar Square would have passed without incident, had not a man of wealth heckled the crowd." His voice was, unfortunately, rather shrill.

"The police have not been able to confirm that story, your Highness," Lord Edward said.

Samantha panicked. Was the queen asking for advice? "We are all worried about the Chartist meeting at Kennington Common, madam. I believe that a light touch is best. It has worked so far."

"We hope you prove to be correct." Victoria turned back to Lord Edward. "Please ensure Lady Samantha receives sufficient protection. Her aunt and cousin were murdered, remember."

"I shall do my best, madam," Lord Edward said.

The interview seemed to be at an end. Samantha curtsied again and carefully withdrew. Lady Spencer led them through the house and along the marble corridor. Samantha was bewildered. "What do we do now?"

"Back to the landing field and the waiting airship. Back

27

in London by sunset," Lord Edward said.

"Do you mean it's over? Nothing more? I wish I could have stayed and dined with the Queen," Samantha said.

"Believe me, you've had a lucky escape, my lady. Amongst the courtiers, dinners at Osborne House are dreaded for their dullness."

They climbed back into the carriage. "Lord Edward, why did you take on the task of introducing me? I thought a girl's nearest female relative had to do it."

"Because I introduced you as chatelaine of the College, not as my cousin."

"Oh. I see." Samantha was thinking further ahead. "I expect my formal presentation in the autumn will be a lot more intimidating."

Lord Edward was irritable. "Don't you understand? You don't need a formal presentation. You were presented just now. There's no need to do it again."

"Oh. I see." She was relieved that she had been spared the stress of all of those duennas judging her curtsey. But she missed the thought of that opulent dress.

"If you had been presented formally, you would have been at the end of the queue. But the chatelaine is far more important than the second cousin of an earl."

"Is the Queen right about my aunt being murdered?"

Lady Mary tutted. "Her Majesty is fanciful at times."

"Look over the evidence for yourself," Lord Edward said. "Then make up your own mind. But these allegations allow me to give you a stronger guard than would normally be justified."

Soho, afternoon of 8 April

Charley Williams, known to his friends as 'Coffee', was working on the Printing Engine. When his friend Dave One-eye arrived, he put his work to one side without regret and made a pot of tea. He had a quiet corner with a fireplace, screened off from his worktable. Tea and iron filings did not mix.

Dave glanced at the machine parts on Coffee's work desk. "I haven't come at the wrong time, have I?"

"No, no. Cleaning the components of the Printing Engine is fascinating work but it's exacting. I need to take a break from time to time."

The noise of the Engine's calculations went on in the background. The loud rhythmic slapping as the locks darted in and out acted as counterpoint to the clanking of the shifting array of bronze wheels. Beyond that he could hear the hiss and whuff of the steam engine that powered it all. But that was somebody else's problem. The clanking of the Engine worried him, because noise meant friction. He wanted to make it quieter. That meant very special metals, light yet durable.

"What's the machine doing today?" Dave asked.

"It's producing the contents of a navigator's almanac. Not a big, heavy nautical almanac. No, Air Navigation Tables. The authorities want to send airships across the Atlantic. It seems the navigators need special calculation tables that'll allow them to make their calculations more quickly." He poured tea into their mugs. "You're probably wishing you'd never asked."

"Not at all. I was wondering what print company would get the contract. But what are you working on?"

"Taking the bloody printer apart and putting it back together again. The central mill does the calculations and puts the result onto punched cards. Then, a day or so later, somebody feeds the cards into the printer and hopes it works."

"Ah. I see." Dave picked up his mug.

Coffee waited for Dave to say his piece. Coffee's mother had been born a slave in Montserrat. He had inherited her skin tone, so he faced constant prejudice. But he had grown up here in London, which gave him the right accent. He wasn't an Irish Catholic escaping the famine or a Russian Jew fleeing the pogrom. They were the two groups who faced the worst prejudice at the moment.

Dave gulped at his tea. "I'm worried about the big meeting on the tenth, to present your petition. In Kennington Common. It could go bad, turn into another riot."

"We've got to make them take notice," Coffee said. "Other petitions have achieved results. Think of Bethnal Fields. The local MP collected ten thousand signatures and the government gave them a public park. If we make enough noise on the tenth, the authorities will pay attention."

"Bethnal Fields was just that, a field. Your petition's about politics. The right to vote. I want the vote too, Coffee, but violence won't achieve it. Violence didn't achieve anything in 1832. I tried it, and what did it get me? I lost an eye and earned a prison record."

Coffee merely grunted.

"Are you going to Kennington?"

"I'm one of the elected delegates for London. Of course I'm bloody well going. And losing a couple of day's pay because of it." Coffee took a noisy gulp at his tea. "Tomorrow I'll be with the other delegates, planning the event. Will you be there?"

"I'll show up and watch from the sidelines," Dave said. "I hope I'm not distracting you from your work. I don't want you to lose your job."

"No, no. If I work too long without a break, I start

making mistakes. I get pay deducted if my work isn't perfect. Long hours and fewer mistakes suits me fine."

"Doesn't the noise get you down?"

Coffee grinned. "I find it soothing. The sound of the future."

Dave scowled. "I think the printing press is the future. The sound of freedom."

The College, 9 April

"Lady Samantha, this is Charles Lloyd," Lord Edward said. "He has been one of my guards for a couple of years. He's good, but he's getting stale. I decided he needed a challenge, so I'm giving him the task of building up your guard team."

Samantha was embarrassed. Lloyd was in his early twenties, fit, and good-looking, with blond hair. His black uniform jacket had been tailored to fit him better. What was the polite thing to say? "I am sure you will do well, Mr. Lloyd."

"Thank you, my lady." He spoke with a clear patrician accent.

"And this is Mr. Smith," Lord Edward said. "He's in the final year of his apprenticeship. He too has worked on my team, but last month he appeared at Bow Street Magistrates' court. Mr. Knight persuaded the authorities to drop the charges for lack of evidence, but he's in disgrace. We decided that he also needs a change."

Samantha glanced at Smith. Judging by his scowl, he resented this appointment. She was appalled. Was a transfer to her team seen as a punishment? "I am sure you will do well, Mr. Smith."

His scowl vanished. If he bore a grudge, it wasn't with her. "Thank you, my lady." He had a strong East London

31

accent. His jacket was dark grey, a size too large. Perhaps he could not afford a good tailor.

An hour later, Samantha followed her maid along a windowless corridor and into the study of Oswald, the lecturer in Distance-Talking skills. He was over sixty, with scant white hair. He was sitting at a writing desk. As she entered, he turned his wheelchair so he was facing her. "Good afternoon, my dear. I hope you will excuse me for not getting up. Please, take a seat. You too," he added to the maid.

"Thank you, sir," Samantha said.

He had a tartan blanket across his knees. He turned his chair to face the desk and smiled kindly. "You may be uncomfortable at the idea of exchanging thoughts with a man. But don't worry. Talking is restricted to words. At first, we use a restricted number of words. For a novice to establish a rapport with a partner, it is necessary for them to touch. A simple handshake will do."

He stretched his hand out across the desk towards her. Samantha hesitated a moment, then rose from her chair and stretched out her own hand. His clasp was firm. She was surprised, and a little disappointed, that nothing happened.

He smiled. "When a pair of talkers wish to re-establish rapport, they usually exchange tokens of some kind. But today my prompt-cards will do. See here."

On the desk were a series of white cards, ten inches long and two wide. Oswald turned them over to show that each contained four or five words. "Together, they make up that magnificent speech of John Donne. It seemed appropriate. Now, turn them so I can't see them, choose one at random, and think through the words."

Samantha chose 'No man is an island' and concentrated.

"You must concentrate, my dear. Remember when you

produced that white light? Do that again. Then think of the words. Then think of the person who made out those cards. Think of each word in turn."

"Should I touch the cards, sir?"

"Yes. I wrote out the cards myself. Think of the labour I spent over them. I've held them and read the words, again and again."

Samantha nodded and tried again.

Oswald smiled. "Five words, that's all I get. The last word is longer than the others, so I could make a guess. Try another."

Ten minutes later, Oswald called a halt. "You're not a natural Talker, I regret to say. To become proficient, you'd have to practice ten times a day, with ten different people. As Chatelaine, you won't have the time. You'll only be able to establish rapport with two or three people."

"I see, sir." she tried to hide her disappointment.

"Has anyone given you the safety lecture? Did your mother warn you about that white light of yours?"

"She said that I should only maintain an intense light for a couple of minutes. But a less intense light could be maintained for longer. Half an hour, if it was no brighter than a candle-flame. Why? Is there a similar rule about Talking?"

"Oh, yes. You should never maintain rapport for more than five minutes. Then take a break for at least two minutes." He gestured at the blue and purple blanket covering his legs. "Did nobody explain how this happened? I tried to find out how long a couple of Talkers could maintain rapport. Five minutes, six minutes, six and a half - then this. My partner was killed outright. So be careful, my lady."

"Oh. I see, yes."

He gave a tight little smile. "Every year, they wheel me out and I give my little speech to the new apprentices. I think of it as a way of atoning for my partner's death."

33

She was silent for a moment. "I did wonder why the guild had so much difficulty in finding new recruits."

"Didn't your mother ever warn you?"

"She said that over-exertion would ruin my complexion and destroy my figure. That was probably more effective than a warning of sudden death. And she said that society disapproved of parlour tricks." She hesitated. "You said I would only be able to establish rapport with two or three people. Will you be one of them, sir?"

"I would be honoured, my lady. I sit here like a spider in a web, listening, listening."

Chapter 3 Kennington Common

10 April

Thousands of Chartists protesters had assembled on the Common, only a mile and a half south of the Houses of Parliament. In the centre of the Common they had built a temporary stage for their speakers. Next to the stage, a long banner dangled from a flagpole.

Lord Edward was standing on the western side of the Common, on the pavement outside the Horns Tavern. This morning he was in command of a contingent of magicians, including a pair of Talkers, to back up the police. He was wearing an elegant frock-coat and silk hat, with his walking stick in his right hand.

He would have preferred more practical clothing. If there was any fighting, that silk hat was likely to be trampled into the mud. But he had to look confident and that included dressing the part. Some spectators had turned up on horseback, but that option was not open to him today.

A dirigible hovered overhead, its propellers turning just enough to overcome the influence of the wind. It would only be needed today if the protesters broke loose from the Common and marched on Westminster.

The Horns Tavern had been chosen as the headquarters of the Police Commissioners because it was on the junction of the Portsmouth Road and Kennington Road. If there was any fighting, it would be here.

Edward's position this morning was awkward. Usually, an earl would outrank a police commissioner. But today Edward and his colleagues were special constables, under orders.

The Metropolitan Police Force was not allowed to carry firearms on their patrols. For emergencies, they had a few flintlock pistols. They could, in a crisis, ask the army for support. But merely asking for support could make the crisis worse. So the Commissioners tended to ask the Guild to provide combat-trained magicians in difficult cases. It was a compromise that suited everyone.

After the Trafalgar Square riots in March, the country's leaders had forbidden both the Chartist meeting and their march to Westminster. But the Chartist Executive had refused to back down. They had made it clear that they intended to assemble in London whether they received permission or not.

Edward, amongst others, had persuaded the authorities to accept the inevitable and give permission for a meeting south of the Thames.

The authorities were not taking any chances. They had ordered a thousand police officers to block the western exits from the Common. Further back there were thousands of troops, under the command of the Duke of Wellington. They were entrusted with the task of blocking the bridges over the Thames. Edward hoped they would not be needed.

As the morning wore on, Chartist groups converged on Kennington from all over London. Many had travelled by train from much further afield. Some groups were less than a hundred strong; others numbered almost a thousand. Each group arrived with its own banner. Edward noted that the London Irish contingent had chosen the harp for its banner.

"It took a lot of organisation to get everyone here, my lord," Edward's talker said.

"Yes. Let's hope they put some thought into getting everyone home again at the end of the day."

They were waiting for Feargus O'Connor, an Irish ex-MP who ran a violently radical paper in Leeds, 'The Northern

Star'. He was, in Edward's opinion, a showy idealist whose abilities lay exclusively in his tongue. He had been involved in the foundation of the Chartist movement fifteen years before. That had collapsed, but O'Connor had managed to get himself elected to parliament and had attempted to resurrect the Chartist movement. When the king in France had been swept away by the Second Republic, O'Connor had been inspired to draft a republican constitution for Britain, with himself as its first president.

Today his ambition was more modest. The Chartists had assembled a petition, with several thousand signatures, demanding the right to vote. O'Connor had promised his followers that he would present it to parliament, and on that point he had refused to back down.

A large carriage, pulled by four horses, appeared at the northern edge of the common and made its way across the grass to the centre of the open space, opposite the tavern. "This will be Mr. O'Connor and his friends, I fancy," Edward said.

"At last," his Talker said.

Edward walked into the tavern to find out if the Commissioner wanted a word with him. The Metropolitan Police had been established by two Commissioners. The barrister, Richard Mayne, provided the legal expertise, while Sir Charles Rowan was an ex-soldier. Mayne was dressed in a sombre morning suit while sir Charles was wearing his dark blue police uniform.

Edward was just in time to hear the Sir Charles give his orders to an inspector. "Tell that fellow O'Connor that you've been instructed to communicate to that gentleman that the Police Commissioners desire to confer with him."

"Yes, sir." The police inspector walked across the Common to Mr. O'Connor's carriage. Someone opened the door to hear what he had to say.

Two men immediately descended from the carriage

and, accompanied by the inspector, began walking across the Common in the direction of the Horns Tavern.

"Why two men, my lord?" the Talker asked.

Edward leant on his walking stick. Stability, not action, must be his watchword this day. "The plump would-be dandy on the left is Mr. O'Connor. The bantam boxer on the right is M'Grath. He's the toughest member of the Chartist Executive. He's probably come along to keep an eye on O'Connor."

A cry went up from somebody in the crowd that Mr O'Connor had been arrested, but one of the delegates shouted that the Commissioners merely wanted to discuss a few details with Mr. O'Connor.

O'Connor ignored this disturbance and waved to well-wishers as he passed, or returned a shouted greeting. His surly minder ignored everyone.

The Commissioners chose to wait for O'Connor outside the tavern, on the pavement. Sir Charles explained in an aside to Edward. "We thought it best if the crowd could see what's going on, even if only the delegates could hear us."

O'Connor walked across the road to the tavern. A few selected delegates gathered in a semicircle behind him. The most distinctive amongst them was a very short man with dark skin. Edward wondered how a man of African blood ended up in the Chartist movement. How had he won his place in the front row amongst the Chartist Delegates?

"Good morning to you, Sir Charles, Mr. Mayne," O'Connor said.

"Good morning, Mr. O'Connor," Mayne said.

Sir Charles chose to be more direct. "Mr. O'Connor, I wish to inform you that the Government has sent troops to take possession of each of the metropolitan bridges. Those troops are commanded by the Duke of Wellington. If the Chartists try to pass, the soldiers will use force to stop them."

"Sir, everyone assembled her today expects to deliver

our petition to the Houses of Commons." O'Connor indicated the crowd behind him with an airy gesture.

Edward and his Talker, careful not to intervene, watched the haggling with interest. The Commissioners were polite and tactful, but firm. They refused to let the protesters advance any further.

O'Connor had an expressive face, allowing Edward to measure his mounting anger and dismay.

"No! I insist. I gave these men my promise."

"That was to them, not to us," Sir Charles said.

"If they are not allowed to proceed, they will turn violent."

"Surely you can persuade them to stay within the law," Mayne said.

Edward was grateful that the Queen was safe on the Isle of Wight. He wished that Lady Samantha was safe there too. The March rioters had pushed all the way to Berkeley Square, smashing the windows of the gentlemen's clubs, before the police stopped them. But he knew that the chit would have refused to go.

*

The negotiations were witnessed by the elected Chartist delegates. Coffee Williams had used his status as one of the elected delegates for London to get a place in the front rank. He listened to the negotiations with dismay. He firmly believed that the working men of London would only gain a hearing if they were decisive. And now O'Connor, who had persuaded the Chartists to trust him, was revealing his true colours. He was too timid to face down the government. He was betraying the cause.

Coffee recognised Lord Edward Radley, patron of the Guild, standing behind the Commissioners. Williams respected and resented Lord Edward in equal measure. This morning His Lordship seemed restless, shifting his weight from foot to foot, his gaze sweeping the crowd as if looking for trouble.

Coffee was a metalworker. He was paid for the work he produced, not by the hour, maintaining Babbage's Analytical Engine. It was a magnificent machine, and Coffee was proud to be entrusted with the task. But his contract obliged him to work long hours. Deductions were taken from his pay if he made mistakes. He had been secretly using magic to improve the quality of the components he supplied.

You couldn't use magic unless you were a member of the guild; and the guild restricted its membership to toffs. If he was caught using magic, he would be sent to Newgate.

Lord Edward, endlessly watching the crowd, paused for a moment. Coffee told himself that Lord Edward was merely curious about his skin colour or his diminutive height. The Earl could not possibly smell out his illegal use of magic. After a moment, Lord Edward's attention switched to O'Connor. Then he returned to that tireless sweep of the crowd.

Coffee let out a sigh of relief. He desperately wanted to move back into the crowd, but that movement was sure to attract Lord Edward's attention. Coffee despised the idle rich, but you couldn't accuse Lord Edward of being idle; when he protected the privileges of his Guild, he was too energetic by half.

*

Edward, standing motionless behind the Commissioners, rested his weight on his walking stick. He tried not to show his impatience as the negotiations dragged on.

Finally, Sir Charles conceded that O'Connor could take the signed petition to the houses of parliament, on condition that he travelled alone.

O'Connor was suspicious. "But will the petition be read, sir?" he demanded.

His question was addressed to Sir Charles, but it was Richard Mayne, the barrister, who replied. "Yes, Mr. O'Connor. Every signature will be examined. You have my word on that."

Edward tensed. "Now we find out whether the fellow's got any backbone," he murmured.

"Sir?" his Talker asked.

"If he has any integrity, O'Connor will accept this compromise. But if he's a coward he'll blame his failure on us and provoke a riot."

"That would lead his men to disaster, my lord."

"Yes, but it would allow him to escape from humiliation."

O'Connor straightened up. "I accept the proposed terms."

Edward turned to his Talker. "Did you get that? Tell them at St. James's."

"Yes, my lord."

*

Edward watched as O'Connor, still accompanied by M'Grath, left the tavern and made their way towards to the improvised platform at the centre of the Common. His re-appearance on the platform was met by the most enthusiastic cheering.

One of the delegates proposed that the meeting should be chaired by Mr. C. Doyle, the Secretary of the National Chartist Association. The motion was gravely seconded by Mr. Adams. The Chairman delivered a short speech of the usual Chartist character, and then, with many flourishes introduced Mr. O'Connor to the assembly. This was the excuse for prolonged cheers from the multitude.

O'Connor began a speech to the assembled crowd, containing many vague generalities about "Liberty" and "Rights of the People", and concluded by urging his listeners to disperse peaceably, as the Government had taken possession of each of the metropolitan bridges, making it impossible for the Chartists to pass without a struggle. He consoled them by the assurance that "the Executive" of the Chartist Association would convey the petition to the House of Commons, and that he himself would present it that evening.

"Your petition will be taken to Westminster and will be read by the authorities, just as I promised you. This day will go down in history. This is the beginning of a new era for Britain ..."

Edward was distracted by his Talker tapping his sleeve. "My lord, the Duke wants to know what's happening now."

When you spoke of 'the Duke', everyone knew that you meant the Duke of Wellington, commander in chief, and responsible today for the defence of the bridges.

Edward looked at O'Connor, in full flow, with the crowd listening attentively. "Tell him that everything's quiet. O'Connor's giving a speech. I'm bored and that I hope to go on being bored. I'll let him know when O'Connor drives off to Westminster."

"If, not *when,* begging your pardon, my lord."

"Send your message, damn you." Edward was nervous and that made him irritable.

Sometimes Edward would spot a ripple in the crowd and he would tense, wondering whether the men were moving towards one of the exits. The most direct route to Westminster Bridge was along Kennington Road, past the Tavern. His guards would tense too, aware to any danger. On each occasion the movement would reveal itself as an example of a spectator jostling his neighbour, forcing that man to move in turn. On each occasion he had been able to relax. So far.

Edward glanced at that diminutive African amongst the Chartist Delegates. For the fellow to persuade his fellow Londoners to elect him, he must have a powerful personality. Judging by the man's demeanour, he was angry, probably at O'Connor's decision to back down.

Another speaker took over and told the crowd it was useless for them, as peaceable men, to engage in a fight for which they were wholly unprepared. He regretted that the meeting had not been held on the other side of the river Thames, as in that case there would have been no bridges to bar their way. He claimed that they had achieved a victory, for they now held a meeting which had been forbidden. He trusted his listeners would follow the admirable advice given to-day by their friend and leader; and if they did, eventual success was certain.

O'Connor came forward again. "Gentlemen! I ask the you, the people gathered her this day, the signatories to this petition, to give me authority now to deliver your petition to Sir George Grey, in Downing Street, on your behalf.

"I shall tell Sir George that the people are determined not to come into collision with any armed force, police or military; and that they are resolved to keep the peace inviolate this day."

The crowd responded to this request with loud cheers.

Edward tried to hide his relief as he watched O'Connor attempt to load the monster petition into a cab. There were so many documents, so many signatures, that one cab was not enough. Finally, the documents were loaded into three cabs and O'Connor gave orders to be taken to the houses of parliament. He proceeded on his way, cheered on by the crowd.

43

As soon as O'Connor departed, the audience began to show just how impatient and angry they were. First, the people at the back, who had been unable to hear O'Connor's speech, showed signs of dissatisfaction with aggressive chanting. This unruliness spread to the delegates at the front. The tendency in the crowd showed itself by rushes from one point to another, shouting slogans, much to the annoyance of the people at the front. Edward also very distinctly heard that peculiar baying cry of East End desperadoes.

"What's that, my lord?" his Talker asked. "It gives me the shivers."

"Haven't you heard it before? That's the cry that young daredevils and thieves of London signal to each other." He had to admit that the cry, mingling with the general uproar, gave him the shivers too.

As this evidence of disorderly spirit grew louder, and spread across the Common, several delegates took it upon themselves to deliver fiery speeches in every corner of the crowd.

Edward heard four men, two of them delegates, squabbling about the propriety of having abandoned the procession.

One of them, whom his colleagues addressed as Spur, was the loudest. "The people here should accompany the petition until we were opposed by the military. Then we'll find out whether British troops will fire on Londoners! That would be illegal, and we'd be justified in a more forceful protest."

"Yes, you're quite right, Spur. Put an end to compromise," a Londoner said.

"Compromise won't get us the vote," the dark-skinned delegate said, in a broad Cockney accent.

Spur was delighted at this support. "Let's go after O'Connor and his petition. See if the troops stop us!" A portion of his hearers violently applauded.

Edward straightened up. If he could hear them, from the far side of the road, then every Peeler in the Tavern could hear them too.

Fortunately, some of the less intemperate delegates interfered. Perhaps they realised just how disastrous Spur's proposal was.

"Remember that the Duke's waiting for us. He'll do 'is duty, 'owever unpleasant 'e finds it."

The diminutive African was the most forthright. "Stow that talk. How many people would get killed if they followed you? And how would that help the cause?"

The crowd was unhappy, but most of them felt that O'Connor had fulfilled his promise. Slowly, they began to disperse.

Edward turned to his Talker. "Tell them in Westminster that the fellow's on his way. I'm to be informed at once if anything delays him."

"Yes, my lord. But Lady Samantha is asking whether we'll be returning to the college now."

Edward looked at the crowd as it broke up into its contingents and streamed away from the Common. He knew he could not relax. This was the point when a minority in the Trafalgar Square gathering had turned ugly. He sighed. "Tell them we won't be able to leave the common for another hour at least."

Chapter 4 Representing the College

Training, Afternoon of 11 April

Edward led Lady Samantha and her four guards into the atrium of the College. He had chosen to wear a Norfolk jacket instead of his formal frock coat. "You need some training in self-defence, my lady."

In the centre of the open space, he turned to face them. "It is not your task to stand in the front rank. At first sight of violence you must run away."

Lady Samantha had a brown complexion, with mouse-coloured hair, very simply arranged. Her countenance was pleasing, without being beautiful, her best feature being a pair of dark eyes, well-opened and straight-gazing. She was also impertinent but, considering the burden he had dropped on her, he considered that to be a good thing. At the moment she was, quite understandably, indignant.

"I am not a coward, sir."

He ignored her objections. "You're too important to risk. Just as I am. Why do you think I have a team of guards to protect me? The greatest risk will be from assassins. They'll take you by surprise."

The lady's guard, Charles, was offended. "Lady Samantha doesn't need any training. We'll stop them from reaching her, my lord."

Edward was impatient. "Are you suggesting your vigilance is perfect, Mr. Lloyd? No?" The boy wilted and Edward turned back to Lady Samantha. "So you must train for speed, my lady, not staying-power, to get your defences up in a couple of seconds."

"Yes, my lord." She was serious now. Edward was relieved.

"I am going to form a shield, an invisible shield. I will form a shape in my mind. You can manipulate light, now you have to manipulate air." He concentrated, muttered "Partum a scuto" and formed the shield. "Did you get that?" He relaxed his guard and repeated the procedure. "Partum a scuto."

"Again," Samantha said. "I need to feel you create it. I feel it inside my head. Does that make sense?"

"Yes." He created the shield twice more, and she nodded. Edward turned to Charles. "Lloyd, I'll form my shield again. Demonstrate it by throwing a couple of tennis balls ... Partum a scuto."

Charles, grinning, threw a ball at Edward as hard as he could. It stopped dead and then dropped to the ground. He threw two more, to each side, to demonstrate how wide Edward's defences were.

Lady Samantha shrugged. "There's no need for more. I can sense it."

"Very well. Imagine you're holding a shield in front of you. Got it?"

"Yes, my lord. Just like Britannia on the coins ... Partum a scuto." She held her left fist in front of her.

Edward took a ball from Charles and lobbied at her. To his surprise, it swerved wide.

"You're doing something right. Very well. Relax a moment. Getting your shield in place will be more important than maintaining it."

A minute later, he judged she had rested enough. "On guard!" He and Charles practised by lobbing tennis balls at her.

To Edward' surprise, each of the balls was deflected to each side rather than being stopped dead. "I've never seen that before."

The girl was contrite. "I'm sorry, I'll try harder."

"No, there's no need to apologise. If you've found something that works, stay with it."

Reception, evening of 14 April

Samantha stood in the centre of the college's lecture hall, wearing her new evening dress. Lord Edward and Lady Mary had arranged a formal reception to allow Samantha to meet the fellows of the College, and Edward's relatives, many of whom were also practitioners. The servants had cleared the hall for the occasion.

There could be no dancing because she, and the rest of the College, was in mourning for her aunt. Her new mourning dress was in a sober navy blue, but it was made of the finest wool. The cut of the skirt was extravagant, ballooning around her, with a great many flounces. But mourning demanded sombre colours, not austerity.

In her childish fantasies she had imagined attending a grand event such as this, the centre of everyone's attention. The difference was that instead of attracting admirers because of her beauty, she attracted attention because of her role.

She was single, so Lady Mary was technically the hostess here today. Samantha was glad of the company but would have preferred someone less boring.

She noticed Lord Edward and a slimmer man standing next to him. "Who's that handsome man in company of the Earl?"

The guest was tall, his jacket was finely cut, and his trousers showed off his muscular legs to advantage. Although Edward, in his formal dress coat, looked dignified too.

Lady Mary looked them over. "That's your cousin.

Third cousin. the honourable Randolph Radley. Actually he's Edward's cousin. He's Edward's heir."

The gentlemen strolled over. Edward smiled. "Good evening, ladies. May I introduce you? Lady Samantha Hampden, this is the honourable Randolph Radley." Cousin Randolph bowed and Samantha curtsied.

"Some say Randolph would have make an excellent Master of the Guild. Far better than poor Archibald," Edward said.

"Unfortunately, I find magic boring, and administration more so," Randolph said.

"However, you do like teaching, it seems," Samantha said.

Randolph noticed Samantha's dark dress and black gloves. "I'm sorry about your aunt, cousin."

"Thank you, sir." Lord Edward and Lady Mary moved away, discussing the dining arrangements. With so many titled people present, many of them touchy about their status, that was a major issue.

"It was strange of your father to leave you in London," Randolph said. "Although staying in that school probably saved your life. Someone hated the chatelaine enough to kill her, and her daughter, but you were invisible."

She thought this was absurd. "You're as fanciful as the Queen. Why should someone kill the Guild's chatelaine but not its patron or its master?"

He shrugged. "Because Edward is guarded night and day. The chatelaine wasn't, until her majesty spotted the pattern and dropped the hint."

After dinner, Samantha and the other ladies followed Lady Mary to the withdrawing room. Samantha was not surprised that Lady Mary was eager to discuss Randolph. "Do you think he's handsome, my dear? Educated, too. He read economics at Edinburgh university."

"Why not Cambridge?"

"He said it wasn't studious enough. Said it was full of snobs. He isn't as wealthy as Edward, of course, and he doesn't have a title, but he does well enough."

Samantha was appalled. Did Lady Mary consider Randolph as a potential husband for her?

Bow Street Police Station, 18 April

Samantha climbed out of the carriage, followed by two guards. She had brought one of the College's maids along for the sake of propriety. Technically, Lady Mary should have accompanied her, but she always had an excuse for avoiding unpleasant duties.

Charles Lloyd had completed his apprenticeship, but had chosen to stay at the College, while Mr. Smith had one year of his apprenticeship still to go. Mr. Smith had a strong London accent. She suspected that both men were impressed by her social rank. One thing they agreed upon was that they should apply for further training, to broaden their skills.

She was shown into the magistrate's rooms. The old man, sitting behind a vast wooden desk, stood up as she entered. His green coat was ten years out of date. In a corner, a fashionably-attired man sat on a wooden chair. A uniformed constable loomed over him.

The magistrate invited her to take a chair, then resumed his seat. He looked hostile. "You're from the College, my lady?"

She remembered her lessons in elocution and spoke clearly. She stated her name and rank. "Yes. I am Lady Samantha Hampden, Chatelaine of the College of magicians. You asked for an expert witness."

"I see, my lady. The criminal here has been practising magic illegally. We caught him selling charms. He said that possession of his papers would allow the purchaser to succeed in any job application. Usually, we ignore these scoundrels. But he got greedy and set his price too high."

"May I examine his documents, sir?" She removed one black glove and touched the paper, delicately.

She frowned. "No. These documents are worthless. This person is not a magic user."

The man in the corner bleated a wordless protest. The policeman growled a warning and the prisoner subsided.

She handed the evidence to Charles, the more experienced of her guards. He frowned. "No, nothing." He hesitated, then passed it to Mr. Smith, who poked the document and shook his head.

The magistrate was unhappy. "So he's done nothing? We'll have to let him go?"

"He has not been practising magic, sir." Was the magistrate asking her advice? "Did he take money for these, sir? Did he claim they were endowed with magic? If so, he's a fraudster. He's been breaking the law ..."

To her relief, Charles intervened. "If you wish to prosecute, sir, you'll have to do so under the statutes for fraud. However, I cannot advise you on that point."

She smiled. "Would it help, sir, if I signed statement that these bits of paper have no value?"

"Yes, thank you," the magistrate said.

Charles told her, in an undertone, that he had never made out a witness statement, so she wrote it out herself. Her governess had advised her how to draft letters of various kinds, but never something like this. Finally, she was satisfied. "Charles, can you add your signature to mine?"

He read it quickly. "Yes, very elegant. And nothing left out." He signed it and handed it to the magistrate.

The old man read it through, then put it down. "It'll do. May I ask why the College send a woman, my lady?" he asked.

She put her glove back on. "They said I had a light

touch. But this petty scoundrel isn't worth the time of my male colleagues. He's already known to us. Good day to you, sir."

The guards escorted her back to the coach. "I'm impressed by your ability to put that magistrate in his place, my lady," Charles said.

"And by your legal expertise," Mr. Smith said.

St. James's Palace, morning of 20 April

The brick façade of the palace was three hundred years old. The interior, ill-proportioned and rambling, had been rebuilt fifty years before. Today, the Talkers assigned to the diplomatic service worked here. There was even a red-coated sentry at the gate. He presented arms as they approached.

Samantha's senior guard, Charles, explained they were on Guild business and the sentry let them through.

Samantha, accompanied by her maid and her two guards, found the young man in an alcove, sitting at a stout wooden desk that had been pushed against the wall. Paper, pencils and pens were laid in front of him. A series of leather-bound books were propped against the wall. He looked consumptive, like so many Talkers. He was wearing the usual magicians' midnight-blue jacket and trousers. Samantha noted that the jacket fitted him to perfection. He was fingering a pipe.

He turned to face her as she approached, then remembered his manners and jumped up. "Please, take a seat, my lady." She took the visitor's chair and he sat down again. He picked up his pipe again. It was empty. She wondered whether he ever lighted it.

"Good morning, sir. Your name is Rupert, I believe. And you handle the discourse with Osborne House. I hope I am not obstructing your work?"

"Not at all, my lady. Everything's quiet at the moment." He smiled. "Just about now, Her Majesty will open the despatch boxes sent overnight. An hour from now, she'll want to check the details and Fred will send me a lot of queries."

"I see. Her Majesty asked me to find a female Talker. Lady Mary was with me, and she gossiped. Are you familiar with Lady Mary?" His mouth turned down, which she took as evidence that he was indeed acquainted with Lady Mary. "The rumours spread, I now have ten applicants. All of them claim to be Talkers. But before I start the interviews, I need to know whether her Majesty wants a lady, to dine at her table, or an upper servant, at her beck and call? Is the Talker at Osborne House a gentleman?"

The young man put down his pipe. "Fred's College-trained, a member of the Guild. He's a gentleman. But there's a strict hierarchy at Osborne. The gentlemen take breakfast together in the breakfast room, but the aristocrats are served breakfast in their rooms. So we don't get to see the Queen. But at dinner, it's the aristocrats who dine together and we're the ones served in our rooms."

"So you don't get to see the Queen then, either."

"Not unless they're short of guests and they need someone to fill the place at the table." He smiled. "But perhaps we're lucky. Her Majesty's dinners are deadly dull. After dinner is worse, though. The gentlemen join the Queen and her ladies in the withdrawing room. Two hours of the most boring small talk imaginable."

She raised her eyebrows. "Lord Edward said the same. Thank you, you've been most helpful. Right. A widow, or a governess, good."

Rupert looked sour. "Fred and I manage well enough, my lady."

"Really? Lord Edward tells me that you complain of being overworked. You're on call twenty-four hours a day. If we send a lady down to Osborne house, she and Fred can take turns."

He was uncomfortable at being challenged. "Well, yes, that's one way of doing it."

The Toledano household, 23 April

The maid-servant who opened the door led Samantha to the dining room. Samantha turned to her guard. "Charles, wait in the hallway, please."

The family were middling wealthy. The father had described himself as a wholesale grocer, several steps above a corner-shop retail grocer. Samantha glanced round. The cream wallpaper was good quality, as were the dark red carpets. The dining table was covered with a pure white embroidered tablecloth. The family stood as Samantha entered. All three looked nervous. Were they afraid of her rank, or dreading her diagnosis? The mother and the daughter were wearing dresses of pale green silk. Both wore their hair in exquisite ringlets that must have taken an hour or more to prepare.

"Good afternoon, my lady. Won't you sit down?" Mrs. Toledano said, and sent the maid for some tea.

The daughter of the household, Alice, had rich black hair but was painfully thin. She said nothing and bent over the embroidery on her lap. Samantha judged the girl to be about her own age.

Samantha wondered how to begin. "Mr. Toledano, I asked for this appointment today because of this malicious gossip about your daughter. They say that your daughter hears voices in her head or is going mad." A quarrel had arisen at Alice's school, she had described the voices, and the stories grew until the College heard about them. "We have a policy of examining such cases."

54

Mr. Toledano shook his head. "My Alice hears voices. But she isn't mad."

Mrs. Toledano was more combative. "Why didn't the college send a gentleman?"

Samantha hid her irritation. "The man who usually does these interviews is an old grouch. I judged him to be quite unsuitable for an interview with a girl of Alice's age. But he did give me some questions to ask."

Alice looked up, but she kept fingering her embroidery. Samantha wondered whether she ever worked at it.

"Alice, is the message that you hear a religious one? Does the voice say you're sinning? Or does it say the world is sinning and you need to reform them?"

Mrs. Toledano was alarmed. "That sort of message would put her in the madhouse."

Mr. Toledano managed a smile. "No, it'd put my girl on speaker's corner in Hyde Park."

Alice shook her head. "No. It isn't a message. It's just young men talking."

Samantha went cold. "Are they bullying you? I've heard of cases like that. Aggressive bullies torturing the vulnerable."

Before Alice could reply, the maid brought in a porcelain tea set on a magnificent silver tray. There was silence until the maid poured out tea for them all and withdrew.

Alice ignored her cup. "No, my lady. They don't know I can hear them. They're asking each other, or themselves, oh, whether their shirts are clean enough. Or whether their jackets would be acceptable if they happened to meet a pretty girl. They – they don't think they'll have any success with the girls. So I'm eavesdropping, you see. And I can't help it."

Mr. Toledano poured out some tea. "Young men often think about pretty girls. Perfectly natural."

Alice looked directly at Samantha. "Behind the men,

there's something else. It's as if everyone in London is whispering at me. So I concentrate on the young men, because their thoughts are clear. That keeps out the whispers."

Samantha accepted a cup from Mr. Toledano. "I see. It is possible to keep the voices out, Alice. I have a series of mental exercises. Like religious devotions."

"I won't have any of that papist nonsense in my household," Mr. Toledano said.

"Mr. Toledano, these exercises were developed by people trying to meditate to keep out mundane distractions. They're quite practical."

Mrs. Toledano put down her teacup. "Alice needs to be kept busy. Something to distract her from -. Marriage would do that."

Mr. Toledano smiled. "Or attending university lectures, perhaps, my lady?"

Alice was working at her embroidery again, making tiny stitches, careful not to look at anyone. "I would like to meet them. These young men. Find out what they're really like."

Samantha was uncomfortable. "They *could* be apprentices at the college. But most talkers are dabblers. They don't even join the college."

Alice looked up. "Oh. I had wanted to meet other, er, magic users. People like myself. Find out whether they have the same problems."

Her mother was upset. "Really? You never told us, my dear. Most people want to avoid magic users."

"I might be able to introduce you to some people at the college," Samantha said. "But if you do meet them, you mustn't say you've overheard them. That would embarrass them. Very bad manners."

Alice smiled at this. "Unladylike."

Samantha smiled back. "Yes."

Alice put down her embroidery. "Could you teach me to Talk?"

"Well, I've only just started myself. Old Oswald tried to teach me, but - we're not really compatible. It would be best if someone at the college -."

"Can't you try?" Alice's eyes were wide, pleading.

"Do you mean here? Now?" Samantha turned to Alice's parents. "Do you object?"

Mr. Toledano was fascinated. He shrugged. "Not at all."

Samantha turned to Alice. "We should start by touching. Shaking hands would do." Shyly, Alice held out her hand and brushed Samantha's fingertips. "Now, shall I talk to you or shall you talk to me?"

"You talk and I'll listen. I know I can do that," Alice said.

Samantha hesitated a moment, then handed over her gold ring. "You must hold something valued by the sender, at least at first. Some Talkers give a book. Now ... listen. Think of the ring and its owner." She concentrated on the transmission exercises that old Oswald had tried to teach her. But what message should she send? She began fingering one of the flounces of her dress. She thought of the coming-out dress she dreamed of. But she would not be presented formally, nor wear that dress. She began mouthing the words. 'I shall never wear a coming-out dress. I am disappointed. I shall never-.'

Alice stroked the ring. "This is your only gold ring. But that's not your message ... Disappointment. I got that. At your presentation? No. Because you'll never get a coming-out dress." She smiled.

Mrs. Toledano gasped. "You've been presented, my lady? At court?"

Alice ignored this and jumped up. "Now it's my turn." She ran out of the room.

Samantha turned to Mrs. Toledano. "I have been presented to her Majesty, madam, but that was at Osborne House, not at court."

Mrs. Toledano put down her cup. "But if you've been presented, does that mean you could present my Alice?"

"Well, no. I couldn't present someone who was merely an acquaintance, you see. Only close family." Samantha sipped at her tea and waited.

Alice returned with a slim leather-bound book. "Take it. And tell me what I think of it!"

Samantha picked up the book and turned the pages. Troubadour poetry? Still holding the book, she began the Talker exercises. She gasped. "It's bosh. You think it's bosh." Alice's words were perfectly clear. "But why did you read it? I see. Your governess made you read it. Well."

Alice clapped her hands. "I did it."

Samantha smiled back. "Yes, you did." She bit her lip. "Mr. Toledano, I would like to offer Alice a place at the college as my companion. I'm lonely up there. I need someone my own age. Someone who isn't frightened by the thought of magic. I have Lady Mary with me, but all she thinks of is her next party and her next dress."

"Just the two of you?" Mrs. Toledano said. "Aren't there any other ladies there?"

"They're all married. They don't visit very often," Samantha said. "Lady Mary has a rule, about the evening meal. Unless there are at least five ladies at dinner, she makes the four of us dine in her room. Alice would make up the numbers."

Alice was fascinated. She and her mother exchanged a look.

"Are there any presentable men at the college?" Alice said.

Samantha frowned. How could she answer that? "There's the students, but they're all so young. Adolescent.

The fellows are all so old. But there's the graduates, doing research." She thought of Charles, waiting outside. All of the presentable men seemed to marry early. "I suppose the best looking man is Lord Edward." The thought surprised her.

"I agree that my daughter needs something to occupy her," Mr. Toledano said. "But not a paid companion. Not a servant."

"But if she stays at the college with me -."

Mrs. Toledano intervened. "Could she stay here, perhaps? And travel to the college every day?"

"She might find it inconvenient. But if she doesn't mind ... I have to attend balls and so on. It's part of my duties. I would expect Alice to attend them with me. Does she have a suitable dress?"

"Yes, certainly," Mrs. Toledano said.

Samantha smiled at Alice. "I need a companion of my own age. But I hope you'll be more than that: a friend."

Chapter 5 The Budget

The College, Breakfast room, evening of 25 April

The senior fellows of the College had assembled to discuss the accounts with Samantha. Once the details were agreed, it would be her task to present the budget to the Chancellor.

Lady Mary was sitting next to her, concentrating on her embroidery and ignoring what was being said.

Samantha had discovered that Lord Edward was responsible for the Guild – the researchers and the self-employed members.

Archibald Knight, the Master of the College, was responsible for the apprentices, the journeymen, and the salaried employees. Most of the money received from the government went to him. Just to confuse things, though, Edward was responsible for a couple of 'practical research' projects too, funded by the government.

Samantha had been dreading this meeting. "Gentlemen, I see that each of you has asked for an increased budget."

Lord Edward smiled at her. "My lady, you will find that all of us always want an increase in funds."

She ignored this sally. "Gentlemen, over the last few weeks you've brought me complaints of outdated research that's wasting us time and your money ... you've said that if this work could stop, you could save a fortune."

"Yes, indeed," Humphrey said.

"But I don't understand. Some of this scholarly research has been going on since my grandmother's day. It hasn't produced any results, but nobody has made any effort to stop it. Why?"

"Mainly because your grandmother approved it. Your aunt was reluctant to change anything," Lord Edward said. "In some cases, we wanted to abolish them years ago."

"But - does nobody have the power to stop this? Could I do it?"

"Yes, of course," Oswald said. "None of this research gets done unless there's a budget. If the chatelaine takes away the budget ..."

The oldest fellow, Humphrey, raised a hand. "I would like to cancel three projects – perhaps you can guess which."

"This research is worthy," Mr. Knight said.

Lord Edward sat back in his chair. "It may be worthy, but they're looking in the wrong place."

"Do I have the authority to do this?" Samantha asked. Everyone was watching her expectantly. She looked at Mr. Knight. Why hadn't he closed down this research? If he thought it was important, why didn't he speak up? He looked bored, not angry at her meddling. Was he passing the buck? Would he blame her if things went wrong? But the research was achieving nothing, good or bad.

"All you need is my signature? Do it, then. Unless you think a, a positive outcome is imminent."

Lord Edward smiled at her. "I would like to continue with the ongoing thunder-flash research."

"What on earth is that?" Samantha said.

"It's a close-order weapon. It's meant to produce a loud bang and a bright flash, but it's harmless. We'll use it to suppress riots. I've always hoped the research would pay off."

"You're an optimist, Edward," Humphrey said.

"I don't want to give up," Lord Edward said. "The improvements are small, but incremental."

"But that research is done by my students. It comes

from my budget. I want to see the back of it," Mr. Knight said.

"The students are more enthusiastic if they're told it is research and not practice," Edward said.

"More cautious too," Humphrey said.

"I'm all in favour of student research. Especially if it gives a practical result," Samantha said.

Mr. Knight sniffed. "What do you know of research, my girl?"

She was annoyed: "I have been attending lectures at the University of London, Mr. Knight. Some of the experiments we have to do are trivial. I realised that their main purpose was to teach the student how to write down his aims and record his results."

Mr. Knight opened his mouth to complain. She was saved by Oswald. "If a student kills himself, the notes will tell us what killed him."

Samantha was appalled. "Will that happen?"

Lord Edward shook his head. "Not in this research, no. We're asking the student to use his power in a more intelligent way, not use more power."

Samantha, relieved, turned back to the accounts. "Gentlemen, you have also asked me for money for new projects. You promised they wouldn't cost anything ... Yet now I see that your budget estimates have increased."

Humphrey smiled. "The budget is a pack of lies, my dear."

Samantha was annoyed. "If you want me to present this to the Chancellor, then at least the lies I tell must be plausible." Humphrey at least looked embarrassed.

She looked round at them all. "Gentlemen, you're trying to bully me into accepting these figures, but somehow you expect me to bully the Chancellor into accepting them."

Mr. Knight ignored her. "You're getting greedy, Humphrey."

Samantha glanced at Lady Mary for assistance, but the older woman concentrated on her embroidery and did not look up.

"It's the Prime Minister who's getting greedy," Oswald said.

"Gentlemen ..." Samantha said, but they took no notice.

"You need to be more aggressive, Archibald," Humphrey said.

Samantha was on the verge of tears. She remembered her lessons in elocution and speaking to an audience. She raised her voice slightly and spoke in icy patrician-to-plebeian tones. "Gentlemen, is it necessary for me to remind you that you are in the presence of a lady?"

Everyone hushed. Samantha waited with bated breath. If she had used that tone in her mother's presence, she would have been thrashed for impertinence. But if her mother had been alive, she would be here today, controlling this meeting.

Lady Mary's stitching was the loudest thing in the room. Mr. Knight looked angry. But nobody contradicted her.

Lady Mary tutted. "Samantha, my dear, a lady should never raise he voice. I am surprised at you."

"I beg pardon, Lady Mary."

"Your predecessor Lady Constance was always polite." Mr. Knight was at his most saturnine.

Lord Edward smiled. "She treated you like a recalcitrant five-year-old, Archibald. It was a pleasure to watch."

"Your behaviour was quite craven, as I recall," Mr. Knight said.

"Is it always like this?" Samantha asked, in an undertone. Lady Charlotte's success was becoming understandable.

Lady Mary spoke in a whisper. "Edward's flattery was quite adroit."

Samantha realised that the men were angry at each other, not with her. She was merely a spectator - or an umpire. Suddenly she realised how this game could be played. If it was played by Miss Hampden, a schoolgirl, she would be open to censure; but Lady Samantha, Chatelaine, was obliged to play boldly.

"Gentlemen, your attention, if you please." She tapped the account book in front of her. "Mr. Knight, the cost estimate for your section over the next quarter is the highest in the college. If you intend to cancel any projects, please let me know the estimated cost."

The Master of the College looked contrite. "Yes, Lady Samantha."

Humphrey raised a hand. "There are three projects that I have been hoping to implement for a long time, but it will take me a couple of months to make preparations. I would like to start them in the next quarter rather than this one."

"That sounds reasonable, Humphrey."

The old man smiled. "Thank you, my lady."

Samantha turned to Edward. "My Lord, your budget estimate has been reduced slightly, for which I thank you."

Mr Knight muttered something that might have been 'crawler'.

"Mr. Knight, do you have anything pertinent to say?"

"No, my lady."

Samantha glanced at Lord Edward, who winked. She ignored that and turned to the account book. "Shall we continue? The biggest single item in the accounts is the orphanages. The records are vague about the precise cost."

Lady Mary paused in her handiwork.

Lord Edward was embarrassed. "These are for children from a poor background who have displayed magic potential.

Sometimes parents of a middling background abandon their children, because the magic they do is dangerous or just embarrassing. The boys are fostered as soon as they're old enough. If they show promise, they usually go on to become apprentices, here in the college."

"And the girls?" She knew there were no female apprentices.

"They're taught domestic tasks and how to run a household. Some of them serve a couple of years as maids here at the College. They know a bit about magic, so they won't be frightened by it ..."

"It seems unfair."

He shrugged. "It's an old tradition. The girls stay long enough to learn how to run a household, then they get married. We give them a modest jointure. What would you put in its place?"

She felt he was hiding something and waited.

He bit his lip. "Some of the girls who work here are exploited by Guild members. In most houses, if a girl gets pregnant they're turned off. But here, because the child might have magical potential, the girl's sent back to the orphanage."

Samantha tried to understand what lay behind his words. "So, once we take them in, they're trapped?"

He shrugged. "We've always done it that way. I don't see how to end it."

She was dismayed. "That's monstrous. It sounds as if these 'orphanages' are no better than workhouses." But she thought that the 'orphanage' part of the project was acceptable. "But - none of this appears on the budget?"

"No. Caring for orphans is not the main purpose of the Guild. The details are all hidden."

Humphrey leaned forward. "There was a theory, seventy years ago, that the child of two magicians would have exceptional abilities. So the Master -."

Lord Edward grimaced. "Must we discuss that here? The theory was discredited years ago."

She decided it was time to change the subject. "Lord Edward, one project that I haven't been asked to close down is this search to find healers..."

Everyone relaxed. Lord Edward smiled. "Yes, my lady. I am eager to find magicians with a skill for healing. According to our theories, it should be one of the spectrum of skills."

Samantha decided this was a forlorn hope. "Anyone who attempted to use his magical energy to heal another person would exhaust himself. The healer would probably drop dead."

"That would certainly explain why we haven't found any," Oswald said.

Lord Edward was stubborn. "This search doesn't cost much. Not in money terms, anyway."

"Perhaps they're looking in the wrong place," Mr. Knight said.

"My lady, the resource involved is tiny," Lord Edward said.

Samantha, against her better judgement, backed down.

Interview with the Chancellor: 27 April

Samantha and Lord Edward met in the hallway of the College, dressed for travelling. They had an appointment at the Treasury with the chancellor. A few minutes later, Lady Mary descended the staircase to join them, wearing a grey cloak over a pink dress. She would accompany them for the sake of propriety.

At that moment, there was a knock on the door and a footman in an unusual livery walked in.

"Yes?" Lord Edward said.

"Lord Edward, sir? I'm sent by the chancellor. He says, sir, that the location of your meeting has been changed to the chancellor's private residence."

"Very well," Lord Edward said, and led the way down the steps.

"But where's that?" Samantha asked, as she stepped into the carriage. She took the forward-facing seat. Lady Mary took her place beside her.

Lord Edward sat down facing her. "Number eleven Downing Street, of course." He used his stick to bang on the roof and the carriage moved off.

The houses of Downing Street were four storeys high, faced with dark brick. Number eleven was the exception in that the ground floor was faced with white stucco. The constable guarding the door saluted the Earl as he descended from the carriage. "Good morning, my lord."

The doorman let them into a modest hallway. The chancellor's secretary was waiting for them. His prim expression, as he ushered them into the small dining room, showed what he thought of females meddling in chancellery business.

The Chancellor of the Exchequer, Sir Charles Wood, was sitting at the table, but he stood as the ladies entered. He had curly grey hair and a prominent nose, but the thing that Samantha particularly noticed about him was his polka-dot cravat.

He bowed. "I am delighted to meet you, Lady Samantha. Please, I beg of you, be seated. But aren't you a trifle young for such arduous duties?"

Samantha sat opposite the chancellor and put her big ledger on the table in front of her. Lady Mary sat at her left.

Lord Edward took the chair to Samantha's right. "You forget, sir, that her aunt and her mother both died suddenly. Her Majesty suspects foul play."

Sir Charles was startled. "Does she, indeed? I hope you

keep her well-guarded, Lord Radley. But can no-one teach the girl her duties?"

Edward smiled. "We could ask Lady Mary to give her a lead, sir."

Lady Mary gave an outraged gasp.

"Well, perhaps not." Sir Charles opened Samantha's ledger and turned to the last page. "I see. You expect to keep within last year's expenditure?"

"Yes, Sir Charles. However, we will not be able to do the same next year."

Sir Charles closed the book. "Never mind the budget. It's because of these Chartist riots, you see. The Prime Minister, Lord Russell, wants a hundred extra magicians, with combat skills, to protect the residences in Mayfair." Samantha knew that this district was the most expensive and exclusive in London, where the aristocrats lived. She was wondering how Lord Edward could find that many men when Sir Charles's next statement drove that from her mind.

"And Lord Russell is prepared to increase your budget to pay their salaries."

Samantha tried to calculate the amount involved. What could the guild do with that money!

"His Lordship sounds desperate," Lord Edward said.

The chancellor ignored this. "My lady, I ask that any increase in your budget would be matched by an increase in the number of magicians on duty in the West End."

Samantha turned to Lord Edward. "Can we find that many men, sir? In that case, Sir Charles, I give my word on that."

"I must stress that these men must be of assured loyalty," Sir Charles said.

Samantha wondered what he meant by that. Did he want the recruits to be gentlemen? Or of independent means? Could Lord Edward find that many?

Lord Edward coughed. "Why does Lord Russell need

this help from us?"

Sir Charles shrugged. "He's afraid of unlicensed magicians amongst the rioters. He believes that only you can stop them."

"He's worried about nothing," Lord Edward said.

"Lord Radley!" Lady Mary was angry. "Back in March, sir, the rioters were breaking windows in Berkeley Square. People were in fear of their lives. We could hear them, if you recall."

Samantha thought it best to intervene. "So all that Lord Russell wants from us is a few students standing in the rain in St. James's?"

"Not students, my lady. They must be fully qualified," Sir Charles said.

"How long will you need these men?" Samantha asked. "Because if it's temporary, less than a year, then it's solely within Lord Edward's remit and not the Chatelaine's at all."

Lord Edward shot her a look, as if to say he wished he had thought of that.

"That is a good question, my lady," Sir Charles said. "I wish I knew the answer."

Lord Edward shrugged. "The Chartists are a broken reed. That fellow O'Connor's a laughing stock. Lord Russell is, ah, worrying unduly."

Sir Charles was not impressed. "The Chartists may have given up, but these fellow-travellers haven't. Have you seen the police reports? The panic amongst the nobility may last a while yet." He sighed. "I think that we had better assume that we will need those guards on duty for at least twelve months."

"Very well, sir," Samantha said.

Lord Edward led the way down the steps and across the flagstones to the waiting carriage. Samantha and Lady Mary took their places. Lord Edward climbed in after them.

He was still angry. "These patricians merely want a

gentleman in a black suit loitering outside their homes. Our men are being asked to act as scarecrows."

Samantha nodded. "That was what I thought. But can we refuse?"

"Not during this crisis, surely," Lady Mary said.

Samantha accepted this. "But where can we find the hundred loyal and experienced magicians that the Prime Minister wants?"

Lord Edward looked up. "What if we transferred men from other duties? We have researchers here who don't do anything apart from dreaming of new ideas ..." He looked at Samantha. "Can we still ask for the increased budget on those terms?"

Samantha considered this. "If the researcher does his dreaming standing in the rain in Downing Street, I suppose my word is fulfilled."

"And what if they refuse?" Lord Edward said.

She smiled. "Then the forfeit their cosy rooms at the college. They can do their dreaming in some other household."

Lady Mary was vehement. "Yes, during this crisis, we could call it their patriotic duty."

Chapter 6 Orphanages

Cable Street, 5 May

Samantha climbed into the carriage and took the forward-facing seat. Her maid scrambled in and sat beside her. The girl had grown up at one of the orphanages, so she was unlikely to be shocked by anything she saw today. Oliver Crow climbed in after her and took the rear-facing seat opposite. One of her guards, Mr. Smith, followed and took his place, alongside Mr. Crow. The coach swayed as Charles, the last of her guards, climbed up to the box alongside the coachman.

Samantha nodded to Mr. Crow, who knocked on the roof and the coach moved off.

She looked at the man sitting opposite her. For years, he had been the College's manager for this disgusting research project. She was angry at Lord Edward for deliberately misleading her about its aims.

Oliver Crow was in his late thirties, slim, dapper, and dressed in Magician's black. His lapel badge indicated he specialised in glamour, otherwise known as charm or compulsion. She hated what this man had done.

He made an attempt at polite conversation. "You seem to have caused chaos amongst the College fellows, my lady."

Despite herself, she grinned. "It's not as chaotic as it looks. A couple of senior fellows asked me for money for new research. I said that was fine, so long as they could save money by scrapping worthless projects."

"So this sudden energy is just the water flowing after the logjam is cleared."

Samantha ignored this remark. "I want to look into this enterprise as well. The Master ensured that this project got precedence over everything else. He persuaded my aunt to throw money at it. Now I'm being asked to justify that, and I can't."

"I see, my lady."

"Each of these houses has ten highly-skilled magicians protecting them at any one time. In three shifts, Mr. Crow. They outnumber the women they're protecting. I can't justify that. The Prime Minister thinks the Chartists are still a threat. He wants me to send every trained magician to Mayfair to protect his aristocratic friends ..."

"Yes, I heard about that, my lady."

Samantha was watching the street outside, trying to judge the mood of the pedestrians. Their destination was in the East End. She spoke without looking at Mr. Crow. "How long have you been responsible for all of these – these orphanages, Mr. Crow?"

"Almost seven years, my lady. I was responsible for maintaining the charm, amongst other things."

Samantha was distracted. "Maintaining them?"

"Complex charms are like other complex spells. They take a powerful magician a great deal of effort to build up, but then a relatively modest magician can maintain them."

Was he weak? "I hope you have now stopped – maintaining them?"

"Yes, my lady. Your instructions were quite clear. But I hope you understand it will take weeks or months for the effects to disappear."

"Yes, I understand."

"The women are annoyed that you stopped their – visitors. Those visits were usually the only interesting event that week."

"I thought those visitors mistreated them."

"Not physically, never that. Most of the visitors were

perfect guests. Entertaining."

"But their whole way of life was degrading."

"It's the only one they know. If you don't approve of that, I suppose we could find a way to marry them off."

"Could you do that?" Samantha shook her head. "No. My mother wanted to marry me off to a stranger. I hated the idea. I won't do it to these poor women."

"Some of the women had favourites. But the charm meant that marriage was unthinkable to them. It was like a fairy-tale, something that didn't happen to real people. Now that the charm is wearing off, well, some of them find it thinkable after all."

"Oh. I see. That sounds promising."

The coach slowed and turned a corner.

She dreaded the answer, but she had to know. "How did the compulsion work?"

Mr. Crow glanced at Mr. Smith beside him, but the guard was concentrating on the people outside. "The most powerful of them gave the women a desire for lots of children. Strong, healthy children with magical abilities."

"I see." Samantha's grandmother had been like that, greedy for grandsons. "Sons rather than daughters, I suppose?"

"The magician who built up the charm thought in the long term. Daughters could give you grandsons."

"Oh. My."

"So, for these women, a miscarriage was a disaster. Heart-breaking. Ah – I suppose you know what a miscarriage is, my lady?"

"I can guess." Her own mother had suffered two, but she saw no need to tell Mr. Crow that.

"Half of the pregnancies in these orphanages end in miscarriages. The average for the mundane community is about one in ten. It's heart-breaking for these women. They were charmed into thinking their sons were vital for the survival of the country, yet they lost one after another. Although, if the pregnancy survives to, to term, the baby has a high chance of survival. I apologise for discussing such a distasteful subject, my lady."

"I did ask, Mr. Crow."

"I hope you don't mind me saying so, my lady, but I think Doctor Cornwell's whole project was a complete failure."

She agreed wholeheartedly. "The doctor's ideas were fashionable once."

"He ignored the evidence that was put in front of him. I visit these women regularly and I listen to what they say."

"And what do you hear, Mr. Crow?"

"The girls' main problem is boredom. The compulsion doesn't allow them to leave the houses. Their main occupations are their children and housekeeping. And reading." The carriage turned another corner. Mr. Crow hesitated, then rushed ahead. "The charms were set up, over sixty years ago, by someone who was old-fashioned even then. He never thought that women would want to read, so he didn't ban it. So when the women asked for permission to read, twenty years ago, there was no way to stop them. You can't amend those powerful charms, you see. You can only dismantle them and then build new ones. The Master at the time didn't think it was worth the trouble."

Samantha had not thought of that. "What do they read?"

"Lord Edward arranged for a subscription to the Weekly Mail."

Samantha sniffed. Her father had once described the Mail as 'mindless pap'. "That's all?"

"Well - whenever I visit a house, I bring them my copy of the London Times. I assumed Lord Edward wouldn't mind."

"I see. Well, I want you to arrange for each house to get

its own copy of the Times. No – get the Manchester Guardian instead."

Isn't that a bit radical?"

"So my father says. No, I've got a better idea. Let them read the Guardian and the Mail and let them compare the two."

Mr. Crow raised an eyebrow. "Yes, my lady."

"What else do they read?"

Mr. Crow hesitated. "The society magazines. The girls are fascinated by them. They've read all about Lady Mary's parties."

"Good God." Samantha would have described the society journals as mindless pap too.

The carriage came to a stop. Charles climbed down from the coachman's seat, opened the door and let down the folding step. "The house's own guards know who we are. There won't be any misunderstanding, my lady."

"Good. Mr Crow, wait until last, if you please."

Mr. Smith climbed out. "Clear." Samantha scrambled down and stood beside him. Her maid and Mr. Crow followed. She had practised this with her guards, to ensure they could leave the coach as quickly as possible without tripping over each other.

The building had a brick façade, darkened by years of soot from factory chimneys. The tall, narrow windows had a coating of grime. Keeping them clean would be a never-ending task.

Mr. Crow led the way across the pavement, climbed the three stone steps and knocked firmly on the door. Almost immediately, it opened and a ten-year old girl in a grey dress peeped out. So they were expected.

"Good morning, Phoebe," Mr. Crow said. "May we come in?"

"Yes, Mister Crow." The child opened the door wide.

Samantha and her maid followed Mr. Crow along a

hallway with a high ceiling. There was a faded green carpet underfoot and a series of three varnished wooden doors on each side, all firmly closed. At the far end was a set of double doors. Mr. Crow opened them and led Samantha inside.

This, Samantha guessed, was the dining room. It had none of the vulgar opulence that she had expected. She had imagined flock wallpaper, heavy curtains and velvet-covered couches. But, of course, the College could not afford opulence. Instead, the walls were painted white. The only decorations were the brass wall-sconces for the candles. The tall narrow windows were covered by lace curtains. Everything was neat and clean. Samantha decided that whoever was in charge here must be a martinet. The long wooden table had been pushed to the far wall, under the windows.

Twenty-five women stood in four rows, facing the door. They were all dressed in sombre grey woollen dresses. The child, Phoebe, scampered past Samantha and took her place in the back row.

Samantha measured up her charges. The five women in the front row were was clearly past child-bearing age. Samantha wondered whether they had spent all their lives here. Two women in the second row were heavily pregnant and three held silent babies. Three more were presumably in the early stages of pregnancy. Behind them were twelve girls, their ages ranging from two to fourteen. They all looked healthy. They stared at Samantha with a mixture of curiosity or fear.

Mr. Crow stepped up to the woman in the middle of the front row, with vigorous white hair. "Lady Samantha, this is Katie. She's in charge here. She makes all the day-to-day decisions."

Katie bobbed a curtsey. "Welcome to Cable Street, my lady."

Samantha thought it bizarre for her to be formally

introduced to this woman. Her training in courtesy took over. "Good morning, Katie. This place looks well-run. You keep it clean. You all look well fed. Healthy."

"Thank you, my lady. We're grateful that you came to visit our home. Lady Constance never thought we were worth her trouble."

Samantha felt a moment's shame. She had come out of curiosity, not to help.

Mr. Crow interrupted. "The old doctor had some strange ideas, but he understood that if you want healthy children you need healthy mothers. He imposed a well-balanced diet. The place is kept warm. The women are kept safe."

"Safe? From their visitors?" But there were none of the cuts or bruises that Samantha had expected. The women did not look cowed. Instead they looked truculent, as if they resented her presence. "What's wrong? Why are you staring at me like that?"

"We heard you were going to throw us out into the street. With only one way to earn a living," Katie said.

Samantha was horrified. How had that rumour reached them? And who had started it? "No, there's no suggestion that you'll be evicted. I had hoped that you'd all learn trades, so you could earn your own way, and set up on your own."

An older woman, standing next to Katie, glared. "But we don't want to leave. This is our home. This is all we know."

Samantha realised that this woman was too old to learn anything new. That was another layer of complexity to this problem. The younger women apparently shared this fear, even if the idea of confinement under Katie's rule was not attractive.

Samantha tried to change the subject. "Do any of them have magical skills, Mr. Crow?" Anything of practical value, I mean?"

"Yes, half of them have very weak powers. None of them are Talkers -."

"You didn't bother to train them? Strengthen their powers?"

Mr. Crow shrugged. "Their powers posed no risk to them or their household. Tradition bans female practitioners. Lord Edward saw no reason to change that."

The usual double standards, she thought. Men with weak powers were encouraged, women with moderate powers were held back. "Yes, I understand. You all look wonderfully healthy."

At that, the older women's expressions changed. They looked like housemaids caught sweeping dust under the carpet. Had Samantha looked like that when her mother caught her trying to hide a book on magic? "What's going on here? What are you hiding from me?" Her tone was more challenging than she intended.

Katie exchanged a look with Mr. Crow. "You're better at explanations than I am, Mr. Crow."

Mr. Crow, who looked equally guilty, coughed. "Lady Samantha, three of the women here have weak Healing powers."

"They're Healers? And nobody told me?"

"Their powers are very weak. They can heal minor cuts and grazes, but even that leaves them exhausted. Lord Edward was only interested in real Healers who could rebuild a man as good as new."

He indicated to the blonde woman in the second row holding her baby. "This is Agnes. She has two sons. This is her first daughter." He turned to two of the slim women in the second row, a brunette and a redhead. This is Bettie. Her first son was taken for adoption a few months ago. And this is Dianna. She suffered a miscarriage, but she's recovering now."

78

"And they're good with colds, don't forget," Katie said. "If we heal the first child who catches cold, it doesn't spread."

Samantha listened with rising indignation. "But surely, with training, their powers could be increased. They could save lives."

"Who's to train them? Bettie here is the most powerful we have," Mr. Crow said.

That gave Samantha pause. She was still thinking through the implications of her discovery. With Healers, she could save lives. People would be thankful for magicians instead of hating them. And if these women could be classified as magicians, even if it was only as apprentice magicians, then they could earn their keep in a way that she found acceptable.

"Perhaps I could take these girls to the Free Hospital. We could find out how much they can achieve with their limited powers. And perhaps we can find a way to increase their powers."

Agnes, nursing her baby, looked more truculent than ever, but Bettie and Dianna were bouncing with excitement.

St. James's Palace, Afternoon of 6 May

Lord Edward accompanied Samantha and Alice to the Talkers' common room in old St. James's Palace. Eight ladies had been escorted into the common room and now waited, standing around the table. Lord Edward looked embarrassed, clearly out of place amongst so many women. Lady Mary had flatly refused to attend.

All of the ladies were older than Samantha. She guessed that they all had a tale to tell. Three widows, an abandoned wife, another living in genteel poverty with her husband, and three spinsters living with their parents, 'on the shelf'. All of them were educated as far as convention allowed. They qualified as ladies and respected Lady Mary as a leader of fashion. All hoped that this adventure would change their lives. Their dresses were as varied, in colour and quality, as their backgrounds.

"Please, ladies, be seated," Samantha said. She took the armchair for herself and the ladies followed her example. Only then did Lord Edward take his place at Samantha's right hand. The Talkers on duty were curious but shyly keep their distance. Only Rupert, in daily contact with Osborne House, and Edward, patron of the Guild, listened in. A male servant brought them tea.

Samantha attempted a smile. "Good morning, ladies. All of you have demonstrated your potential as Talkers. You have already worked out who works best as your partner. I will need one member of each team here, while the other will be stationed with her Majesty. I asked you here today so you could see the place where you would work."

The dowager Baroness Inismore was wearing the most expensive purple dress. Her son was a member of the Irish peerage. "When are you going to tell us who will go to Osborne House, young woman? And why do you need so many teams?"

Samantha gathered her courage. "It would be unfair to keep you on duty without a break. That would disrupt your social lives. I am told that her Majesty's ladies-in-waiting serve one month on duty and three months off. So I had planned to follow a similar pattern." The unspoken reason for so many teams was that she expected at least three of these women to fail.

The dowager looked displeased. Samantha wondered whether she always looked like that. She was rescued, unexpectedly, by Rupert. "You must understand that her Majesty visits Sandringham and Windsor. It would be most helpful if a Talker could travel there, a few days in advance of her Majesty, to prepare for her arrival."

"Don't we do that now?" Lord Edward asked.

"Yes, my lord, but the Talker has to be diverted from other duties. It would be most helpful if one of these ladies could be assigned to that task." Rupert smiled. "And the Queen is buying a palace in Scotland. They intend to visit the place in the autumn. Someone will have to travel up there."

"It appears that we will have a lot of travelling to do," the eldest widow said. She sounded pleased.

The dowager straightened up. "Before we go any further, young lady, I wish to make it clear that we have all decided that we wish to be treated as professional magicians. We are nor amateurs or – day workers."

Samantha felt as if a trapdoor had opened under her feet and she was falling, falling, probably with a snake pit at the bottom. She wondered whether the ladies had really discussed it amongst themselves or whether this dreadful old woman had bullied them into it.

One of the unmarried ladies leaned forward. "I believe it is illegal for magicians to accept payment unless they are members of the Guild."

Lord Edward was annoyed. "The Guild cannot bestow on you the status of professional magicians. You have not received any training."

The dowager glared at him. "Young man -."

Samantha hurried to interrupt. "Can't we take these ladies on as apprentices?"

Lord Edward frowned. "The Master would hate that."

"My lord, we must do something to give these ladies a legal status. If the worst came to the worst, we could create a new Guild for them."

Lord Edward smiled. "The Master would have a stroke if you told him that. But things aren't that desperate. Yes, we can take them on as apprentices. And pay them an apprentices' salary."

"A salary? Not a wage?" the eldest widow was suspicious.

"Certainly, madam," Lord Edward said.

"We all want to study," the dowager said. "Starting with the safety aspects. From what Lady Samantha told me, I nearly killed myself in my attempts to Talk."

Lord Edward nodded. "Certainly. I'll give you a reading list."

Samantha tried to regain control. "I had planned to send you to Osborne House, Lady Inismore, for a period of one month. Before you go, however, there's the question of your dress. At Osborne House, her majesty might invite you to dinner. So you will need to take your evening dress with you."

Lady Inismore nodded. "That will not be a problem, Lady Samantha."

Samantha looked round the table. She guessed that some of these women were on the edge of poverty. They could not afford splendid new dresses.

"At Osborne House, you will be representing the Guild. I could buy dresses for you -."

"I will not accept charity," the abandoned wife said. The other women, by their expressions, seemed to agree.

Rupert turned his pipe over in his hands. "The male apprentices get a suit of clothes when they arrive. It's day wear, but perhaps the same principle applies ..."

Samantha tried again. "If the Guild supplied the cloth, could you make it up?" The male apprentices wore grey trousers and black jackets. "I suggest a grey skirt and black jacket." The women still looked doubtful. "You could pay me back, after you've worn the outfit at Osborne House."

Once again, the dowager disapproved. "Grey? I do not wish to be mistaken as a servant ..."

"You could discuss the style amongst yourselves," Samantha said. "Lady Mary says that a spencer jacket is quite fashionable. And she likes the idea of contrasting colours. The cut of the jacket would be stylish, of course."

The dowager was impressed. "Wait - do you mean Lady Mary Clifton? The one who's in the fashion magazines? Do you know her? Well!"

Samantha brazenly exaggerated her relationship with Lady Mary. "Yes, she's a cousin."

She smiled at the other ladies. "I would like you to come here regularly, once a week, to practice your skills and get to know the routine here."

"Excuse me, Lady Samantha," Lord Edward said. "But I would like to send two of these ladies to Windsor Palace for a couple of days, to examine the accommodation available to them. I suspect that her Majesty will be moving there in two or three months."

The College, evening of 6 May

At dinner, Old Oswald asked how Samantha's day had gone. She mentioned her visit to St. James's Palace.

Mr. Knight was seated two places to the left of Samantha, with Mrs. Knight and Lord Edward in between. He leaned forward to talk across them. "Lady Samantha, Edward has been telling me of the demands made by these women. He says they want us to treat them apprentices. And he says you agreed."

"Well, yes, sir."

"What were you thinking of, you foolish child? Why didn't you ask your betters before you made this absurd decision? Apprentices? I refuse to accept them in this hall. Everyone knows women haven't the tenacity to last a four-year course."

Samantha was mortified. Mr. Knight's voice was rising. Half the room could hear. The students at the long table turned to look. Why couldn't he choose a private place for his reprimand?

Mr. Knight took a gulp at his wine. "Even worse, if they pass their finals, we'll have to concede them a place at the high table."

Lord Edward spoke quietly. "Haven't you just contradicted yourself, Archibald?"

Mr. Knight ignored this. "And then the whole story will get into the newspapers. We suffer enough notoriety already. What were you thinking of, girl? You've embarrassed the whole College with this absurd notion."

Samantha wished he would burst into flames and disappear. She realised that she knew the fire spells. She could set his coat on fire. Her powers were not very strong but his waistcoat would have a nice hole in it.

"You ought to tell these women that their demands are impossible," Mr. Knight said.

Samantha imagined summoning up the energy and saying the words. The temptation grew. She could not stand it any longer. She jumped to her feet and ran from the room.

In the atrium she stopped, breathing hard. For a blessed moment she was alone. Five minutes later, Lord Edward walked in, followed by Samantha's maid.

"Are you all right? Lady Mary burst into tears and fled to her room. I thought you'd done the same."

Samantha looked up. "No. Do you think I've embarrassed the College, my lord?"

"Not half as much as Archibald has done, right now."

"But the newspapers ..."

"They're going to hear about these female Talkers whatever we do. I only hope that we can report a boring success rather than a scandalous failure. Besides, much worse can happen. The pair of us could return to Osborne House and tell her Majesty that we can't find a single female talker."

She shuddered. "Yes. Those women want some sort of recognition and status. It seems a reasonable request."

"Yes. This would be a lot simpler if their request wasn't reasonable – we could just say no. Lady Samantha, probably half of them will drop out. But one or two of them will prove stubborn enough to stay the course. Ah - I asked Oswald to give them his safety lectures. He agreed."

"But the Master refused to teach them."

"He mainly teaches the first year students. He shows them *how* to study. Your ladies seem to be past that stage. Just give them a reading list and let them get on with it." He frowned. "Archibald deserves a flogging for speaking to you like that. He ought to apologise in front of everyone."

"No. That would embarrass me all over again."

"You're sure?"

"Will he do it again?"

"I'll make sure he doesn't. He needs to understand that you're doing this at the Queen's request. It's not some whim of your own."

"Yes."

"He also needs to remember that if he offends the Chatelaine his budget could vanish."

Green Road Orphanage, 7 May

The carriage came to a stop outside a building on the misnamed Green Road. Charles scrambled down from his place beside the coachman, unfolded the steps, and held out a hand to help Samantha down.

Samantha hesitated, then accepted. She wanted to prove that she did not need help. But it was rude to ignore an act of simple politeness. Alice followed, and Charles gallantly helped her down too. This time, Samantha thought it was safe to bring Alice with her. She was confident there was nothing here to shock the girl.

The smoke from the chimneys was prevented from escaping by the fog. The grime attached itself to everything.

Mr. Crow led them into the house and along a familiar plain corridor. Even the carpet was the same faded green. He ushered them into the house's dining room.

The twenty-eight women waiting for them were standing in four rows, mature women at the front, children at the back. Three were heavily pregnant and two silently nursed babies. They were all dressed in plain grey woollen dresses.

The women in the front row all had vigorous white hair. Mr. Crow stepped up to the woman in the centre of the row. "Lady Samantha, this is Nancy. She's in charge here. She has two sons and two daughters." Mercifully, he did not go on to list the woman's miscarriages.

Nancy curtsied to her guest. "Good morning, Lady Samantha." She spoke with a cockney accent.

"Good morning, Nancy." Samantha measured up Nancy and realised that she was in trouble. The woman knew what she was going to say. Did these communities of women have a network of secret Talkers as well as Healers?

She took a breath. "Nancy, I was at Cable Street two days ago. Yesterday I took Katie's healers to visit the charity hospital. They helped care for lots of children. Mr. Crow says you have three Healers here. I want -."

"I don't care what you want, Lady Samantha," Nancy said.

Samantha, astonished, glanced at Mr. Crow. Weren't these women supposed to be under a compulsion to obey? Perhaps the long-dead magician who created the spell had thought that obedience did not require politeness.

Mr. Crow shrugged, equally bemused.

"All of our Healers have gone through a pregnancy," Nancy said. "They decided that they could best use their skills by helping other women with the same hardship."

"Other women? Outsiders? You –."

"Yes, my lady. We help the local community. As midwives, you understand. The problem cases."

Samantha was still trying to understand the implications. "You go out to them?"

"Them as needs our help comes to us," Nancy said. "We don't go outside."

That was clever, Samantha decided. The charm must have included a compulsion to care for children and pregnant women. Nancy had twisted that to include the local community, not just women coerced by the college. Samantha wondered whether the Green Road Healers had decided to help the local women or whether Nancy had made the decision for them.

"But – nobody ever noticed?"

"Who notices what women do?"

Who indeed? "So you run a - midwife charity"

"It isn't a charity. We don't approve of charities here. Money that's thrown at the poor by their 'betters' usually gets wasted. No, we help each other. Mutual assistance."

Samantha decided that there was something wrong with Nancy's East End accent. Was she exaggerating it to annoy her upper-class visitor? Samantha was irritated. She refused to give up.

"Nancy, I took Katie's healers to the charity hospital yesterday. They did a lot of good, despite being so weak. They helped children, healing their cuts and bruises. With a bit of training they could grow stronger, save lives. I – the hospital - needs every healer I can find. But one of them, Agnes, refused to enter the hospital. She said it was a sink of putrefaction. I thought – if I could send her here, from time to time, to help you out, perhaps you could occasionally send some of your Healers to the hospital?"

Nancy did not like that at all. She was as stubborn as

Samantha, and knew that any compromise would erode her authority. Samantha glanced at the women in the second row. She smiled. Two of the women smiled back, clearly delighted at the thought of escaping from Nancy's control for a few hours, even if it meant visiting a hospital.

Alice stepped forward. "Perhaps we could discuss it over a cup of tea, Nancy?"

Chapter 7 Whitechapel Hospital

20 May

Samantha followed the apprentice Healer, Bettie, into the hospital's operating theatre. She had expected a foul stench and blood-splattered walls, but instead she found a small rectangular room with a scrubbed wooden table and three tiers of varnished wooden benches along each wall. High windows let in the afternoon sunlight. Perhaps students attended important operations, but today the benches were empty.

Alice had begged for permission to wait in the corridor outside, under Charles's protection. Charles was looking bleak too, so Samantha had agreed.

"I thought I would hate the operations," Bettie said. "But once you start the healing, it's fascinating. Hello, Doctor Jones."

A tall, elegant man turned to face her. He was presumably a gentleman, but he had taken off his jacket. He began rolling up his shirtsleeves.

"You must be Lady Samantha. The Guild's Chatelaine. I'm Simon Jones, the surgeon. I'm grateful for these Healers you've found for me." He smiled.

Samantha decided that he could be quite charming. "I never thought that they could do anything as complicated as a surgical operation, doctor."

"Oh, I do the surgery, they do the patching up. But, working together -. Their skills have limits, yes. I'm pushing them as far as I can, to find out how we can make full use of those skills."

A big brute of a man with a swarthy complexion entered the room, pushing a trolley on which a man lay. The brute lifted the patient onto the wooden table. The man's lower right leg was covered in bloodstained bandages.

"Thank you," Jones said. He turned to Samantha. "This fellow's foot was crushed in a factory accident. The bones were reduced to splinters. I would have to push each bone back together before the healer could start work. It's just too intricate for your girls. I'm going to have to amputate, with the assistance of your girls. Usually, the most dangerous part of the operation would be stitching the wound back up again, but I won't have to do that because the girls will do their magic for me. For my purposes, an artery stitched together is just another three-inch wound. Quite within your girls' capabilities."

Samantha swallowed. "I see."

"With your girls' help, he'll be ready for his peg leg in two or three weeks. Without them, it would be a month at least."

"What's your – success rate?" She did not want to mention the dread word 'gangrene' with the patient listening.

"Very high." He smiled. "Some might call it miraculous. Whatever your girls do, it's more than just sticking wounds back together."

The two Healers, Bettie and Dianna, helped each other to put on clumsy paper pinafores. To Samantha's surprise, Jones allowed himself to be tied into one too.

Samantha smiled. "I heard about this, but I didn't really believe it."

Jones grinned. "You get one too. Your girls refused to get blood on their dresses. They said it smelt of putrefaction. So I had to dig out cotton pinafores for them. But your girls wanted me to wash them every day. I decided it was cheaper to buy paper ones and burn them."

Bettie tied the waist band of Samantha's pinafore.

"Even the cords are just twisted paper, my lady."

The big brute who had pushed in the trolley attached broad leather straps across the patient's shoulders and waist, pinning his arms to his sides. Then he fastened the man's ankles.

Samantha watched, appalled. "Doctor Jones, who is this man?"

Jones looked up, surprised. "He's the Lascar. He came from India originally. His name's Solomon or something, but nobody can pronounce it properly, so it's simplest to call him that."

The man looked at Samantha. "It's pronounced Sal-man, Doctor Jones." He sounded resigned.

"That's it." Jones used scissors to cut the man's trouser leg away. More delicately, he trimmed away the bandages.

"Stand back, my lady." He put a wad of leather into the man's mouth. "Bite down, hard. Ready everyone?" Salman leaned forward and held the man's leg down. Jones picked up his scalpel and made the first incision.

The man on the table spat out the wad and screamed. Everyone ignored him, even Bettie. Samantha was shocked. "Shut up!" The man ignored her. She stepped forward and looked down at him.

"Stop that!" The man opened his mouth and screamed again.

Samantha, on the edge of panic, realised what she had to do. She hated to use a compulsion spell, but ...

"Look at me. I am a magician. I can enter your mind and take over control. You will feel me doing it. And you are going to hate me for it. That hatred is the most important thing in the world. The only thing in the world."

The screaming stopped. Samantha looked up to see that everyone was looking at her in astonishment, even Salman.

Fear made her curt. "Get on with it, doctor. I can't keep

91

this up for long."

She looked back down at the man on the table, who stared back. She knew she was doing something right, but what? Hatred, that was it.

"The dragoons. You hate the dragoons," she said. The man nodded. Everyone in the East End of London hated the dragoons. "That hatred is the most important thing in the world. You hate Lord Russell. He sent in the dragoons." The man nodded. "You hate the government. They supported Lord Russell." Another nod. "And you hate Le Marchant, because he's responsible for Home Affairs."

The man looked uncertain. Perhaps the ignorant fool had never heard of Le Marchant. "And you hate the Guild, because they support the Home Office." The man nodded. "You hate the College of Magicians. And so you hate me, because I'm the Chatelaine of the College."

The man looked up at her. "No," he said.

Samantha felt another twinge of panic. If her compulsion stopped working, the man would realise he was on the operating table and he would start screaming again. Jones murmured something to Bettie about the artery and the Healer murmured an acknowledgement and leaned forward.

Samantha stared down at the man again. "You hate the magicians, yes? Everyone hates the magicians. They work alongside the dragoons. And you hate the dragoons ... and Lord Russell. And the politicians ... And the magicians. They back up the dragoons. That hatred is the most important thing in the world ... And I'm a magician. I'm in your mind, twisting your thoughts. You can feel it. And you hate that." The man nodded. "So of course you hate me. Because I'm twisting your mind. Right?"

The man looked trustfully up at her. "No. I can't hate you, lady. You're beautiful."

Samantha lost her temper. "Listen, fool! My name is

Lady Samantha Hampden. My father is a government official. I'm the Chatelaine of the College of Magicians. If I tell you to hate me then you'll damn well do what you're told and hate me!"

The room was silent. She looked up to see that everyone was looking at her. "You can stop now," Jones said. "We're finished. Thank you."

Bettie leaned forward and stroked the stitches on the man's stump. As she did so, the ugly red inflammation faded to a more healthy-looking pink. She looked up at Samantha. "I can't heal it completely, but the doctor says that because of us, it'll take twenty days to heal rather than thirty."

Dianna looked exhausted. "We could come back tomorrow, and encourage the healing along, but there's always more injured people arriving."

"You're not too tired?" Samantha asked. She was responsible for these girls.

"They have to pace themselves," Jones said. "Three operations a day, with an hour in between. Or a score of deep gashes and cuts. Perhaps more minor cuts and grazes ... Speaking of operations, can you come back and do that again next time? It made my task so much easier."

Samantha was horrified. "Out of the question. I have an appointment with the Cabinet tomorrow. The Master of the College wants more resources; he needs my support ..." Yet she couldn't let these poor men go on suffering, not when she could prevent it. "Bettie, are there any girls with Charm in Cable Street?"

"There's Hettie," Dianna said. "She's ever so jealous of us coming here."

The Lascar, Rahman, began undoing the straps that held the patient to the table. Samantha walked over to him. "Mr. Rahman, how did you come here? To London, I mean?"

He smiled. "When my father died, the moneylender said I had to pay my father's debts. So I jumped on a ship going to London. When I got here, I tried to find a place on a ship going home again. While I waited, I found a temporary job." He smiled. "I'm still here."

The Toledano Household, 21 May

They all smiled at each other over their teacups. For Samantha, this was a bizarre contrast to the horrors of the day before.

Samantha summoned up her courage. "Mr. Toledano, Alice has been a great help to me in all sorts of ways. She accompanies me everywhere."

"Alice has told us what it's like in the college. All those young men. She says you need her company," Mrs. Toledano said.

"Yes, madam. But the Master of the College has given me permission to find a Talker of my own, to relay my messages back to the College, or to St. James's." She swallowed. "I would like your permission for Alice to be trained as my Talker."

Mr. Toledano frowned at his daughter, who smiled demurely back. "Alice needs something to occupy her, that is true."

"She tells me all about the young men she meets at the College," Mrs. Toledano said.

"Mother!" Alice said.

Samantha cradled her fragile cup in both hands. "My proposal is that I recruit Alice as a hired companion," Samantha said. "That would formalise her status at the College. As my talker, she would have to stay there twenty-four hours a day."

"No, my lady," Alice said. "I want to sign on as an apprentice, on equal terms with all the others. And study

94

magic."

Samantha was annoyed. "You didn't tell me you wanted to be an apprentice. It's a big step. Too big."

"An apprentice? No," Mrs. Toledano said.

Mr. Toledano coughed. "My dear, you have to admit that Alice is a bit flighty. And she did say she wanted to keep the whispering at bay. Working there seems to be therapeutic. I think that she needs the discipline that a course of study would bring."

"But I want my Alice to get married, not train as an apprentice," Mrs. Toledano said.

Samantha recovered her wits. "We could allow for that. If Alice married, her apprenticeship would end."

"I hadn't thought of that," Alice said. She looked from her mother to Samantha and back again. "All right," she said.

Samantha was suspicious. Alice had given in too easily.

"But what will she wear? Will she have to leave her fine dresses behind?" Mrs. Toledano said.

"Alice would have to accompany me everywhere. So she would have to dress accordingly. Just as she does now."

Alice disapproved. "The queen's talkers chose grey and black. Can't I wear the same?"

Samantha nodded. The talkers had chosen a neat enough outfit. "Although that's for day wear. If I attended an appointment that required I wear an evening dress, Alice would too,"

Green Road Orphanage, 24 May

Mr. Crow led Samantha and Alice up the steps to the Green Road orphanage. A twelve-year-old girl with brown hair, wearing a plain grey woollen dress, opened the door for them.

"This is Dora," Mr. Crow said. "She's fairly new here.

When her fire-starting skills developed, six months ago, her parents sold her to us." He glanced at Alice. "Does that shock you? Do you mind me telling your story, Dora?"

Dora closed the door behind them and smiled a gap-toothed smile. "I was working in a bar. It was a bit posh, they sold brandy. If anyone spilt any, I'd set it on fire. They used to laugh."

"I heard about it, you see," Mr. Crow said. "I thought she might set the place on fire. And back then, I was under orders to, er, recruit any magic users. But when I approached her parents, they said they'd sell her to a brothel unless I outbid them."

Alice gasped.

"You needn't be worried," Dora said to Samantha. "They were bluffing. What house would take a girl who could turn the customers into toast?"

Mr. Crow smiled. "Men who visit brothels sometimes have unusual tastes, but I doubt if any have that one." Dora grinned at this sally.

Samantha was shocked. "Dora, are you happy here? Less unhappy than you were at home?"

Dora frowned in concentration. "It's boring. Dusting and washing and cooking. Less interesting than working in a pub. But at least no-one threatens to hang you as a witch." She grinned. "But there's no brandy."

Samantha smiled back. Dora clutched her hand. "They say you asked one of the Cable Street girls to help defend her home. Apprentice pay and everything. I'd like to do that. Allowed to practice my skills."

Samantha nodded. "See to it, Mr. Crow. Find out if her skills are adequate."

"Yes, my lady."

Dora, satisfied, turned and made her way down the plain corridor with its familiar faded green carpet.

Samantha paused. "Mr. Crow, a moment, please. Last

time we were here, Nancy let slip that she knew why I had come. And now Dora has heard about Lucy. Do you think that these houses have a Talker too?"

"It's possible, my lady. But how would she find a recipient in the other houses? She would have to meet them in person, or at least receive a gift from them. And if somebody knew how to bring a gift, why bother with a Talker? If it's happening at all, my guess that the use of charm is involved."

"You knew about this, didn't you?"

Mr. Crow shrugged. "I had my suspicions. But what was the point of asking questions? They would just lie to me. And Lord Edward didn't want ... complications."

"No. I need to know. These evasions have got to stop."

Dora ushered them into the house's dining room. This time the visit was less formal. The women looked up, then continued their daily routine of cleaning, dressmaking, and laying the table for dinner.

Nancy the housekeeper, standing aloof from this bustle, bobbed a curtsey. "Would you like a cup of tea, my lady, Mr. Crow?" She led the way to a corner. Three faded armchairs were positioned around a low table bearing a tea set.

Samantha seated herself. "Thank you. Nancy, I would like to speak to the girls who can use a compulsion."

Nancy did not waste any time on denials. "Yes, my lady. We have two girls who've meddled with charm, no more than that. Dora, could you fetch Janet and Carol please?"

"I'm worried about Dora," Nancy said. "She boasted about her skills until she learned she was no different from the rest of us. She boasts of that bar she worked in. Now she wants to protect us! She's eager to learn her letters, though. And she doesn't skimp her chores, I'll grant her that."

Samantha poured some tea into her cup. "Mr. Crow,

that is one thing I don't want to change. If a child with magic skill is abandoned by her parents, I want you to take her in."

"How can I judge when a girl is at risk from her own parents?" He sighed. "I'll do what I can, my lady."

Nancy poured some milk into her tea. "You could offer to pay for the girl's schooling. And if her parents say no ..."

Dora returned, accompanied by two young women. "These are Janet and Carol," Mr. Crow said. Janet had rich black hair while Carol was a redhead.

Samantha subjected them to a cold look. "When I first came here, Nancy said she knew why I had come. And now Mr. Crow says he knows how you carry messages from one house to another. Well?"

Both women adopted a crestfallen look. Neither attempted a denial. Guilty as charged, Samantha thought. She wondered how she had done it. Was she using some form of compulsion without knowing about? Did she have Lady Mary's patrician arrogance? Or had they surrendered as a result of the outrageous half-truths she had told?

"They meant no harm, my lady," Nancy said.

"Perhaps. But I want to know how they did it," Samantha said. "Well?"

"Charmers have a spell that makes people ignore them," Mr. Crow said. "Apprentices call it the invisibility charm, but of course it's nothing of the sort. It merely tells passers-by that we aren't the people they're looking for, move along, go about your business." Janet nodded in acknowledgement.

"Charmers use the spell when they're asked to follow a suspect," Mr. Crow said.

Samantha shook her head. "But how did they get out? I thought the charm told them to stay indoors, inside the – house."

"So did I," Mr. Crow said, sipping at his tea.

Janet shook her head. "No, miss. My lady. It isn't like

that. The charm tells us to stay inside the community. We mustn't leave."

"We don't want to leave. We're safe here," Carol said. "But these ten houses – they're all part of the same community. They all have the same purpose. Serving our country."

"Yes. So you see, there's nothing to stop us from going from one house to another, because we're not leaving the community," Janet said.

"They're barrack-room lawyers, every last one of them," Samantha said.

"So it would seem," Mr. Crow said.

"How long has this been going on?" Samantha asked. Both girls looked blank. "Since forever," Janet said. "Cook did it, but she said it got boring and cooking was more interesting."

"The girls at Cable Street, they get better fashion magazines than us, so we do a swap," Carol said.

"I want this to stop, right now. The streets are too dangerous," Samantha said.

Mr. Crow raised a hand. "My lady, you do us an injustice. Most parts of the East End are just as safe as the streets of the West End. Well - if you avoid the side alleys. And if you travel in daylight. I believe that young ladies such as yourself are allowed to walk around the West End?"

Samantha was annoyed. How had they come to be discussing the proper conduct for young ladies? "Only if they have an escort. A servant. Or two girls together." She exchanged a glance with Alice.

Everyone watched her in silence until Alice coughed. "What are you going to do, my lady?"

Samantha took a sip at her tea. How could she stop these women running errands? "The first thing to do is visit the post office. Arrange for regular collections. I want each of these houses to be able to send letters to each other. Yes, and to me at the College as well."

"But there's no fun in that," Carol said.

"What you're doing is too dangerous. And I'm responsible for you," Samantha said.

Mr. Crow sipped at his tea. "I'm afraid they're going to defy you, my lady. You told me to remove the compulsion. In a few weeks its effects will have worn off. You could ask me to reintroduce the spell. Or you could thrash them every time they get caught."

Samantha knew that was what her mother would have done. "No, not that. But I want them to be safe. Perhaps, if they travel in pairs -."

"Ah." Carol grinned. "It's always more fun travelling together."

Mr. Crow smiled. "What she means, my lady, is that when two apprentices operate the glamour as a team it takes twice as much skill. So it's always fun if you can get it right." He took a sip at his tea. "That gives me an idea. I'd like to test each of these girls, going outside with each in turn, working as a team. Unless they can perform better than me, they'll have to stay indoors." Carol grinned at this.

"They could perform better than you?" Samantha asked.

"I'm probably stronger than them, but I haven't tried teamwork in years."

Samantha nodded. "But I don't want them travelling in the dark. If they're caught out late, I want them to travel home in a cab."

Nancy interrupted. "My lady, the healer from Cable Street, Agnes, visits us regularly now. Just like you agreed. She's escorted by a magician, of course. And my two younger healers visit the hospital regularly. And now you use charm to keep away the pain. I wish I'd thought of that."

"Well, yes, I was forced to improvise," Samantha said.

Nancy gestured at Carol and Janet. "These two can use

charm spells, even if they use it for the wrong reasons. I wondered whether they could learn the trick of charming away pain. So they could use it here."

Samantha sipped at her tea and tried to work out exactly what Nancy was asking. "You want Carol and Janet ease the pain of women in labour? And to learn, you'll allow them to visit the hospital? Share the workload?"

"Just to learn, my lady. And to keep their practice in."

Chapter 8 Buckingham Palace

Afternoon of 28 May

Samantha had been told it was essential, for the dignity of the college, that she attend this reception at Buckingham Palace.

Portraits of princes and dukes in army uniform hung on the walls. The carpet had an intricate pattern in shades of maroon and scarlet. The crystal chandeliers sparkled.

When Lady Mary received her invitation, she had complained that this was not the sort of activity that would be attractive to leaders of fashion such as herself.

She had grumbled until Lord Edward had pointed out that the rules forbade an unmarried woman to attend these functions alone. The Chatelaine was obliged to attend and Lady Mary was the most appropriate person to accompany her. Samantha was glad of the older woman's company but wished that Alice could be at her side too. She was certainly less boring.

The elections in France had produced a reactionary government. Lord Palmerston, the colourful Foreign Secretary, had formally recognised the new elected government. The French had responded by sending a new ambassador.

"That man Palmerston is atrocious," the Queen said.

"Yes, your Majesty," Samantha said. She was standing next to Lady Mary but it was clear that the Queen was addressing her complaint to Samantha.

The Queen had travelled by airship to London the day before to attend this reception. Lord Edward had told

Samantha that the Queen intended to return to Osborne House as soon as she could.

"Palmerston is supposed to be *our* foreign secretary. He is supposed to listen to *our* advice. But he recognised the new government in France without asking us."

Samantha tried to find something tactful to say. "I am assured that the new French Republic is moderate in its views. It has no intention of starting a new war, madam."

"But it's a *republic*," the Queen said. "That poor King Louis was chased into exile. He's my guest in Buckingham Palace as we speak. How can we approve of a republic? And now their ambassador has arrived in London, at Palmerston's invitation. And we have to welcome him as if we mean it."

"Yes, madam."

"And what makes matters worse is that we and dear Prince Albert are held responsible for Palmerston's actions by the other Courts of Europe."

Samantha realised that most of those kings and princes were related to the Queen in one way or another. "Yes, madam."

Samantha was wearing a sleeveless court dress in midnight blue wool that was worth a fortune. Her petticoats rustled as she walked. It made her feel deliciously extravagant. And it had been paid for by the College. She told herself that the cost was fully justified. She was representing the College today. The colour of the dress complemented with the black gloves she was wearing as mourning for her predecessor.

In her childish fantasies she had imagined attending a grand event such as this. Unfortunately, her dress was quite restrained compared with those worn by older, married ladies.

Lady Mary gave Samantha a discreet nudge. She took the hint and moved on, to allow the Queen to explain her indignation to somebody else.

Samantha looked round for Lord Edward. He was supposed to be in the reception somewhere.

Lady Mary was not happy. "You should have been more tactful, my dear."

"You could have helped, my lady," Samantha said, more waspishly than she intended.

They were approached by the new French ambassador. He was in his late forties or early fifties. His formal suit was expensive, elegant, but hardly the latest fashion. He paused at a discreet distance until Lady Mary welcomed him with a curtsey. Samantha followed her lead.

He bowed to Samantha. "You are from the College, madam?"

"Yes, sir."

"You have the ear of your Queen, I believe?"

She decided that discretion was the best approach here. "Well, I've only spoken to her Majesty once or twice."

"You are too modest ... Your – College maintains law and order, yes?"

"That is among the College's duties, sir."

"We expect trouble, soon, from the riff-raff in Paris. They make insatiable demands for the money of honest Frenchmen. But never fear, the people of France shall destroy them." He took a step closer. "Britain also is under threat. You must be on your guard against your Chartists here in London. Crush them if need be."

"They are certainly a hazard," Lady Mary said.

Samantha was aware of the danger but was annoyed at being lectured to by this foreigner. "The Chartists have asked the establishment for certain favours. They have no desire to overthrow the establishment."

"The urban poor are totally untrustworthy. You must be vigilant," the ambassador said.

"Yes, sir." She noticed Lord Edward, with an elegant

man standing next to him. Both were dressed in formal evening tailcoats. She recognised the second man as Edward's cousin, the honourable Randolph Radley. Although she had to admit that Edward looked dignified too. He carried his suit very well.

The gentlemen strolled over. They exchanged bows with the ambassador, who said his farewells to the ladies and moved on. "Good afternoon, ladies," Lord Edward said.

Cousin Randolph smiled. "Edward is forced to perform his duties as Earl of Culham today. He is most unhappy. Some say I would make a better earl than Edward. He never attends debates in the House of Lords."

Lord Edward looked embarrassed. "I wish you could stand in for me, Randolph. I never seem to have the time. My Guild duties keep getting in the way. And my official duties make it difficult for me to dabble in politics."

"It is unfortunate that, for the Earl of Culham, the two roles cannot be separated," Randolph said.

"If only they could," Lord Edward said. "What was the ambassador saying, my lady?"

"He had the audacity to lecture me on how to deal with the Chartists ..."

"He predicted trouble from the Paris mob," Lady Mary said. "He almost seemed to gloat at the thought of crushing them."

"I expect we'll have to do that in London too," Randolph said. "The Chartists are plotting a violent uprising."

Samantha was upset. "I had hoped the matter could be resolved peacefully." She wondered whether she could tell him of the confidential police reports she had seen. Lord Edward shook his head.

"How is your hunt for Chartist conspirators getting on, Edward? Can we expect any arrests?" Randolph asked.

Lord Edward frowned. "The Chartists want the right to

vote, that's all. The police are hunting the extremists. But they're keeping a low profile."

"The conspirators want to provoke the rabble into perpetrating acts of gross destruction. The ambassador was right. No compromise is possible. Either we destroy them or they destroy us," Randolph said. "But if you will excuse me, I must speak to ..."

Samantha watched him go. "Is he right, sir? That violence is inevitable?"

Lord Edward looked grave. "No. London isn't Paris. I agree with you. A tiny minority would profit from violence, but a peaceable resolution is possible. Cousin Randolph seems to be growing more reactionary."

Lady Mary tutted. "Why do you say that? He's a charming young man. Educated ... he studied economics or something at Edinburgh. Athletic, too."

They said their farewells and made their way towards the exit. "Why did Cousin Randolph want to know about arrests?" Samantha said.

Lord Edward shrugged. "He was teasing me. He knows that I'm not at liberty to disclose confidential information."

In the hallway, they found Alice, Charles and another guard waiting for them. Charles was wearing his best guild uniform.

Alice was wearing a fine woollen skirt and fitted navy blue jacket, as close to the male talkers as she could manage. They straightened up as Edward, Lady Mary and Samantha approached.

"Do you have any messages, Alice?" Samantha asked.

"No, my lady. And nothing for Lord Edward. I would have sent Charles if anything came up."

Edward turned to the second guard. "James, tell the coachman to be at the door in five minutes."

"Yes, sir."

Cousin Randolph entered the hallway and noticed the

group. "Leaving early, Edward?" He took in Charles' uniform. "In the guild, I see. Guarding Edward? No doubt you will go far."

"Thank you, sir, but -."

Randolph ignored Alice and turned to Edward. "I didn't believe it when I heard that you had given Samantha her own Talker. But it seems to be true."

"Her Majesty told us to provide Lady Samantha with a guard. Charles here is one of them. And we thought it best to give her a Talker to keep her in touch with us at the College."

"It seems excessive ... Paranoid."

Samantha was annoyed. "Alice acts as my chaperone - and confidant."

Randolph's eyes widened. "She acts as your confidant?"

Lady Mary stiffened. "I would take on the task, but as you know my other duties keep me far too busy."

"Yes, I know, my lady," Randolph said.

Samantha noted that he was deliberately ignoring Alice. Perhaps he was too much a gentleman to speak to a grocer's daughter. A glance at Alice told her that her friend had reached the same conclusion.

"Randolph ..." Lord Edward said. "I hear you've been invited to give lectures at here at London University. And your chosen topic was the benefits of living in a republican state."

Randolph smiled. "Quite true, Edward."

Samantha was surprised. "Isn't that dangerous for you, sir, in these troubled times?"

He raised his eyebrows. "My dear girl, if that fool O'Connor can publish a republican constitution, surely I can give a lecture? Besides, the purpose of the lectures is to make the students think. If they disapprove, I ask them to explain why." He smiled. "Don't you agree, cousin, that a republic would be an improvement? Abolish the house of lords and

107

hereditary peerages?"

Lady Mary cried out at this. "Is that what you want, cousin?"

Randolph shrugged. "The problem is how to get from here to there. The cost would be too high. People would resist. There would be thousands of deaths. No."

The guard, James, returned. "Your carriage is waiting, my lord."

Randolph bowed to Lady Mary and then, more abruptly, to Samantha. "Good night, ladies."

Lady Mary and Samantha climbed in first, taking the more comfortable forward-facing seats. Lord Edward and Alice sat facing them.

Alice was still hurt from Randolph's conduct. "Is your cousin like that to everyone, my lord? He reminded me that I was a grocer's daughter. Without even saying anything."

Lord Edward turned. "Remember, Miss Toledano, it works both ways. Do you really want to include Randolph amongst your acquaintances? If he approaches you in the future, you can ignore him. Give him the cut direct."

Alice, fascinated, cheered up a little. "Oh. How would I do that?"

Lady Mary smiled across at her. "Ignore him, my dear. A gentleman should not approach a lady without her permission. At the worst, ask him whether you have been introduced."

Alice bit her lip. "I don't want to presume, my lord, but - can I call myself a lady and tell him to keep his distance?"

This was met by an embarrassed silence. It was finally broken by Lady Mary. "You have the manners of a lady, Alice. I have never been embarrassed by your conduct."

"At worst, your father is as prosperous as Samantha's," Lord Edward said. "Her father is a diplomat, so he receives a salary from the government. As you do, as an apprentice" Lord Edward smiled. "Your education is as good as

Samantha's. I might even say your manners are better than hers."

Lady Mary protested as this but Samantha merely laughed.

The College, evening of 28 May

Lord Edward led Samantha and her four guards into the atrium of the College. He was wearing a tweed shooting jacket with large pockets. He was hatless, which told Samantha he was up to no good. "You need to practice your training in self-defence, my lady."

Samantha wondered why he thought extra training was necessary. She had been given just enough time to change into an old rusty-black woollen dress.

"Although we must hope that you will never put these lessons into practice. You're to rely on your guards. That's what they're for."

"Yes, my lord. I've been thinking about this. I want to add something to the training. These guards protect me, but we need to train as a team. Any attacker will try to take my guards by surprise."

Charles was offended. "We'll stop them, my lady."

Lord Edward was impatient with this. "I've told you before. Your vigilance is never perfect. And her Ladyship is right. You must train as a team, so you don't get in each other's way. My lady, you must always be able to get your defences up in a couple of seconds."

"Yes, my lord."

"How to do it, though?" Lord Edward frowned. He walked to the centre of the atrium. "My lady, stand there. Charles, what's your defensive pattern? A diamond formation? Now, all of you, walk towards me."

"I'll take point," Charles said. Then, grinning, he

109

walked forwards. Samantha and the others kept up.

Lord Edward produced a couple of tennis balls from his pocket and negligently tossed one in the air. He caught it and threw it as hard as he could. Charles was taken by surprise and the ball hit him under the ribs. He stopped, too winded to even swear.

"Charles, you are now dead." Lord Edward threw the second ball at Samantha.

Samantha had been expecting something, but not this. She had been preparing the spell to create a shield. In a panic, she tried to snap it into place. "Partum a scuto."

To her surprise, the ball was merely deflected and hit her arm. "Ow! That hurt."

"You did better than Charles. But not good enough."

Charles had recovered is breath. "I'm sorry, I'll try harder."

"You'd better. Or you'll be off this team." Lord Edward walked to the far end of the atrium. "Turn around, everyone, and walk towards me. Smith can take point. Charles, you're rear-guard."

Lord Edward watched as they approached, his face expressionless. He waited until Smith was nine feet from him, then took two steps to his right and threw two tennis balls in quick succession, one at Smith's flank, and one at Samantha.

Both were expecting trouble. Smith used his shield to stop the first ball, while the one aimed at Samantha went wide.

"Well done," Lord Edward said grudgingly. "We'll try again tomorrow."

Samantha was offended. "My lord, you must not go easy on me. That might put my life at risk."

"My dear girl, I threw that ball squarely. Your shield seems to deflect projectiles rather than stopping them."

That evening at dinner, the French ambassador's arrival was the main topic of conversation. Samantha kept quiet about the Queen's remarks and instead described the ambassador's comments. She did not hide her indignation.

"The ambassador is right," Mr. Knight said. "The Chartists need putting in their place. There's been too much talk. We should have dispersed that meeting with a cavalry charge."

Conversation at the high table stopped. Samantha felt obliged to fill the silence. "The Chartists are asking for the right to vote, sir. Most of them are artisans or tradesmen of some kind. They merely want something that many of their neighbours already have."

"How could that be, my lady?" Lord Edward's tone was one of polite enquiry.

"A householder qualifies for the vote by owning property. So a prosperous man who rents his home is excluded."

Mr. Knight was stubborn. "These men have insulted their betters. They ought to be prosecuted and transported."

Samantha reminded herself that Mr. Knight was Master of the College. Should a young lady let an older gentleman have the last word? But everyone seemed to be waiting for her response. "The Chartists have politely asked for a concession, sir. And when their request was rejected, they quietly accepted it."

"Their Executive hasn't given up, though," Lord Edward said, and the conversation turned to other things.

Albion beershop, evening of 5 June

Charley 'Coffee' Williams and a few like-minded men gathered in the upstairs room of the Albion beershop on the Bethnal Green Road. He – and the others – were angry that the government had ignored the Chartists' Grand Petition.

Mcrae proposed Peter McDouall as chairman of the meeting. Coffee felt that McDouall was a good choice. He had been a delegate at the first Chartist convention and had fled abroad with a price on his head after the general strike of 1842. He was tall, prematurely aged, and balding. He wore as sombre blue suit, while his shirt collar had fashionable high points.

"Thank you, Mr. Mcrae. The agenda this evening is our preparations for an uprising." McDougal unfolded a map of London. "We need to formulate a series of possible plans of attack."

"We need as many men behind us as possible," Mcrae said. Instead of a collar and tie, he had chosen to wear a bright red neck-cloth. "We've told the faint-hearts we're going to present a petition. The Chartist Committee arranged for a large crowd to assemble in Bethnal Fields to demand the right to vote. But instead we'll march across Soho to Seven Dials. They'll be waiting for us and they'll put up barricades as soon as we bring in the reinforcements.

"When?" McDouall asked.

"On Whit Monday."

"And where will the barricades go up?" McDouall asked.

Mcrae pointed at the map. "Here – the Strand, Ludgate Hill, Cheapside and other City streets." His finger moved across the map. "From Clerkenwell to the Barbican and Hatton Garden. To cause a distraction, we'll set fire to theatres and other buildings. We'll get our weapons from pawnbrokers' and gunsmiths' shops."

"We need more distractions," McDouall said. "Across Waterloo Bridge at Kent Road, we'll attack the police station. If they send the artillery from Woolwich, we'll stop them and seize their weapons."

"Questions?" Mcrae asked.

Coffee was appalled. "That sounds far too complicated. Too many people doing things at different places. It would have more chance of success if we kept it simple."

McDouall shook his head. "We accept that half of these will fail. But we need to distract the police. If they concentrate their numbers, they can stop us before we've begun."

Chapter 9 Bethnal Fields

Bonner Gate, Monday 12 June

Samantha rode through Bonham Gate at the western end of Bethnal Fields and stared at the large open space beyond. The widely scattered trees prevented her from seeing the far side of the park, but it was easy to see that hundreds, if not thousands, of men had gathered there. Alice rode one length behind her. She looked uncomfortable after so long in the saddle. Samantha's usual guards followed.

Fifty feet beyond the gate was the Regent's Canal and the elegant Bonner Bridge over it. On the near side of the bridge, a line of twenty policemen blocked the path. Samantha realised that the canal provided a more formidable barrier than the park railings.

A dirigible hovered over the trees in the distance, its propellers turning just enough to overcome the influence of the wind.

Behind the row of policemen, a horseman wearing the uniform of a police inspector used his superior height to observe the crowd.

A young man in a long raincoat and top hat stood at the inspector's stirrup. He was trying to light a pipe. Samantha noticed that another man, dressed in a shabby suit and top hat, was leaning against one of the ornamental gateposts.

Samantha urged her horse forward. "Good morning. I'm looking for Chief Inspector Bearsbridge."

The rider turned. "I'm Bearsbridge. And who might you be, young woman?"

"I'm Lady Samantha Hampden, from the College. This is Alice Toledano, my Talker. You said you needed another Talker here, and there was no-one else left but us."

"This is no place for a lady," Bearsbridge said. He was a big man, over six foot in height, and barrel-chested, yet he sat his horse with an easy grace. He had a powerful voice and Samantha felt that he could make himself heard across the park if he wanted to.

"You said the Fields have too many gates to be covered by three talkers."

"Yes, but if I knew your Talker was a girl I would never have asked her here."

She thought of old Oswald in his wheelchair. "Everyone else is busy. If you had given a couple of hours' notice, we could have found someone. But you wanted a Talker at once." She tried to sound positive "Where do you want to send us?"

"You'd better stay under my eye, young lady. Clarence here can go to the Royal Gate, at the north end of Grove Road."

Clarence, the young man with the pipe, did not seem to be upset by this change of plan. Perhaps he wanted to escape the inspector's eye. "Alice, we've never established rapport, have we? Can we do that now?"

"Of course." She leant down from the saddle and they shook hands. "You need a token ... I'll want it back later." She delved into an inner pocket and produced the embroidery that she never seemed to finish and handed it to Clarence.

"Thank you." He tapped the tobacco out of his pipe and handed it over. He turned and, escorted by a squad of police constables, headed across the park. Alice put the pipe into the pocket on the right side of her saddle.

Bearsbridge gestured at Samantha's guards. "Couldn't any of these fellows send reports for you?"

"These men are here to guard me," Samantha said.

"There's Charles, I suppose. He can establish rapport with two of the talkers here."

Charles was outraged. "Lady Samantha! My duty is to protect you. Four of us aren't enough."

Bearsbridge subjected him to a glower. "I have a thousand constables here, young man. If they can't protect the ladies, how can you?"

Charles refused to give in. "Who would take command in my absence?"

"There's Mr. Smith. He has the experience. He worked on Lord Radley's team. We must hope that nothing will happen, of course," Samantha said.

Charles and Smith exchanged a measuring look.

"Is this young man the best you have?" Bearsbridge asked.

"He isn't a trained Talker, you understand. But he can establish rapport with ten others."

"Eleven," Charles said. I can talk to Miss Toledano as well."

"Indeed?" Bearsbridge said. "Then the lady should be the one to stay here and you should go."

Alice urged her horse forward. "Let me know you are safe, Mr. Lloyd. Every hour on the hour."

To Samantha's surprise, Charles seemed to accept this. "Every fifteen minutes, Miss Toledano."

"Very well. If I'm not busy," Alice said.

"At the south-western corner of the Fields is another bridge, by the Cricketer's gate," Bearsbridge said. "You can just about see it from here. But I'll rest a lot easier with someone watching it. My sergeant will escort you."

"Yes, sir." Charles tipped his hat to Alice and rode off.

Samantha turned to Bearsbridge. "Have you seen the evidence that Lord Radley mentioned?" The police had two informants amongst the extremists, but sometimes they told different stories.

"I have indeed, madam. But it is not a matter to be discussed in public. This fellow here is a news reporter."

Samantha glanced at the newspaper reporter, leaning against the gatepost, just within earshot. He caught her gaze and tipped his hat to her.

"Yes, I see." She would have liked to discuss the evidence with the police inspector, but she knew that she had to be discreet.

According to the informants, the conspirators had formulated a series of secondary attacks across London. While these attacks were diverting the police, another conspirator would subvert the thousands of protesters assembled in Bethnal Fields and order them to march across central London to the West End. The protest would turn into a riot, setting light to public buildings and ransacking gunsmiths' shops.

The demonstrators had assembled in Bethnal Fields just as the Chartist Committee had planned. But the police, present in large numbers, blocked the exits.

"My orders are quite clear," Bearsbridge said. "I must not divide my force, no matter what reports I receive from you people."

"I understand," Samantha said. With so many potential trouble spots, the guild's supply of Talkers was spread thin. When the inspector had asked for another talker here on Bethnal Fields, Samantha had seen no option but to accompany Alice here. Alice had agreed that it was preferable to waiting at the college, wondering what was going on.

Chief Inspector Bearsbridge harrumphed. "I ask you to promise one thing, my lady. If trouble does break out, I want you to get clear as fast as you can."

Samantha looked across the Fields at the hundreds of watchful policemen. They were trained in dealing with riots. If trouble did break out, two girls would just get in the way.

"Of course, inspector. We'll call for help, then get out of the way."

"Good girl ... The Chartist Committee had dissolved itself, you know. They've made it clear that any violence from now on won't be part of the Chartist movement."

The reporter edged forward. He was annoyed. "How did you find that out, Chief Inspector?"

Bearsbridge was smug. "It's public knowledge. Your paper will put it in its next headline."

"But you knew before we did," the reporter said.

Bearsbridge ignored him. "There's still more agitators that we haven't identified. It's said that one of them's a man of property."

"That sounds unlikely, sir," Samantha said. "The agitators hate all property owners."

She looked out over the Fields. "It all looks peaceable enough. Has there been any trouble so far?"

"Not here on the Fields. The latecomers are still trickling in, through the eastern gates, you understand. It's only the western gates they can't use."

Alice began the task of contacting the other Talkers. "Clarence says the protesters are good-humoured. They're listening to speeches from agitators or glaring sullenly at everyone."

To Samantha, the crowd seemed to be constantly in motion, drifting towards one of the exits or back towards the speaker's platform.

The policemen had been ordered not to provoke trouble. For the most part, they lounged at their ease, waiting for orders and watching the speakers. Only at the gates were the policemen drawn up in a line. But Samantha feared that a single word from one of the conspirators could change everything.

Alice dismounted with Smith's help, using the parapet as a mounting block. She walked round to stand at

Samantha's stirrup. She did not have much practice at riding and she tired easily. "I wish we could move. It's less tiring than standing still, somehow. Samantha – haven't you got a proper riding dress?"

Samantha smiled down at her friend. "A riding dress is so impractical, my dear. When you dismount, the hem drags in the mud. You have to pick it up and carry it. I thought that, today, I might need to have both hands free."

"But – with the hem hitched up, your boot is showing. It's so unfashionable."

Samantha grinned. "It's a very nice boot. Made by London's best bootmaker."

Alice tensed. She placed her hand against the horse's flank and stared down at the road. "Samantha, that was a message from Lord Edward's team. They've checked out the Albion public house in Bethnal Green, but none of the suspects was there. So they're moving on to the next place on the list."

"Thank you, Alice. Can you tell him that all's quiet here?"

"I did, my lady."

Bearsbridge listened with interest. "It sounds as if we've got them on the run. Can you tell the people at St. James's Palace that all's quiet at the Bonner Gate on the west side of the park?"

"Of course, sir." Alice leant against her horse, as if she gained strength from the animal. She muttered a few words under her breath. "They said thank you for keeping them informed."

"And what does your Talker at the south gate have to say?"

Alice smiled. "He says he's annoyed at being asked so often. He says it's going to rain."

Bearsbridge looked up. The smoke from London's chimneys was merging with the low cloud. "You don't need to be a magician to know that. Let's hope that a spot of rain is the worst thing to happen today."

A few of the demonstrators gathered at the eastern end of the bridge to shout insults at the line of policemen. The policemen stolidly ignored them.

Bearsbridge was embarrassed. "Should I intervene to stop them, my lady?"

Samantha shook her head. "That might provoke further trouble. We knew what to expect when we came here."

Alice smiled. "They'll have to try harder than that. I've heard worse at Billingsgate market."

"We'd better stop, lads," one of the hecklers said. "There's proper ladies listening."

Bearsbridge urged his horse forward onto the bridge. "The lady says you'll have to try harder than that. She's heard worse from the fishwives at Billingsgate."

Samantha was horrified at this provocation but the men merely laughed.

"Alice, did your parents take you to Billingsgate?" Samantha was shocked.

She grinned. "No, of course not. My maid and I sneaked off there once. But don't tell my father."

One of the men stepped up to the bridge. He took off his hat. "What are proper ladies doing at Bethnal Fields? If I may presume to ask, my lady?"

His tone and manner were polite so Samantha responded in kind, speaking slowly and clearly so that everybody could hear. "We're from the Guild of Magicians. We're here to send reports back to St. James's Palace." When she had taken lessons in elocution she had never imagined this.

A man at the back said there was no such thing as magic but his companions hushed him.

Another man doffed his hat and stepped onto the

bridge. "You magicians send messages to the Queen. Can you send one for us? We're all her loyal subjects here. It's just the government we want to change."

Bearsbridge was outraged. "The Guild doesn't waste their time on the likes of you!"

Alice plucked at Samantha's sleeve. "Rupert at St. James's says the Queen is anxious. She wants to know what's going on here. Any word is better than silence."

"But she doesn't want a petition, surely? Won't we get into trouble if we send one?"

Bearsbridge turned towards her. "It's always best if you can get the blighters talking. Once they've done that, they're less likely to resort to violence. Besides, there's no chance we'll have to send a message. These fellows will spend six hours arguing over the words, then they'll give up."

"Are you sure?" Samantha urged her horse forward so she was at the highest point of the bridge. The men looked up, expectant. "If you can agree on the wording of a message, I will ensure it is sent to Osborne House." This was welcomed with a cheer. She raised her right hand. "But the message must be less than forty words long. Otherwise the messenger will get a migraine."

Samantha urged her horse back a pace. "Alice, can you tell Rupert that the people here want to send a petition?"

"Of course, my lady."

The men began a lengthy debate amongst themselves. The reporter watched with distaste. "Should you pander to this rabble?"

Bearsbridge was watching the crowd with approval. "With a bit of luck they'll be arguing all day."

Alice scrambled back into the saddle, using the low wall of the bridge as a mounting-block, solely to relieve the boredom.

Samantha noticed more men approaching the bridge. She was dismayed. Were they planning a breakout?"

121

"Chief Inspector, why are those men coming here?"

The inspector shrugged. "Perhaps we're less boring than the speech-makers." The newcomers merely joined the crowd, waiting peaceably.

Twenty-five minutes later, a demonstrator wearing a blue tweed jacket stepped forward and doffed his cap. His companions gave way to him. He had very dark skin and was short, no more than five feet tall. He seemed to make up for his short stature with a vibrant energy.

"I've seen you before," Bearsbridge said. "Williams, isn't it? And what brings you here today?"

"I came to make a speech, Chief Inspector, sir. And very well received it was too. But having made it, my time's my own. So I came to see what the fuss was about. The lady's presented us with an interesting problem."

"Yes, indeed," Bearsbridge said.

Williams grinned. "Beg pardon, sir, madam, but could I ask you for a sheet of paper? It seems none of us thought of bringing any."

Bearsbridge, in a show of good humour, produced a notebook from an inner pocket, and tore a sheet out of it. He handed it down to a constable, who gravely passed it to Williams.

Another half-hour went by as the men argued amongst themselves. Finally, the dark-skinned man stepped forward. He was grinning. "Here you are." A constable took it and handed it up to Samantha.

Samantha was disconcerted. She had hoped the crowd would argue all day. She read the message through. It was closely-written, grammatically correct and managed to convey a declaration of loyalty within the limit she had imposed. She handed it to Alice, who scowled in concentration and read it aloud.

Samantha turned to her listeners. "The message is now at St. James's Palace. A new Talker has to send it to Osborne

House."

"But will the Queen read it?" the spokesman asked.

"I can't promise you that. All I'm certain of is that the Talker at Osborne house will get it," Samantha said. The man nodded and stepped back.

The low cloud turned to drizzle. She was glad that she had brought a riding cloak – unfashionable but practical.

Samantha tensed. The crowd in the distance was moving again. But, instead of a random flow, the men were drifting towards the western tip of the Fields.

Seriously worried, she turned to the inspector. "Are they going to force their way through?"

Bearsbridge snorted. "It's more likely they want a look at you, my girl."

"Nonsense. It's more likely they've come to listen to Alice's message."

"Then we'd better hope there is one, my lady," Alice said.

Samantha was appalled. "I hope my intervention hasn't made things worse."

The reporter snickered. "A bit too late to think of that, madam."

Bearsbridge subjected the man to a glare before turning back to Samantha. "Your presence has changed the nature of the equation, certainly. But I think you have changed it for the better."

It appeared that the inspector was right. A swirling pattern emerged in the crowd as men edged forward to catch a glimpse of her, then allowed themselves be elbowed aside so other men could come through. They pulled back from the bridge, forming a semicircle, so more men could get a look. The men bantered amongst themselves, but none of them made any attempt to talk to her. The police officers and Samantha's guards looked stolidly back.

As the crowd shifted, she caught a glimpse of Williams

in the second row. He waved impudently at her, but she thought it best to ignore him.

She wondered whether they were going to get an answer from Osborne House. And how would these men show their disappointment? Her impulse seemed more reckless with every minute that passed.

After half an hour, Alice tensed. She leaned forward and patted her horse's neck. "Inspector, can you take a dictation?"

"Certainly, miss." The inspector obligingly pulled out his notebook and wrote down the message for her. "Her Majesty has read with interest the missive from her loyal subjects."

Bearsbridge handed the note to a constable, who walked across the bridge and handed it to the dark-skinned demonstrator.

He stepped forward, turned to face his companions and read it out in an orator's voice. They were disappointed.

"That's all?" a tall man asked.

Bearsbridge was angry. "You sent a message and got an answer. That's more than most gentlemen in England can say. And you've probably done more good for your community than anyone else gathered here."

"We're all loyal and law-abiding, inspector. Why won't you let us through?" the dark-skinned man asked.

"That's what they said at Trafalgar Square. Before the riot broke out." Bearsbridge held up a hand. "I'm prepared to admit that most of the men at Trafalgar Square that day were law-abiding. When they promised to go home, at sunset, nine out of ten did go home. It was the remainder who caused all the trouble. Nine out of ten of you here are law-abiding. But if I let those one in ten get through, there'll be mayhem."

This was received in a glum silence. They knew the inspector had a point. The spokesman turned to Samantha and doffed his hat. "What do you think of our Charter, my lady?"

His voice had lost its mocking tone. He seemed genuinely interested. All of the men in the group turned to stare up at her.

Samantha felt a twinge of panic. She knew that she could not simply ignore them. She had to keep them talking. "My thought is that ... you're asking for too much, too soon. One request at a time would have more chance of success ... and I certainly don't want annual elections." Inspired, she grinned at them. "What I want to see on that charter is votes for women."

The protesters were indignant. "Politics is mucky work."

"Not at all suitable for a lady," the dark-skinned man said.

"The Tories want to protect *you* from that mucky work. They're depriving you of the vote for the good of your souls. Or so they say. But if you can handle it, so can I."

"Ladies haven't got the head for that sort of thinking," another man said.

"The Tories say you have no head for thought. If I don't deserve the vote, you don't either."

The men were indignant at this. Samantha smiled at them. "I thought you were a parcel of revolutionaries. But I mention votes for women and suddenly you're a bunch of Tories." As she hoped, they laughed at this.

"Do you want to go into politics, miss?" the spokesman asked.

"I could tell you what I think of politicians, but I have to remember that I'm a lady."

The reporter was indignant. "Is it the act of a lady to bandy words with this rabble?"

"Rabble, are we?" the spokesman said.

Samantha stared down at the reporter. "We're not

bandying words; we're engaged in a debate."

Bearsbridge might disapprove of Samantha's presence, but he disapproved of the reporter even more. He grinned. "The Bethnal Fields debating society."

He spoke louder than he intended and the nearest protesters heard him. They laughed. Then they turned to pass the joke back.

Samantha noticed a man worming his way through the crowd. He could not afford a coat, but instead wore a threadbare navy jacket, a long woollen comforter, and a battered top hat. He wore a patch over one eye. Finally, he stepped clear and tipped his hat to her.

"Good afternoon, my lady. My name is David Farringdon. As it happens, Bonner Ward *does* have a debating society. Would you like to attend one of our sessions?"

"No! I mean, I'm always too busy. I couldn't find the time." She saw that he looked disappointed. "Besides, do you and your colleagues want someone like me disturbing your comfortable meetings?"

"I'm sure they would welcome you."

Samantha doubted that. "Well ... if your society sends an invitation to me at the College, addressed to me, I'll try to find a gap in my schedule."

"Thank you, my lady. Good day to you, inspector." Farringdon tipped his hat to them and stepped back into the crowd.

"Now there's an interesting fellow," Bearsbridge said. "Dave One-eye is known to us. He's an agitator. He was active in the thirties, and went to prison for it. And now he claims to run a debating society." He laughed.

The drizzle turned to rain. Alice tensed. She leaned forward and patted her horse's neck. "Inspector, I've just received a message from St. James's Palace. The Talker in the dirigible says they'll have to give up because they've seen

126

lighting."

"Very well," Bearsbridge glanced up at the dirigible hovering over the trees. "It's a nuisance, but we don't want it bursting into flames. I just hope it won't be needed."

At two pm, a cab drew up outside the gate. A man stepped down and walked through the gateway. Bearsbridge turned in the saddle to see who it was. "Good lord, it's Mr. Mcrae. I hope you'll excuse me, ladies, if I do not introduce you."

"Isn't he a gentleman?" Samantha asked.

"Not quite, no. But the real reason is that he's dangerous." He turned to Alice. "Young lady, could you tell your colleagues at the other gates that Mr. Mcrae has arrived. And – make it clear that he's alone."

"Certainly, Inspector." Alice reached for her pocket book.

The reporter was fascinated. "Mcrae? They say he's the toughest man on the Chartist Executive. Perhaps he'll give me a word."

Mcrae stopped, just inside the gate. Samantha realised that the man was dismayed. Was it the number of policemen guarding the bridge? The policemen on standby, sitting on the grass, turned to face the new arrival.

"Good afternoon, Inspector. A pleasure, as always." Mcrae took off his hat. He gestured to Samantha. "Who are they, if I may ask?"

Bearsbridge shrugged. "I asked the guild to send me every available man. So they sent me these two. I've got one of their Talkers at every gate." All day, he had been talking mild tone. Now he spoke more forcibly.

Samantha judged that Mcrae could pass as a gentleman if he wished. His coat was made of the very best wool. Its fit suggested an expensive tailor. She received the impression that Mcrae exercised regularly. He would be a dangerous man to know.

She had turned in the saddle to get a better view of him. Her horse misunderstood this and turned, so she was blocking the path. She leaned forward to reassure the animal. When she looked up, she realised that Mcrae was staring at her – not the behaviour of a gentleman. But was her conduct any better?

Embarrassed, she turned to look at the gate. A man, fashionably dressed, was standing in the road next to Mcrae's cab. His scarf was pulled up over his mouth to protect him from the smoke. He realised she had notice him, turned, and hurried off.

"Aren't you overdoing things, Inspector?" Mcrae gestured to the scores of watching policemen. Some of them stood to get a better view.

Bearsbridge was losing control of his temper. "You could take it as a compliment to your talent for organisation."

His tone of voice unsettled Samantha's horse. It started to fidget and she had to lean forward and pat the animal.

Mcrae took a hasty step back. "I regret that I cannot stay, inspector. Good day to you." He bowed and turned towards the gate. The reporter hurried forward, but Mcrae snarled wordlessly. The reporter flinched back and Mcrae walked back to his cab.

Bearsbridge watched the cab drive off, then turned to Alice. "Young lady, would it be possible for you to tell your colleagues at the other gates that Mr. Mcrae has now departed?" His voice was now back under control.

"Very well, sir."

"Are you tired, Alice?" Samantha asked.

"Perhaps, a bit. But I'm within my limits. I'll tell Clarence at the south gate and ask him to pass it on."

"Things could get interesting," Bearsbridge said. "If he's able to motivate the crowd ..."

Instead, the rain worsened. There was a flash of

lightning to the west.

The men in the crowd realised they had no hope of reaching the West End. They gave up and drifted towards the far exit.

"Good, good," Bearsbridge said. "But I and my men have to stay on duty, to ensure that the crowd disperses as it should."

"I understand, inspector," Samantha said.

Bearsbridge gave an order and a squad of policemen walked across the bridge. The retreating men took no notice, so Bearsbridge urged his horse forward. After a moment's hesitation Samantha followed. This ride, across the grass of the Fields, was the best she had experienced all day. Alice, Mr. Smith, and her two other guards trailed after.

Bearsbridge led his men across the Fields as the crowd withdrew. He was careful not to get too close. He turned to Alice. "Please let the others know that I am moving east towards the Crown Gate," he said. "It's somewhere to the south of us. And tell Clarence and your fellow Charles that they should join me there if it is safe to do so."

Halfway across the Field, they encountered a group of men and women, hanging back. Samantha's guards tensed, expecting trouble.

As Bearsbridge approached, the crowd divided to allow the riders to pass. Samantha guessed that these people were younger than the men around the Bonner Bridge.

"That's the lady, a real lady, just like they said," a man said.

"You talk to her then," a young woman in a cheap print dress said.

The nominated spokesman approached. He doffed his cap. Mr. Smith turned to Samantha for guidance, and she nodded her permission. "Excuse me, miss, are you really a magician? Could you show us?"

Samantha leant down. "Yes, I am, but it would frighten

the horse. I'm trying to find the south gate, the Crown Gate."

The boy pointed. "It's over there, miss. But you mustn't go in a straight line because it's low-lying, muddy. Especially after rain, if you take my meaning. You have to go round it, north-about."

"I see. Thank you. Could you show me the way?"

He hesitated. "Yes. All right." He turned and strode off.

Samantha urged her horse after him and they headed off together, with the boy's companions following behind him.

The Crown Gates came into sight. "There you are, miss." The boy waved, as if he had created the gates himself.

"Thank you," Samantha said. The gates were elegant wrought-iron affairs. The canal here was a hundred yards south of the road, so the police were standing outside the gate, guarding the road, not the canal. The Talker was waiting for them next to the sergeant in charge. Samantha noted that the Talker was wearing a practical waterproof coat, quite unlike her fashionable cloak. They exchanged nods.

Clarence walked across the park towards them. "The Royal Gate is free, inspector." Gravely, he and Alice exchanged tokens once again.

"I only need these talkers now, lass," Bearsbridge said. "You can go home to tea."

Samantha glanced at Alice, looking as miserable as she felt. For once she did not resent Bearsbridge's condescension. She was quite happy to leave. "Thank you, sir."

"And – I thank the pair of you for what you've done today."

The College, morning of 13 June

Samantha was in the Chatelaine's study, going through the account books. She was trying to catch up on the work she had abandoned the day before. Alice was working at her embroidery. She hoped to establish rapport with more people soon and needed talismans to exchange with them.

Both girls looked up as Lord Edward walked in. He was carrying a broadsheet under his arm. Samantha thought he looked angry about something.

"Good morning, my Lady. Have you seen the newspapers this morning?" He held them out.

Samantha took the top one. One lurid headline read 'Schoolgirl saves the day'. Alice stood so she could read over her shoulder.

Samantha was horrified. "Do they give my name?" She knew that a lady should never allow her name to appear in the papers.

"No, look," Lord Edward said. He pointed to sentences that referred to 'Lady S' or 'The Baronetess'.

"Will people be able to recognise me?"

"Yes, my Lady."

"I'm ruined, then."

"It isn't that bad. They say you're a heroine." His tone was grim.

"Are you going to punish me?" she asked in a fade-away voice.

He was amused. "My dear girl, I have no authority to punish you. If I raised my hand against you, your father would have me thrown in jail. Now, if I had written to your father ... Besides, I have received a letter from Chief Inspector Bearsbridge. He has apologised for his hasty demand for a Talker yesterday. He regrets that the two of you were discomposed. He accepts full responsibility for everything that happened."

131

"Oh. That was kind of him." Samantha tried to recover her composure. "That's all very embarrassing. If I had known that he wouldn't need his Talker until two in the afternoon, I could have stayed here and asked Oswald to find a volunteer."

Now he looked confused. "Why two o'clock?"

"That was when the agitator arrived. Bearsbridge refused to introduce him to us."

Lord Edward waved that aside. "But he couldn't have known that in advance ... He asks me to thank you for your initiative. He commends your courage."

"But I didn't do anything. There was nothing to be afraid of. Except - when I saw all those men walking towards the western end of the field, I thought they were going to rush the gate. But they just wanted to hear Alice's reply from Osborne House."

"Ah, yes. Your message. Rupert told me it was all his fault for encouraging you."

"Was it wrong of me to send it? Bearsbridge said they would never agree on the wording. But when they did, I felt honour-bound to send it."

Alice waved a hand to indicate the account books. "Lord Radley, we thought that going to the Fields would be slightly less boring than checking these books. Except that things got more - complicated."

"And was it boring?" Lord Edward asked.

"Most of the time," Samantha said.

Alice smiled. "I've explained what happened to my father, but he still doesn't quite understand."

"Ah, yes. I may end up explaining my actions to Lady Samantha's father," Lord Edward said.

The town-house of Lord Lovelace, afternoon of 14 June

Samantha and Alice followed the maid into the elegant morning room of Lady Augusta King. The maid bobbed a curtsey. "Lady Samantha Hampden and Miss Alice Toledano to see you, my lady."

The room was elegantly furnished. The large window looked out over the street. Lady Augusta was sitting at an elegant coffee table bearing a large leather-bound book.

She rose to shake hands with her guests. She was dainty, in her mid-thirties. She was wearing a silk dress in shimmering sea-green, and her hair was up in curls that must have taken her maid an hour to arrange. "Good afternoon, my dear Lady Samantha. Would you like some tea?"

"Thank you, my lady." Samantha was nervous. Lady Augusta Ada King was also Countess of Lovelace and the only legitimate child of the notorious Lord George Byron. According to some, she was also a mathematician of genius.

Lady Augusta's manners were perfect. Her governess must have been exacting. Her movements were sweeping, graceful. Samantha calculated that she must spend a couple of hours every morning getting dressed. How did she get anything done? Perhaps she solved differential equations while her maid was brushing her hair.

Samantha received the impression of controlled energy. Lady Augusta was a leader of fashion, but apparently that was not enough. Her father had the energy to bring democracy to Greece. Lady Augusta had already earned a place in the history books by writing those algorithms for Babbage's machine. What did she plan to do next?

Next to the leather-bound book, strategically placed, was the latest edition of London's favourite society magazine. The gushing headline mentioned 'the latest daring fashions as modelled by a certain titled lady'.

Lady Augusta noted Samantha's interest. "Isn't it absurd? They claim that I am now the leader of fashion. And they manage to say so without mentioning my name."

"The notion is not absurd at all, my lady. I am sure that Lady Mary will be put out." Samantha could not quite keep the satisfaction out of her voice.

"Do you think so, my dear?" The laughter lines around Lady Augusta's eyes were crinkling. She was stroking the embroidery on her dress. "You're so young! Have you come out?"

Her tone was honey-sweet. Her friendliness was genuine enough, but she was trying too hard. She wanted something from Samantha, very badly indeed.

"I haven't entered society, not really. But I have been introduced to her Majesty. Lord Radley took me to Osborne House especially."

"Ah." Lady Augusta eyed her with new interest. "You must be wondering why I invited you here. It's all about the weather, you see."

The maid walked in, carrying a tray with three cups. Lady Augusta began fingering the decoration on her cup.

Samantha accepted a cup of tea from the maid. "Pardon, my lady?"

"The Board of Trade are worried about bad weather, because it keeps sinking ships. They asked Babbage – you know Mr. Babbage; I trust?"

"I know about him, of course. But I haven't met him yet."

"He holds the most *interesting* literary salons. That's apart from the *other* things he does. Well, the Board of Trade asked whether he could use his Engine to predict storms. So Babbage asked me whether such a thing was possible. Mathematically speaking, of course."

Samantha exchanged a glance with Alice. "Of course,

my lady."

"So I analysed the problem and discovered the most *exquisite* problems. I concluded that it could be done, provided the Engine was provided with enough data ...

"I've written these *beautiful* algorithms and now I need to test them. With real data. I asked the admiralty to reopen their semaphore telegraphs to Liverpool and Plymouth, but they told me they could only justify the cost in wartime." She paused to take a sip at her tea. "So I asked some volunteers to send messages by train. But the trains are so slow."

"Slow?" Samantha asked.

"Sometimes the bad weather arrives before the train does! So I thought of you."

"I see. And you want the Guild's Talkers to provide that data." Samantha considered her resources. "The College has magicians all over the country. Some of them are interested in research. We could ask them to send in reports -."

"No, my dear. That would not be sufficient." Lady Augusta leaned forward, her ringlets swaying. "The Analytical Engine will need data from a *hundred* sources. So we need data about the weather, from as many sources as possible, all round the Atlantic. Otherwise the predictions will not be reliable enough."

Samantha gaped. "A hundreds sources? You mean a hundred Talkers?"

Lady Augusta opened the book, which proved to be an atlas. "Look. All round the Atlantic. To the south-east there's Madeira and the Azores. Owned by Portugal, unfortunately, but I'm sure they can be persuaded to help us. Then, in the south-west there's the Lesser Antilles and the Bahamas and Bermuda. All usefully British. I'm sure they all have garrisons or naval stations or something. A military Talker could provide us with the data we need.

"Then there's the American colonies. They could provide support for the data-collectors. Further north there's

Greenland and Iceland. Less hospitable, but their data will help complete the pattern."

"Yes, my lady." Samantha had read about monomaniacal scientists, but she had never expected that the first one she met would be a titled lady dressed in the height of fashion.

"But of course we need more data sources closer to home." Lady Augusta turned a page of the atlas. "Land's End in Cornwall, Abergwaun in Wales. Then, in Ireland, Cape Clear, Slea Head, Kerry Head, and, oh, as many as possible. Then, in Scotland, there's the Western Isles. And the Shetlands."

Samantha put down her teacup. "My lady, do you know what that would cost?"

"I *hate* it when people say that," Lady Augusta said.

"I hate having to ask it, my lady. But the reason I have any influence in the College is because I know exactly what things will cost. Or, to put it another way, do you know who will pay for it?"

"I had assumed your Guild would pay for it."

"I'm afraid not. All of those Guild members would have to be paid. Their salaries would add up to a pretty sum. And they would expect to be paid extra if they were sent to somewhere in the end of nowhere."

"Oh, I had assumed you would recruit them locally. They would only do a few minutes' work every day."

Samantha considered this. "I had assumed that you wanted hourly reports."

Lady Augusta's smile was warm. "Babbage's Engine can't handle *that* much data. Four times a day would be the most we could handle."

Samantha wondered how she could tactfully dismiss the idea. "Our Talkers have to be of proven loyalty. They handle information of strategic importance."

Alice put down her cup. "But this isn't strategic

information, surely? It's, ah, gossip about the weather. It only becomes useful after the clever engine has made its prediction."

Lady Augusta beamed at her. "There you are."

Samantha realised that Lady Augusta's idea might be workable. "But how could we locate and train that many Talkers? Besides, there's an armed insurrection going on in Ireland at the moment. They support the Chartists."

Lady Augusta's shrug set her ringlets swaying again. "I'm sure you can manage, my dear."

Samantha had always scorned the heroines in novels who indulged in hysterics. But right now the idea was very tempting.

Alice leaned forward. "My lady, did you say that the Board of Trade was involved?"

"Oh, yes, my dear. They're worried about all these ships being wrecked in storms. They want us to predict storms so that ships will stay in harbour. Perhaps they could provide some of the money we need. I hoped that the admiralty could give some material help, but they did not reply."

Samantha took a sip at her tea. "I think I can get the Admiralty to give us their support."

Lady Augusta was surprised. "You think they will fund it?"

"No, they won't pay us. They won't even thank us. But if commercial vessels in London receive your predictions, and naval captains are left out, they're going to bang their fists on the table and demand to be included in the Board of Trade's reports."

Lady Augusta eyed her with respect. "Lady Samantha, you are a most dangerous person."

"Why, thank you, my dear Lady Augusta."

*

That evening at dinner, Samantha vented her feelings. "She asks the impossible. Recruiting the scores of Talkers that Lady Augusta asks for would be as difficult as solving one of her algorithms."

Lord Edward smiled at her. Was there no sympathy in the man? "It isn't quite that bad. We have Talkers at the most important naval bases, Portsmouth, Plymouth and Harwich. I could ask them to send you reports."

Old Humphrey smiled. "We have Talkers in Liverpool and Manchester, but that's a temporary measure, because we have Chartist trouble there."

Mr. Knight looked sour. "Did you mention Ireland? Because of the insurrection, we have Talkers in Dublin and Limerick, working with the army ..."

"Yes. They'll be recalled as soon as the violence is over, but they might help as a temporary measure until you can get your permanent meteorologists in place," Lord Edward said.

"So it's my problem, is it, my Lord?"

Lord Edward grinned. "None of us here has the courage to deal with Lady Ada of Lovelace."

She sniffed her disdain. "Lord Edward, who's in control of the Computing Project? Surely not Lady Lovelace?"

"I don't think anyone knows the answer to that," Lord Edward said. "Mr. Babbage is the engineer. He designed the engine, but he seems to regard it as a monument to his genius. He doesn't want it to *do* anything. However, Lady Lovelace realised that if Babbage wanted to get the engine built, he would have to show that it would pay for itself. She knows half of the scientists in the British Society. Yes, and understands what they're talking about."

"Oh. My," Samantha said.

"So she wrote to her friends, asking whether any of their projects could be assisted by the Analytical Engine."

Mr. Knight leaned forward. "The story I heard was that she asked whether there were any projects that couldn't get under way because of a lack of computing power."

Edward shrugged. "Either way, she obtained a list of worthwhile projects. All of them, taken together, would take a year for the engine to work through. So she sent Babbage off to the Chancellor with a request for money. The machine got built and they're working their way through Lady Lovelace's list."

"But if they haven't completed the list, why is Lady Augusta asking me about the weather? Oh! She said they wanted to build another engine."

Lord Edward nodded. "The lady needs a new list of worthy projects."

Samantha remembered her original grievance. "But she wants me to recruit a score of Talkers all along the Irish coast!"

He shrugged. "You can't be expected to do anything until his insurrection is over. Then you'll have to find a trustworthy person and delegate it."

Lord Denman Public House, evening of 14 June

Charley 'Coffee' Williams and his companions gathered round the table in the upstairs room of the 'Lord Denman' in Great Suffolk Street, in Southwark, south of the Thames. The room had dark oak panelling. The curtains were drawn and the candles in the wall-sconces were inadequate.

Mcrae was last to arrive. He looked round and spotted Charley, sitting in his corner. "What the hell do you think you were doing on Monday, Coffee?"

"That's Mr. Williams, if you please. Or Charley. Only my closest friends call me 'Coffee'." He shrugged. "You were late, Mr. Mcrae. The crowd was bored. I was bored. They'd been told that they were going to present a petition. So I wrote it down for them. Why were you so late?"

Several of the other men tensed. They wanted to know that too.

"I wanted the march to reach Seven Dials at dusk." Mcrae's tone was neutral.

"You should have organised an afternoon meeting, then."

Mcrae shrugged. "The Chartist Executive arranged the meeting, and the timing. I couldn't change that. But – have you heard? The Executive took a vote to disband the general committee. So they won't be overseeing preparations for any more rallies."

Coffee nodded. He could guess that the Executive was well aware of the violent nature of the committee's plans, and had panicked. Perhaps the members of the Executive had become aware of police spies in the midst of the conspiracy.

"The Executive has left London," Mcrae said. "They haven't the guts to do what's necessary."

"That's unfortunate. They organised those rallies for us," Coffee said.

"These mass rallies are more trouble than they're worth, Mr. Williams. We'll have to restrict our plans to men of similar mind to ourselves."

Coffee was annoyed. He looked round at his companions. "Those rallies gave us legitimacy. We were acting for the common people, not for ourselves. They gave us a political agenda. It was a but vague, but it was there. What agenda do you have, Mr. Mcrae?"

"You know my agenda. Truth. Freedom. The vote for every man. We can work out the details after we've won," Mcrae said.

"That's all a bit vague, Mr. Mcrae," a bald man said.

The man sitting at Coffee's right stood up. "I will not

do anything that isn't supported by the Executive."

"If you don't like it, you can leave," Mcrae said. He looked round. "That applies to all of you."

Coffee hesitated barely a moment, then stood. "I shall leave you to your discussion, then, gentlemen."

"Can't you wait until you've heard what we have to say, Williams?" the bald man complained.

"If I don't leave immediately, somebody's going to accuse me of spying," Coffee said. He wondered, belatedly, whether any of these men was a police spy. If so, the fellow had a tale to tell. "It's better all round if I go now. Good day, gentlemen."

Charity Hospital, Whitechapel, 16 June

The corridors of the Free Hospital were painted white, but they were badly lit. Samantha thought the gloom was depressing. The surgeon gallantly escorted her to the northern exit. There had been no major surgery today, but the girls had been eager to demonstrate how they could heal minor cuts. Now they were putting on their navy-blue jackets as they walked along, preparing to leave. The brick-built entrance hall was grimy. Seven people were waiting to speak to the receptionist.

Three men dressed in cheap suits were loitering just inside the doorway. Their leader moved forward as she approached. "Lady Samantha?"

The speaker was wearing an eye-patch. Samantha's guards tensed. Everyone else came to a halt. She recognised the speaker. "Dave, is it? Do you have a problem?"

Dave gestured to the women behind her. "We're all grateful for what these girls are doing, but we object to them being escorted across Whitechapel by these guards of yours. It's almost as bad as a squad of Peelers tramping through

141

here. It's an insult to this law-abiding community."

"I see." Samantha knew that these combat-trained guild members regarded escort duty as a chore. And, besides, Edward wanted to transfer these men to West End.

"We'd be happy to go to work without any escort," Bettie said.

Samantha rejected the idea. She felt responsible for their safety. "Bettie, I could send you all in a cab -."

"Do you know how to find a dependable cabbie?" Dave asked.

She was annoyed by the man's impertinence. "Dave, are any dependable men of this – community – prepared to give up their time to take over the task of escorting these girls?"

He was quite taken aback. He glanced at his companions "Well - I can find a few dependable men. They're handy with cudgels -."

Alice gasped. "Not cudgels, no."

"Yes, Alice, I agree." Samantha turned to Dave. "To people like Sir George Grey, men with cudgels mean riots, which means civil unrest, which means, to Sir George, that they have to send in the army. So your companions will have to defend my apprentices with nothing more than their manly bearing."

Dave didn't seem to like that. "Well - my colleagues are skilled craftsmen. It's quite lawful for them to walk to work with the tools of their trade. Hammers and mallets and such like."

Samantha thought Dave was being over-confident, but none of his listeners contradicted him. She felt she had no choice. "Very well. I agree. But these girls aren't used to these streets or outspoken men. I would expect you to behave like gentlemen while you do this."

She was surprised that everyone grinned at this, even the surgeon. "What's wrong? What did I say?"

You explain it to the lady, doctor," Dave said.

Doctor Jones suppressed a smile. "My, lady, the only reason a young gentleman visits this part of London is to cause mayhem. Getting drunk. Daredevils who think it's a great joke to start fights. Some of them end up here."

"I'm tired of healing gentlemen's cracked heads," Bettie said.

"Some of them end up in the magistrate's court. These, er, craftsmen have probably seen gentlemen at their worst," Doctor Jones said.

Samantha remembered, too late, that the East End was notorious for its brothels. Was that what Dave was grinning about? She was angry at herself. "Then let's say, Dave, I want you and your companions to behave the way gentlemen are supposed to behave."

Dave smiled. "Behave better than gentlemen?"

Samantha was still angry. "Could you manage it for an hour a day?"

Dave was serious now. "I think we can manage that, eh, lads?"

There was a murmur of assent. "Aye."

Chapter 10 Repercussions

Osborne House, 20 June

This time Samantha and Lady Mary had brought their overnight bags and their evening dresses. Samantha had been given a cramped room in the Household Wing. She put on her evening dress, with the assistance of a maid. Samantha and Lady Mary had been invited to dine with the Queen, a rare honour. Samantha gave her dress a final check and stepped out into the corridor.

A maid of honour escorted them downstairs. Samantha guessed that one of the Ladies in Waiting would have to dine in her room that evening to make way for her. The woman was probably grateful of her escape.

The windows of the dining room looked out onto the terrace. They were left open and Samantha noted that some of the ladies sitting round the table were uncomfortable in their flimsy low-cut evening dresses. The Queen, however, seemed impervious to their plight. Samantha noted that the Guild's female talker was not present – she was probably dining in her room too. Lord Edward was sitting opposite her, but the rules forbade them from talking to each other. Her partner's dinner-table conversation was dreadfully dull.

The Queen finished her meal before everyone else and rose from the table. The ladies dutifully stood and followed her into the withdrawing room. Samantha looked round. The most striking features were the four marble columns and the cut-glass chandeliers. The deep red carpet had a floral pattern worked in yellow and blue. Samantha dreaded this. Lord Edward had told her just how boring the Queen's after-dinner conversation was.

The Queen seated herself in an elaborately carved high-backed chair and indicated that Samantha should sit on the sofa opposite. She smiled. "Now, my dear, tell us about the message from Bethnal Fields." Her voice was light and musical.

The Ladies in Waiting clustered around. Samantha realised this was not going to be boring at all. The Queen's manner was friendly, but Samantha felt a trickle of sweat between her shoulder blades despite the cold.

"Yes, madam. The police inspector asked the Guild for an additional Talker. And – my companion was the only one available. If the inspector had given us a few hours, I could have found five or six, but in the circumstances ...

"I could not send my Talker alone, I had to accompany her. I thought it would be an outing for us both, quite unobjectionable. After all, nothing happened. We just waited at the boundary all day long."

The Queen nodded. "Yes, of course. Nothing happened. Please explain the message, my dear."

"Yes, madam." Lord Edward was still in the dining room, no doubt drinking port with the other gentlemen. He could not help her. "Well - the demonstrators asked why I was there, most politely, you understand. So it explained I was a member of the Guild and my colleague could talk to St. James's Palace. They asked whether I could send a message to Osborne House.

"The inspector said it was his policy to keep aggressive men talking. Once they could be persuaded to talk politely, it was unlikely for them to resort to violence."

The Queen considered this. "So they were polite to you?"

"Oh, yes, madam. And - the Talker at St. James's said that you had asked to be kept informed." Samantha noted that the Ladies in Waiting were listening with interest.

The Queen smiled. "Well, so we did, my dear, but we did not expect that."

Prince Albert walked in, followed by Lord Edward. The Queen greeted them, then turned back to Samantha. Her eyes narrowed. "Now, we were advised that you made some comments about votes for women. How could you have the audacity to say that? Elections are such beastly affairs. Any lady who wishes to be involved in such a thing deserves to be flogged."

Samantha looked round. The Ladies in Waiting were sympathetic to her plight, but they could do nothing to help.

Edward stepped forward. "You see, madam, the chosen subject of a debate should be slightly daring. Otherwise it becomes boring."

"Debate, you say? In Bethnal Fields?"

"Yes, madam. It was all very polite," Samantha said.

"So your comment about suffrage was merely a - debating point?"

Samantha was weak with relief. "Yes, madam. These Chartists were impudent enough to want the vote for themselves, but not for women ... I told them that they were really Tories after all."

The Queen laughed. "Yes, we see, yes, very good. My dear, why didn't you bring your Talker with you today?"

Samantha hesitated. "Well, madam - her father is in trade." The high sticklers of society refused to associate with anyone with the merest whiff of trade.

The Queen understood what Samantha meant. "Does the girl have good manners? If so, we would welcome her. we are not a victim of this odious snobbery."

"Yes, madam," Samantha said. She decided that boredom really had a lot to be said for it.

146

College dining room, 22 June

Alice had chosen to dine at the College instead of rushing home. She said her mother was eager for her to spend more time amongst the young men of the College.

Edward finished his first course and put down his knife. "Lady Samantha, is there any truth in the story that you're the author of this bon mot about gentlemen?"

Samantha was bewildered. "What's that, my lord?" This afternoon she was wearing a dress of black wool.

"You're said to have asked some workmen in the East End to behave the way gentlemen are supposed to behave, not the way they do behave." Everyone else at the high table paused to listen.

Samantha was mortified. "How did you hear that? Doctor Jones - I'll kill him!"

Everyone at the table laughed. "So it's true then? How did it happen?" Edward said.

"Oh, yes," Oswald said. "Do tell us, please." Everyone else smiled.

Samantha realised that she could not disappoint them. "Well, I didn't like these girls walking to the Free Hospital alone. It's only half a mile, but ... So I arranged for one of your teams to escort them.

"Well, they didn't like such a boring task. And the local people didn't like a squad of magicians tramping through their streets either. Alice heard that bit." She paused to take a sip at her wine.

"So a local man, the leader of the print workers' guild, complained. He said my men weren't as bad as Peelers, but still ... Samantha smiled at the memory. All of her listeners, Alice included, were listening avidly.

"Well, I said I wanted them to behave like gentlemen." She paused for effect. "That was a mistake, of course, because far too many fine gentlemen visit the East End for all the wrong reasons. Why, some of the apprentices here -."

Alice recognised her cue. "Stop. I don't want to hear any more."

"So I asked them to behave the way gentlemen are supposed to behave."

Everyone at the high table laughed.

"I don't know how it started," Lady Mary said, "but tales of your bon mot have been spreading across every drawing room in the West End."

Samantha was mortified. "It wasn't a bon mot or anything. I just got angry."

"There's a saying that the insults that hurt the most are those that have some truth in them." Alice smiled.

"But this is terrible. Doctor Jones - he's been bandying my name in public."

Edward leaned forward. "That may be a bit harsh. Lady Mary, in your opinion, has the doctor caused offence?"

Lady Mary put down her glass. "He hasn't, well, cast assertions upon dear Samantha's character. I agree, he should have been more circumspect. But if you asked him to apologise you would simply make things worse."

Samantha was embarrassed all over again. "But, Lady Mary, do you say that you've heard it too?"

"Oh, yes. You can hear it in every drawing room in London."

"Good lord. I never meant -."

"So, now I'm waiting for the next brilliant set-down," Edward said.

"Lord Edward, it wasn't brilliant at all. I just got angry at my mistake and said whatever came into my head."

Edward took a sip at his wine. "And now it seems you're a raconteur. But does this escort of craftsmen work as you hoped?"

"Oh, yes, perfectly," Alice said.

"Hush, please. I was worried that the local

troublemakers might stop the – craftsmen – to show how tough they were. But we've had no problems. The girls are Healers, after all, going to the hospital." She smiled. "In fact, the only problem was that the craftsmen got smug, boasting that for an hour or two they could behave better than gentlemen."

"And that Lady Samantha trusted them," Alice put in.

"Hush, please, Alice. So another group of workers complained and they asked to share in the escort duty."

"The problems you have to solve," Edward said.

Samantha shrugged. "It was easy enough. I knew these craftsmen were taking time off work, without pay. They might lose their jobs. So I suggested the second group could escort the girls home in the evening. So honour was satisfied."

"It's not your task to bargain with these, er, craftsmen, my lady."

"Lord Edward, it's the task of the Guild to maintain order and protect society. To my mind that includes protecting the people of the East End too. If a few minutes' negotiation prevents a riot, it's worth it."

Chapter 11 News from Paris

St. James's Palace, afternoon of 25 June

Four pm was approaching. Edward, Samantha and Alice gathered in the 'Embassy' room of St. James's palace to listen to the next hourly report from Paris.

Edward had put a map of Paris on the wall. The reports from the embassy suggested that all of eastern Paris had been barricaded, with the fiercest fighting on the rue du Faubourg-st-Antonine. Edward had carefully noted these on his map.

"According to the embassy reports, the government's troops controlled the centre of the city from the start. They were expecting trouble," Edward said.

Rupert and several other Talkers gathered round Albert's desk. Over the last two days, this had become an hourly ritual. The desk faced the wall. A bookshelf, fastened to the wall, held a series of leather-bound books.

Albert, one of the 'Foreign Office' Talkers, glanced at the clock. "Excuse me, sir." He pulled the notepad across the desk, then opened a slim book of poetry. He looked up. "Have you any questions for me, sir?"

"Well – has anything changed since the last report? Are the embassy staff safe? Is the ambassador all right?"

"The embassy's nowhere near the fighting, sir."

"I know that, Albert. But ask anyway. I want positive confirmation. Tell him that the Queen is most concerned about the ambassador."

"Oh. Right." He closed the poetry book and frowned in concentration. He picked up his pencil and began writing on the message pad in large letters.

'*Big news - archbishop shot – barricade – green branch – critical – staff safe - ambassador safe - George safe - tired. Gunfire constant – thousand casualties - government propaganda.*' He put down his pencil, then frowned and picked it up again. '*A thanks q for her concern*'. He sighed.

"What's the latest news, Albert?" Edward asked.

"The government says that the Archbishop of Paris tried to negotiate with the rebels. He arranged a ceasefire, then climbed up the barricade to talk to them. He carried a green branch to show he came in peace. But the government troops broke the ceasefire, the rebels fired back, and the archbishop was wounded. He was carried clear, but his situation is serious. Apart from that ...

"Gunfire is constant, sir. To the east. The government bulletins emphasise that thousands of rebels have been killed or wounded but they refuse to lay down their arms. So the government feels justified in its actions. General Cavaignac is bringing in thousands of troops by train. George thinks he's been planning this for weeks." He smiled. "And the ambassador thanks Her Majesty for her concern."

Edward smiled. "Right. I'll ask Rupert to forward that to Osborne House."

"Thousands of casualties. Could it happen here?" Samantha asked.

Edward was bleak. "Only if the government's very stupid and breaks all its promises."

"It hasn't made any promises," Albert said.

Samantha thought of all the proposed new laws being haggled over by the politicians, but said nothing. She sat at the desk and began translating Albert's notes into an elegant communiqué. "Will that do?" She turned her draft round so that Edward and Albert could read it.

Edward looked it over. "Yes. Copies to be sent to the

PM at Downing Street and Palmerston at the Foreign Office by hand. Rupert can send it to Osborne House."

"We'd better let the newspapers see it too. An archbishop is big news. They're bound to complain if we ignore them," Samantha said.

She heard the footsteps of several people in the corridor outside, walking fast. She turned to look, just as the first person strode into the room. He was dressed in the height of fashion, a dark blue frock coat. Samantha's mouth dropped open as she recognised him as Lord Palmerston.

He was quite old – about sixty - but still had an athlete's fitness. He was said to ride or swim every morning before breakfast. He was the sort of likeable rogue who created the juicy gossip that an unmarried lady was not supposed to know about. He had taken a series of married ladies as his lovers: first Lady Jersey, then Princess Dorothy de Lieven, before beginning his affair with Lady Cowper. When the husband died, they finally married. According to the most delicious rumours, he had expected to present his new wife at court, but Prince Albert had said no. Looking at him, Samantha thought that all the rumours could well be true. She was relieved when he ignored her.

"Good afternoon, my lord," Edward said.

"Good afternoon, Lord Edward." Palmerston turned to the map of Paris on the wall. "So this is how things are going. Is this up to date?"

"It has the latest information that reached the embassy. But the staff are out of touch."

Palmerston tapped the eastern section of the map. "According to this, the rebels control half of Paris. But General Cavaignac must have made some advances. Can't this Talker of yours go out and inspect these barricades for himself?"

"No, my lord. I can't agree to that. He's the only Talker we've got in Paris. If he suffers an accident, our source of information is gone."

"Taking a look at the barricades can't be that dangerous, surely?" Palmerston said.

Samantha, wordlessly, handed him her communiqué. He took it and read it through. His eyebrows rose. "The archbishop? Wounded? Why haven't we got more Talkers in Paris?"

Edward smiled. "Because you refused to pay their salaries, my lord."

"I see." Palmerston waved the note. "Has anyone seen this yet?"

"No, my lord." Samantha said. "I was about to make out a fair copy. But Downing Street has to see it. And so does Osborne House. And if the editor of the Times doesn't ..."

Palmerston was exasperated. "Lord Edward, who is this chit?"

"Oh! Lady Samantha Hampden, may I introduce to you Lord Temple, Viscount Palmerston." He went on in a less formal tone, "Lady Samantha is the new Chatelaine of the College."

"Enchanted." Palmerston sketched a slight bow. Samantha's curtsey was equally slight.

"Isn't she young for the task?" Palmerston asked.

"Lady Samantha's aunt died unexpectedly, you see, and Lady Samantha had to step into her shoes."

"I see. My condolences, madam."

"The Queen said that she suspected foul play," Rupert said.

"Did she indeed?" Palmerston did not sound very impressed. "Did you hear that the French government had closed down the airmail service between Paris and London? Dirigibles are banned from the capital until further notice."

Edward glanced at Albert, who shook his head. "No, my lord."

"Their ambassador delivered the letter in person. I had

to sign a receipt before I could open it. And the fellow told me that permission to restart the mail service would be delivered the same way." He scowled. "So if anything happens to that Talker of yours, all we've got is the postal service. No, I can't risk him."

"When did the French courier leave Paris, my lord?" Samantha asked.

"Are you asking whether the fellow left Paris before the fighting started? I thought of that myself. My guess is that the government issued that proclamation to the populace and despatched that courier to London at the same time."

The College, late afternoon, 26 June

Edward gave the order for an additional session of self-defence training. Samantha guessed that he was disturbed by the latest news from Paris. The rising had been crushed in four days of fighting. Some people were asking whether London would be next.

The newspapers were at last providing details of the uprising. Londoners, the poor in particular, were voluble in their indignation of the cruelty of the French government.

Samantha had thought up a complication to her self-defence training. She and Alice would walk across the college atrium, surrounded by their guards, and another team would feign an attack. Edward was there to act as umpire.

On this occasion her backup team were defending her and the primary team, led by Charles, were the attackers. A few of the maids had taken a few minutes off work to watch the fun.

Samantha and her team walked past Charles, who

154

smiled but did nothing. Samantha looked over her shoulder to keep her eye on him. Then Charles' number two, up ahead, made a feint. Her defenders blocked his attack without much trouble. Charles waited until Samantha and her guards were distracted, then rushed at them, effectively taking them by surprise. He threw a tennis ball at each.

"You're dead, you're dead."

Samantha noticed the movement, squeaked in surprise and turned to face him. She concentrated on getting her shield up. "Partum a scuto."

Charles ignored her. Instead he grabbed Alice and roundly kissed her.

Alice put her own hands each side of his and tried to pull them away, but without effect. She panicked, shifted her weight to her left foot and brought her right knee up into his groin. The movement was perfectly executed and was delivered with all the force that panic could provide. She was hampered by her skirts, but the blow was effective and Charles collapsed, writhing.

Everyone gathered round the recumbent man. Samantha bit her lip. It would be quite wrong to laugh.

Alice was mortified at this over-reaction. "I shouldn't, I shouldn't. Oh, don't be angry! Please forgive me!" For the moment, though, Charles was incapable of saying anything.

Edward pushed his way forward, angry. "Loosen his clothing, someone. Put him in the recovery position. How did you fools let him through? If you were that sloppy in combat you'd be dead." He turned on Samantha. "And what were you doing, my lady?"

"I got my shield up. But he ignored me."

"So at least one person did the right thing." Edward was not happy at admitting that. He turned on Alice. "What were you thinking of, girl? Your over-reaction is unforgivable."

"I'm sorry, my lord. I shouldn't, I shouldn't have done

155

it."

Samantha was annoyed. "Aren't we supposed to be training for a real assassination? Are you saying, my lord, that if I'm attacked, Alice must not hurt the poor weak assassin?"

"I said -." Edward bit his lip. "I hate it when you're right."

Mr. Smith stepped forward. "My lord, you tell us we're training for the real thing. All of us can kill an attacker. So the rules forbid us to use magic or improvise." He gestured to the figure on the ground. "Charles improvised."

"You hate him, don't you?" Edward said.

Mr. Smith shrugged. "A trace of envy, perhaps, my lord. If I had done this, what punishment would you be devising for me right now?"

Charles groaned. Aided by his friends, he sat up. He had recovered enough to talk. "I'm - sorry. Don't - blame Alice. I just wanted to - show how much I liked her."

"So you can talk, can you?" Now that Charles was recovering, Edward transferred his anger to him. "You like her, do you? Then you chose the wrong time and the wrong method to show it. I'd say you got what you deserved."

"Yes, my lord."

Edward turned back to Samantha. "Alice should learn self-defence. That way your team will know how to anticipate her reactions."

"Please, I don't want to – to touch anyone," Alice said.

Edward glance down at Charles. "Well, perhaps it's unwise to let your opponent get within arm's reach. Don't you have any magical defences?"

"Nothing, my lord. I'm a talker. All I can do is a were-light."

"Show me," Edward demanded.

Alice held out her hand. "Partum a luce." She produced a feeble light.

Edward was not impressed. "It could startle him, I suppose. Singe his whiskers. I want you to practice that. At least your team could anticipate your response ..." He turned back to Charles. "At the next practice session, my man, give Lady Samantha and Alice a tennis ball each. If anyone gets within range, she can hit him with it. That'll remind everyone that she's a member of the team." He turned to Alice. "That is, if you want to stay with the team. Now you know you're also at risk?"

Alice raised her chin. "I'll stay with Lady Samantha, my lord."

"Good girl."

Hospital Fields 27 June

Gretchen was supervising the girls on the second floor of the silk weaving factory. Most of the surface area was taken up by the iron frames of silk looms. Alfred had to raise his voice to make himself heard over the constant rattle of the looms.

In this section the woven fabrics were rolled up and stored on shelves, one on top of the other. It enabled her to enjoy the bright colours and intricate patterns. She knew that the other women considered her young for the task of supervisor. She had won the post because she had learned her numbers as well as her letters and knew how to put both to good use. She had married early, to a silk-weaver. He had died of consumption two years later. She was not eager to repeat the experience. In some ways she was better off as a widow. She held a responsible position, rather than being an unpaid assistant.

Although she admitted that Alfred was attractive. He, too, had learned his numbers. He was said to be an activist in the socialist movement. He was certainly a troublemaker,

157

always complaining about working conditions. He was said to be a member of the Chartists' executive. That danger added to his attraction.

Right now he was grumbling about the morning's visitors, a group of upper-class customers who had strolled around the upper floor an hour before. Gretchen shared his resentment, but thought it wise to remain silent.

"They get in the way, slow everyone down, and they buy nothing. And if they damage the stock, we get the blame." He wore a natty maroon waistcoat over a crisp white linen shirt. His neck-cloth was bright red.

"They didn't damage anything. And if the foreman sees you dawdling, you'll be in trouble."

"He sent me to complain about the purple twill on the last batch. It's too purple, he says."

"Too purple, is it? Well, I know what he means." Gretchen sniffed. She smelled something. "Is that smoke?" She turned and walked between two looms to where the foreman for that floor, Mr. Heap, was talking to the factory manager, Mr. Stevens.

Mr. Heap was wearing a light green suit and a matching bowler hat, while Mr. Stevens was elegantly turned out in a dark grey suit, wide bow tie and a top hat.

Gretchen gave an apologetic cough. "Beg pardon, Mr. Heap, but I can smell smoke." People looked up from their tasks, although the looms continued in their work.

Mr. Heap carried a length of rope in his right hand. He had told her once that if a length of cord was too thin it would cut a slacker's skin. A heavy rope only caused bruises. He had told her more than once that her girls would move faster if she used a ropes' end on them.

The foreman glanced at the racks of shelves at the far end of the building. "Some slacker dropped a cigarette." He turned to Alfred. "Put out the fire. Find another couple of men if you have to. We've got sand buckets. The rest of you -

158

get back work." He thwacked his length of rope against his palm.

Mr. Stevens sniffed. He nodded towards the rear of the warehouse. The smoke was visible now. "No, no. it's got hold. Clear this floor, get everyone clear. Stop the looms and get clear."

Some of the workers dropped what they were doing and ran for the stairs. Others were slower on the uptake. One of the girls turned to Gretchen. "Should we save the stock?"

Gretchen, now thoroughly alarmed, pushed the other girls towards the stairs. "Forget the stock. Out with you!"

She glanced round and shared a look with Alfred. Was he going to rescue her? She was tired and frightened and needed a helping hand tight now.

"You're doing good work! Keep it up," he shouted, and turned away.

She was indignant. How could he abandon her? Then his words sank in. If she was doing good work, saving lives, then she needed to keep at it. The smoke was getting worse. At least there were no flames.

Gretchen was amongst the last to reach stairs. She was still harrying the laggards. The stairs were very wide, with no bannisters, to allow men with wide loads to carry their burdens up and down. This flight of stairs was clear. One floor down, the workers on that floor were trying to leave too.

She lifted her skirts and ran down one flight of stairs to join Alfred at the top of the next flight. Panic was spreading among the shoving crowd. The wide doors, and the view they gave of the courtyard, were a symbol of safety. The people at the back were pushing those in front of them. One person, near the bottom, tripped. The people immediately behind, pushed by those above, fell over him.

The heap of people blocked the stairs. Everyone started screaming. Gretchen was appalled at the disaster below her.

The smoke was getting worse, which increased the panic.

"We're trapped," Alfred shouted in her ear. "Unless we use them as stepping stones – and kill them while we're about it."

Gretchen thought a moment, then sat on the edge of the step. She slid over the side. She landed safely but fell to her knees. When she tried to stand she ripped her skirt.

She ran to the doorway, pushed her way clear, and looked back. Some people were jumping over the bodies in their desperation to escape the smoke. Out in the courtyard, a lot of people were coughing. She took several deep breaths of cold, clear air. Then a sense of duty led her back to the doorway.

The manager looked on, appalled, at the bodies at the foot of the stairs. Some were groaning. He started pulling bodies clear. "Where's that bloody foreman?" He turned to Alfred. "Come on, give me a hand with this."

Alfred did not hesitate. Together, they pulled first person clear. "Can you walk?" Mr. Stevens said. "Good. Get into the courtyard."

They turned to pull the next victim clear, a girl. Alfred pulled her to her feet. She sagged against him.

"You can't walk?" Mr. Stevens asked. He turned to Gretchen and the girl beside her. "You and you - carry her. Make room so we can get more free."

Gretchen was annoyed at his high-handed attitude, but he was quite right. She helped carry the woman into the courtyard. "Lay her down. Away from the smoke."

She went back for more. Each successive victim, further down the pile, was worse than the last. More and more volunteers joined the manager and Alfred at their task.

Gretchen grabbed hold of a girl who was wringing her hands. "Run to the Free Hospital. Ask them to send a doctor or a nurse – or anyone. Warn them they'll have a lot of visitors soon." The girl nodded, glad of something to do, and ran off.

The last three victims made no sound. They found the foreman at the bottom of the pile. He was still holding his length of rope.

"He probably tripped over his shoelaces," Alfred said.

Mr. Stevens had lost his fine hat and had ripped his stiff collar off. It made him look human. He followed her out into the courtyard and looked at the row of victims. "Is their clothing tight? Open their collars."

Alfred ventured up the stairs and reported back. "There's plenty of smoke, sir, but no flames at ground level or the floor above. We could pull the stock out. It'll give the fire less to catch on to."

Mr. Stevens bit his lip. "Do it. But see to it that each man only spends a minute in there. Don't let anyone breathe that smoke for too long."

Alfred and his team were interrupted by the arrival of the fire brigade, with their steam-driven water pump. They told everyone to get out of their way and began unrolling their hoses.

Gretchen was distracted when the healer from the Free Hospital arrived with a doctor. She led them to the spot in the middle of the courtyard where the wounded and the dead lay in rows.

Half an hour later, the doctor made his report to Mr. Stevens. "Three people were crushed to death, sir. Six more are suffering from cracked ribs. Several more have respiratory problems. From the smoke, I think, not the crush."

Alfred turned to Gretchen. "Are you all right? You didn't breathe any of that stuff?"

"I tried not to breathe too deep."

"We're going to need a new foreman," Mr. Stevens said. "Alfred, you thought fast in there. Do you want the job?"

Alfred used his red neck-cloth to wipe his face. "No, sir.

I won't use a whip on anyone. If a man won't work unless he's whipped, then he won't work anyway."

Mr. Stevens waved this aside. "Use your own methods of persuasion, then. We'll see how you get on."

Alfred nodded. "Very well, sir."

Gretchen realised that made him a more interesting prospect. "If you accept, you'll have to buy a new hat."

He grinned. "You'd only marry a man who wears a bowler, eh?"

She blushed. "This is no time for levity."

Chapter 12 The Coaching Inn

Whitechapel, 28 June

The old Roman road cutting through the East End was a ribbon of posterity. The shops and public houses on each side of the road served the prosperous travellers, not the local population, and provided one of the few sources of steady employment. It was rumoured that protection gangs demanded a ransom from each pub to be left alone; but as long as the ransom was paid, lesser criminals dared not touch them.

The 'Princess Caroline' pub, named after King George the Fourth's dead queen, had once been a coaching inn. Now it had a fine Georgian façade, with sash windows and a well-proportioned doorway. Samantha walked inside, accompanied by her guard John Smith, who knew the area well. She was followed by Alice and another of her guards.

She had learned that the larger, more genteel, public houses such as this were segregated, with a saloon bar for women and couples. For her, this was a first. She and Alice were both wearing fine woollen dark grey skirts and spencer jackets in midnight blue.

They were met in the hallway by a tall, plump man wearing a spotless white apron over trousers and shirtsleeves. He took in the ladies' fashionable dress. "Good morning. I'm Mr. Chard, the manager. Are – are you Lady Hampden? I was told to expect you."

"Lady Samantha Hampden, yes. I've come for a private meeting."

He pointed. "The private room is up those stairs, my

lady."

"Thank you." She turned. "Mr. Smith, Mr. Lloyd, come with me, please." She led the way up the stairs.

The room faced south, with the tall sash windows letting in the sunlight. It was smaller than she had expected, with room for only ten chairs around the table. The walls were decorated with sporting prints. Several bottles and glasses stood on the table. Four men were waiting for her, sitting at the far end of the table. Samantha knew they were craftsmen, but today they were wearing jackets over linen shirts. They were all sporting clean red neckerchiefs.

They were tough men, of middle age or older, worn down by hard work and the worry of providing food for their families. Dave One-eye stood as she entered. After a moment, the others did too. "Good morning. Lady Hampden, these are Fred, Harry, and Charley."

Fred had sleek black hair. His top hat rested on the chair at his side. Harry pondered his options, then removed his bowler hat and placed it on the table in front of him.

Samantha recognised Charley from Bethnal Fields. He had very dark skin, as if he had some African blood, and was short, about five feet tall. He wore a cloth cap. Samantha nodded and sat down facing them, and after a moment Alice sat beside her. The two guards stood by the door.

"You can call me Frederick," Fred said.

Dave ignored this. He gestured at the guards. "Why are those boys here?"

"I wanted to come alone, you see. My guards usually stand behind me and scowl at anyone who looks suspicious – which is everyone. That ruins an honest conversation. I told them to stay behind. They refused."

Dave smiled thinly. "I thought magicians were supposed to obey the Chatelaine?"

"Yes, but they're also supposed to protect me. So we compromised. Two of them'll stay outside and scowl at

164

passers-by, while these two will stay out of earshot."

Frederick smiled. "We're in the printing trade, except for Charley here. But he's been dying to meet you. He works on Babbage's engine, you see. He heard you and Lady Lovelace have been scheming together."

"Yes. Lady Lovelace wants to predict the weather. She wants a bigger machine, but -."

Charley sat up. "What! That's wonderful news, if it's true."

"They want a bigger machine, but getting the government to pay for it is another matter."

"Yes, that's true, miss."

Dave glared at them. "If you two're going to spend the rest of the day talking about that damned machine, I'm going home."

Samantha laughed. She looked round. "Did you book this room just for me? I hope it didn't cost too much."

"Don't worry, I told Chard to send the bill to you. I don't think he believed me, at first."

She was amused. "That was not the act of a gentleman, Dave."

Dave picked up a beer bottle and poured the contents into two half-pint glasses. He pushed the glasses across the table towards Samantha and Alice. "You don't mind beer, I hope? My lady - Why have you come to us?"

"You know what the people say, what they're feeling. People listen to you. It's about the Factory Safety Bill. There are so many accidents, the newspapers approved of the Bill, and I had such high hopes. But the government lost the vote in parliament. The Prime Minister could have watered it down, tried again ..." She took a sip at her beer to hide her emotions. The stuff was bitter.

"But the opposition told the Prime Minister that the bill would increase the costs of factories. And if prices went up he'd lose the next election. He made that sound worse

165

than watching London burn down."

"You *heard* him?" Frederick asked.

"Lady Samantha meets all sorts of interesting people," Dave said.

"None as interesting as you, Dave," she said.

He ignored this. "Why did you want to speak to me – all of us?"

"You're my – barometer. Do we have stormy weather ahead? I need to know how the people will react to the news. How bitter are they?"

Dave pursed his lips, considering the question. "Londoners are a cynical lot. They don't put much store by politicians' promises ... Charley?"

Charley the African shrugged. "My guess is that Londoners won't care. Not until another factory burns down or the roof collapses - and children are orphaned. Then they'll remember the promises the politicians made and there'll be a riot."

"So there's nothing you can do, miss – my lady?" Frederick asked. "Can you think of anything?"

"We can hope that the Prime Minister tries again and a watered-down bill gets passed. We can hope there are no more factory accidents ..."

"They aren't accidents, you know," Dave said. "Factory owners take out insurance and then the factory burns down."

"Nonsense, Davey. Those fires are caused by human stupidity, not by cunning," Frederick said.

Davy took a swig at his beer and put the half-empty glass down on the table. "There's a pattern to those fires. There's very little structural damage, so it's easily repaired. It's never the finished product that goes. No, it's the raw product and the workers that burn. And, each time, the owner collects the insurance."

The other men tensed. Samantha, appalled, expected Dave to launch into another tirade. Instead, he took a modest sip at his beer.

Samantha turned to Charley. "Mr. Williams?"

"I agree with Fred. Those fires start in badly designed workshops. But it's easier to get angry about the employer's greed than about everyone's clumsiness."

"Factory owners are greedy," Harry said. "They skimp wherever they can. They hate the Factory Bill. But I don't believe they'll set fire to their own factories."

Samantha took a cautious sip at her beer.

"Charley here is a magic-user," Frederick said. This earned him a glare from Charley.

"Playing with magic can be dangerous," Samantha said. "You can injure yourself, or the people around you, in all sorts of ways. And if you over-exert yourself, your heart stops."

"You can get hurt in other ways too." Dave's tone was sour. "If your magicians' guild thinks someone is using magic for gain, they throw him in prison."

"They rarely bother. Not unless someone boasts too loudly. It's fraud that they disapprove of." She told them about her visit to Bow Street. The story seemed to amuse them.

She put her glass down on the table. She saw that her glass was almost empty. "Well, it's been an interesting visit. I thank you for your time."

"We haven't really told you anything. It's as if we've been wasting your time," Frederick said.

"I told you, I wanted to know if we have stormy weather ahead. You've given me a clue. A bit like Lady Lovelace's weather reports."

Chapter 13 Berkeley Square

30 June

Edward was walking home from St. James's palace. Some high-sticklers disapproved of such exertion, saying that a gentleman ought to travel by coach, but he felt that he needed the exercise. This afternoon he was wearing his most elegant frock coat of blue and green plaid. The garment was tailored to emphasise his shoulders.

Robert, the guard taking point, dropped back. "I feel terribly exposed out here. Everyone in the square can see us. Makes me feel like a deer in the hunting season."

"Nonsense. We know all the passers-by." He paused to raise his hat to a passing lady.

Robert waited until the lady was out of earshot. "What about a man with a gun, in one of those houses?"

Edward was amused. "We know everyone on this side of the square. And who could hit us from the far side? Besides, I need the exercise." He could see the College doorway ahead.

He saw a flash, away to the right. Before he could turn he felt a punch on his right side that knocked him off his feet. He heard a gunshot. Only then did he feel the pain. He thrust his hand into his coat, under his ribs. He hissed at the pain and withdrew his hand. He tried to focus his eyes on it. His gloves were wet with blood.

He could hear his men shouting. "Sniper – ricochet – east side of square – could fire again – keep him down!"

Edward was finding it difficult to concentrate and had no intention of getting up, so this seemed superfluous.

"How could he get that lucky? Perhaps the bastard used a rifle –."

"Never mind that, get him indoors – you two carry him, we'll shield you."

Edward had no desire to be carried anywhere. It seemed simplest to stay where he was. He wanted to say so, but it seemed he was just too tired. It seemed easier to let himself be carried.

His team half carried, half dragged him up the steps and into the entrance hall. He felt himself being lifted onto a sofa. They were shouting again. "Sniper – slightly short but ricochet injured him. And close that door!"

The men around Edward were talking in an undertone. They were angry, on the edge of panic. He was relieved when he heard Samantha's voice cut through the babble. "What's happened here?"

Idiot girl, he thought, couldn't she see what had happened? The babble returned as everybody tried to explain. He expected her to swoon or something, but it seemed she was made of sterner stuff. "Who's in charge here?"

Good question, he thought. Once more she cut through the babble. "Is *nobody* in charge here?" Another awkward question. It ought to be him, and in his absence, the Master, and in *his* absence ...

"I see. Does anyone here know anything about nursing or first aid? Mrs. Hudson? Then fetch her at once." She sounded angry. He was glad she wasn't angry at him. Edward wanted to say this was no place for a girl, but he knew she would ignore him. He was too tired to argue.

"We will have to inform the authorities, the magistrate in Bow Street," Samantha said.

Edward cursed. Did the chit never rest?

"The College prefers to remain discreet," Robert said.

"But you can't hush this up. You aren't that powerful.

169

Or are you? Somebody fired a gun in Berkeley Square. Everybody must have heard it."

Edward concentrated. "Tell them, the authorities. But - only the facts. No speculation."

He closed his eyes and relaxed. He listened, amused, as Samantha and his guards worked out how little they did know. A gun had been fired. Was it attempted murder? Were they certain that Edward was the intended victim? Were they even certain that murder had been intended? Finally, Samantha wrote a description of the incident and told one of her guards to deliver the message to Bow Street.

Then Mrs. Hudson arrived. Edward knew she was competent. Her hands were gentle. "Lots of wounds in his side, my lady. Most of them are minor, but judging by the blood, some's serious. I'm sorry, my lord, but if I want a good look I'll have to remove your coat. And that means getting you to sit up."

"You will have to lift me up," Edward said. He knew it was going to hurt.

Samantha intervened. "I don't want to move him, Mrs. Hudson. The coat's ruined anyway. Cut it off him. I've always hated it."

He wondered why he hated his coat. It was his favourite. There was a delay, then he heard scissors crunching through good wool, and the remains of his coat were peeled back.

"And the shirt too?" Mrs. Hudson said. The scissors crunched again. He heard cries of dismay from his men.

Mrs. Hudson was calm. "Well, I can deal with the minor abrasions but ... there's two deep punctures. There may be something still in there."

"Right. Surgeon's work," Samantha said. "Charles, go and fetch the doctor and a Healer from the Free Hospital. Go by coach, so you can fetch them back that way."

Edward heard somebody rush off. He endured in

silence while Mrs. Hudson put temporary bandages on the serious wounds. Then she set about the task of cleaning the minor ones.

"Should we fetch the local doctor?" Samantha asked. Somebody explained that the local doctor spent most of his time making house calls.

"How are you, Edward? Well enough to speak?" Samantha asked.

"This is no place for a girl," he said, mainly to find out how she would respond.

"Don't try to get up, Edward." Her tone was crisp.

"Yes." He did not feel like talking.

"We must expect them to try again You'll have to change your routine, be less predictable. Travel by carriage from now on. Or at least change your route. And wear an apprentice's black jacket. Or buy two jackets, in different colours, wear a different one each day. Perhaps your guards should change too ..."

Edward ignored this. His thoughts were running in a different direction. "Perhaps the Queen was right about your aunt being murdered ... Perhaps your mother's death was part of the pattern ... why should a murderer target the Chatelaine and ignore the patron of the Guild?"

"Don't try to talk. You did say that the patron of the Guild was better protected."

"Did I? Yes ..." Edward felt there was something important that he had to say. "Can you tell which house the shot came from? Carry out a search. But be polite about it." The sharpshooter was probably long gone. But they might find some evidence.

The door opened and Edward turned to look. Charles walked in, followed by a tall, elegant man. A woman in a grey skirt and blue jacket followed.

Samantha turned to face the newcomers. "Hello, Doctor Jones, Dianna." She sounded surprised. "I'm delighted to see you, Doctor Jones." Edward noted the warmth in her voice. That bothered him.

"Good afternoon, Lady Samantha. Charles told me that your local doctor had no experience of working with Healers, so I thought I'd better accompany Dianna." The doctor had a self-assured tone that annoyed Edward.

Jones took off his jacket and carefully removed Mrs. Hudson's bandages. He spent some time examining the wounds. "Yes. I'll have to cut out that shrapnel. Can we move him to a table? A trestle would do."

Edward tried not to cry out as six men, working as a team, lifted him onto the table.

The surgeon rolled up his sleeves. "I've forgotten to bring a Charmer with me, but I suppose this place is full of them." This was greeted in silence.

"The College has only a score of experienced lecturers. None of them uses glamour," Charles said. "Only Lady Samantha has any experience in that sort of thing."

"Can you fill in, my lady? You've done it before," the surgeon said.

"No, I couldn't. Not Edward." She sounded distraught.

Edward hated the idea too. He did not want Samantha poking around in his mind. "I can manage without."

The surgeon was not pleased. "I am sure you're manly enough to bear the pain, but it'll make my task easier if you're not writhing around in agony. You'll recover faster too. I don't know why." He turned away. "Turn him on to his side, please." That procedure took Edward by surprise and made him cry out. He found himself facing the far wall. The fireplace had a mirror over it.

"Is there nobody else in the College who can do this?" Samantha said. "How long would it take to find someone?"

"We have plenty of students who've practised compulsion spells, my lady, but none have used it to block pain," Charles said.

"I'll do it," Samantha said. She pulled up a chair and seated herself so she was level with Edward. "Look into my eyes, Edward. I am virtuous, just like those ladies that the troubadours sing about. You admire my virtue, just like those troubadours. Your admiration is the only thing in the world."

Edward could feel the compulsion taking over his mind. Her technique was quite elegant. "I can't spend the rest of my life thinking that!" He felt something poking in his ribs that he tried not to think about.

Samantha's gaze was unflinching. "Don't worry, it wears off after an hour or so. But you must concentrate on my virtue. Your admiration of my virtue. Your admiration. It's the only thing in the world." Her tone remained level, commanding.

Edward thought she was really very good. He wanted to use his own skills to fight back. But if he tried too hard, that poking around his hip became impossible to ignore.

Samantha frowned. "Pay attention, Edward. Concentrate on how much you admire me. Nothing else matters. Do you really think you can stop me? You're bleeding to death. You're getting weaker with every passing second. So listen to me, just this once. Concentrate on your admiration."

The trouble was, he did admire the chit. Not her virtue so much, but her bravery. Her ingenuity. Listening to her voice was soothing. He did not want her to stop. "Yes."

"You are powerless. Admiration for my virtue is everything. You cannot resist -."

You can stop now," Jones said. "I've got the shrapnel and cleaned the wound." Edward thought his timing was terrible.

"Don't stop, don't stop," Dianna said in her broad cockney. I need to close the second wound."

Edward stared at Samantha. "Your resolution," he

173

prompted.

"Resolution? Very well. You admire my resolution. It's the only thing in the world ..."

Edward considered this. "Yes. Some would call it stupidity."

"Stubborn, I would allow. But not stupid. Pay attention. You admire my – resolution ..."

"There, I'm done, my lady. You can stop now," Dianna said.

"You must not move for the next twenty-four hours," Jones said. "If you do, the wound will re-open and the Healer will have to do it over again."

Edward tried to remember. "I have an appointment with Sir Charles Grey at the Home Office."

"Then Sir Charles will have to come to you," Jones said. "And for the next week you'll have to travel by coach."

The next morning, Samantha and Alice were sitting together in a quiet corner of breakfast room. Alice looked up. "Here comes trouble."

Samantha's guards walked across the room towards the ladies. All four of them were dressed in black. Samantha was surprised. She had cancelled her usual morning visit. And Charles and Mr. Smith rarely acted together.

"Sit down, gentlemen. Yes, Charles, what can I do for you?"

"My lady, you told Lord Edward yesterday that he'd have to change his ways. You will have to, as well."

Samantha poured herself some more tea. "In what way?"

"The killer will be looking for a lady climbing into a

coach. You must travel by cab in future."

Mr. Smith leaned forward in his chair. "That would still mean you would have to walk down the front steps in view of everybody. It would be far better for her ladyship to get in the coach while it's in the stableyard."

Charles was annoyed. "But if the ladies walked across the stableyard, they would get their skirts dirty. That would be demeaning."

Samantha shared a glance with Alice. The hostility between these two men worried her.

Mr. Smith refused to back down. "Getting shot and dragged through the front door would be even more demeaning."

Alice smiled. "My lady, I suggest that you use both methods, on different days. You should be unpredictable. Also ... You could dress differently. Perhaps you could wear a plain grey dress."

Samantha was shocked. "If I dressed plainly and you didn't, that would make you the target instead of me."

"No, my lady, I just want to confuse the assassin for a couple of minutes, until we got into the coach. Or ... you could dress like Lady Mary."

Samantha pursed her lips. The men exchanged a glance. They knew what Samantha was thinking: she would rather be mistaken for a servant than Lady Mary.

Samantha turned to her guards. "Charles, if I have to dress up, you should too. Four men in black stand out too much. Charles, have you got a tweed jacket?"

Charles was outraged. "But - that is not suitable for your service."

Alice had no patience with this. "If it keeps the lady alive - it's suitable."

Charles stood up, nodded curtly, and walked out. Mr. Smith and the others followed. Samantha watched them go. "Alice, Charles and Mr. Smith hate each other. Do you know why?"

Alice sipped at her tea. "Isn't it obvious? Charles went to Eton, until he was expelled. Mr. Smith went to an East End ragged school. The difference was that Charles refused to learn anything, until he came here, while Mr. Smith learned everything he could."

"How did Charles get himself expelled? Did he cuckold the housemaster?"

Alice smiled. "My dear lady Samantha! Nonsense. He set the chapel on fire. Quite by accident. Or so I hear."

Soho: The Analytical Engine, evening of 1 July

Charley 'Coffee' Williams led Dave into the engine room. Both were wearing white gloves. "They don't want any dirt getting into the engine ..."

Dave looked it over. "Yes, it's a splendid bit of workmanship. I hope you won't get into trouble."

"I often work late, so nobody will take any notice." He gestured to the bundles of cards stored on the shelves, next to rows of boxes which Dave assumed held more cards.

"These cards don't just store numbers; they can store names." He picked up a bundle tied up with red ribbon. "Each of these contains the details of a conspirator who's been trying to buy guns. But if the police ask me if I've got a list of the conspirators, I can say no."

Dave grunted. "Even more important, to my way of thinking, is that if the conspirators come looking, they won't find it."

"Yes. But these cards also contain my estimate of when each man wants to act, I mean, how long they're prepared to wait. And also my estimate of how likely they're to be swayed by the others." He fed the cards into the hopper of the engine, then adjusted a clutch lever. The machine began clanking away.

Dave was startled. "Somebody's bound to come running."

Coffee grinned. "Don't you worry. This machine runs night and day. There's always a queue. When they built it, mind you, they were worried there wouldn't be enough customers to make it worthwhile." He watched as the cards were fed into the engine.

"This machine almost didn't get built. When Babbage tried to build the first one, the Difference Engine, the money ran out. The government had coughed up ten thousand quid but the machine was only one quarter built. Mr. Clement, the engineer, refused to do any more unless he got paid and the government refused to pay any more" He stroked the frame of the Engine. "But a Swedish engineer, Mr. Scheutz, he built his own machine, complete, at a tenth of the cost. What's more, he did it on schedule."

Dave grinned. "How did he manage that?"

"Mr. S built to a price while Mr. C built to a standard. But Mr. Babbage couldn't find anyone to buy it. Lady Lovelace asked her scientist friends, but no luck. Most of them could use it for a day or two for odd tasks, but no-one wanted to use it full time – or pay for it. But the lady added up the days and found it came to more than four hundred. So Babbage told the government he had found a year's worth of customers ..." He led the way out of the engine room to his private alcove.

"Did you hear about that shooting?" Dave asked.

"Do you mean Berkeley Square? They say it was done with a rifle. The sort that toffs use to hunt deer. Funny, that. The toffs have more to fear from each other than they do from us."

"I thought it might have been ..."

"One of my old friends?" Coffee grinned. "No, not if the story was true about the rifle. French-made, they tell me.

You know how difficult it is to get hold of one of those things." He put the kettle on the stove.

Dave was impressed. "French-made? There can't be more than a dozen of those in London."

"And the police know where to find every one. If I can do it, so can they." He made some tea for them both.

"You know why I dropped out, Davey?" Coffee asked.

Dave was sympathetic. "I suppose you realised that violence would do more harm than good. It took me ten years to work that one out."

"No." Coffee waved a hand towards the Engine. "I realised that if the rioters marched from Whitechapel to Berkeley Square, they'd have to come through Soho. And if they wanted to loot the homes of the rich, why not smash the ten-thousand-pound Engine?"

Before Dave could think of a reply, the Engine fell silent.

Coffee led the way back into the engine room. He squinted at one of the dials. "Fifty-nine days from now. August 28." He pulled a lever and reset the dials to zero.

Dave frowned. "You forgot the police. They'll be making their own guess."

"And they'll be tempted to jump early, rather than leave it too late. So, around the 20th, London will get interesting."

The College, 2 July, 9 am

Samantha was talking to Edward in the breakfast room when a visitor was shown in by one of the maids.

"This is Detective Sergeant Underhill to see you, my lady, my lord." the maid sounded flustered, perhaps because she was in the presence of a real detective.

Samantha got up to welcome the visitor, but Edward

178

remained seated. "You will excuse me if I do not stand, sergeant. I've been told that if I exert myself the wound might re-open."

"That's all right, my lord." Underhill was of medium height, and thick-set. He had a west country accent. Samantha noted that his manner was deferential.

Samantha asked the maid to bring some tea, then resumed her seat. "Please, sit down, sergeant."

"Thank you, my lady. I was asked to tell you, sir, that the commissioner had considered sending his most experienced inspector, but then changed his mind, because he thought that might attract unwanted attention from the press. But he said I was bright enough and wasn't set in my ways of thinking."

Edward smiled. "I'm sure you'll do well enough, sergeant. What have you discovered so far?"

Underhill produced a notebook, but barely glanced at it. "The fellow fired from the attic, just as you surmised, my lord. The building is a set of gentlemen's apartments, not a family residence. He carried his weapon in a standard carrying case. He encountered three people, all of them servants. All of them said he was well-dressed, well-spoken. Tall and thin. But - none of them could describe him. I did wonder whether they had been bribed, my lord."

Edward cursed, under his breath. Samantha had to pretend she had not heard.

There was a knock on the door and the maid entered, carrying a tea set on a silver tray.

"Excellent," Samantha said. She poured out tea for everyone. "I suspect that he didn't use bribes. Most worrying."

"How is that, miss?" Underhill asked.

"Well - how to explain?" Edward said. "Magic users can use a spell to put a compulsion on people. The magician can't tell people to forget they saw him, but he can tell them not to look at him. I'm afraid this assassin could be a magic user."

Underhill was astonished. "Surely not, sir."

Samantha concentrated and spoke clearly. "Your nose is itching, sergeant."

Underhill rubbed his nose for almost a minute before he was able to stop. "Was that your doing, my lady?"

"Yes, sergeant. It works best if the victim is unprepared. So if I told you that your ear itched ..."

Underhill clenched his right hand and then relaxed it.

"Was that really necessary, Lady Hampden?" Edward was cold.

"I was thinking that if the sergeant attempted to arrest a magician, the magician might tell him to jump in the river."

"Could that work?" Underhill asked.

Edward frowned. "If you arrested him on London Bridge, you might jump in before you realised what he was doing. But if the river was a mile away, the glamour would probably wear off before you were halfway there."

Samantha took a sip at her tea. "I was hoping that if the sergeant knew what to expect, he might be on his guard."

Underhill did not look grateful. "That complicates things, sir. I was thinking of an East End agitator. Well ... Is there anyone in the guild who wants your job? Some sort of feud?"

Edward rubbed his chin. "The role of patron isn't very powerful. Who would want it?"

"Is there anyone you've offended, my lord?"

Samantha decided that she had to speak up. "The Master of the Guild."

Edward smiled. "Well, yes. But everyone's offended the master. I suppose you'll have to look into it, Sergeant. His name is Archibald Knight. But I suspect it'll be a worthless task."

Underhill glanced at Samantha. "Any other offended persons? Some husband, mebbe?"

Samantha tried not to giggle. "The sergeant is thinking of lord Palmerston."

"That's not my style, sergeant," Edward said gravely.

"Unfortunately, use of magic is not restricted to members of the guild," Samantha said. "There are lots of illegal users across London."

The sergeant glanced down at his notebook. "So that brings us back to agitators."

"But why would they concentrate on the College?" Samantha said.

Underhill looked surprised. "The guild is seen as a bastion of the establishment. Your magicians support the police. There aren't many of you, but you're regarded as more powerful than the police. Sinister ..."

"I see."

"That riot in March. We assumed they were heading for the gentlemen's clubs. They're another bastion of the establishment, patronised by the richest men in England. But the rioters could have been heading here instead."

"I see. Thank you, sergeant," Edward said. "What sort of weapon did the fellow use?"

"Some sort of hunting rifle. One of my men found a minne ball on the pavement. The very latest technology. Those things cost a fortune, which suggests our man had money."

"Could you trace him, sergeant?"

"I'll ask in the gun shops for recent purchases, but I'm not hopeful, my lord. Those rifles are a French invention. He could have gone to France to buy it."

That evening, after dinner, Lady Mary led the ladies into the withdrawing room as usual. Alice seated herself alongside Samantha. She seemed flustered.

"Yes, Alice?"

"I want to ask a favour. Can you tell me, truthfully, who do you think is the most handsome man in the college?"

It was easy for Samantha to guess what had prompted the question. But she gave the question some honest thought. Finally, she blurted "Lord Edward."

"But he's old." Alice sounded shocked.

"You asked me to be truthful." Samantha felt obliged to defend her choice. "He's not that old. He's - fit. Athletic. Educated. A good teacher. And the students are so young." She smiled. "It's easy to guess why you're asking." Alice merely blushed.

"Can we expect a development? Will your father be asking someone – the traditional question?" She adopted a pompous tone. "Can you support my daughter in the way that she is accustomed?"

Alice became sombre. "I'm accustomed to being an apprentice. I like it. Studying magic. I don't want to give it up."

"Well – you can still visit. The married men bring their wives to dinner. Does he want you to stop studying?" To distract her friend, Samantha voiced one of her own fears. "Lord Edward seems so - solitary. Distant. It seems unhealthy – unnatural."

The distraction worked. Alice leaned closer and spoke in a whisper. "Solitary? Nonsense. Haven't you heard the scandal? He's got a mistress. Or he used to. He quarrelled with her. Or so I overhear. She walked out on him."

Samantha was filled with a rage that she identified as jealousy.

Alice grinned. "So he's going to be looking for a replacement."

She hunched her shoulder. "You said that to provoke me."

Chapter 14 Lewes, Sussex

5 July

Samantha's coach, travelling south from London, stopped at a farmhouse just north of Lewes. Samantha told Alice and Bettie to wait in the coach and followed her guard, Charles, up the neat gravel path to the front door. The door opened as Samantha reached the porch. A woman in her thirties, in a rough woollen dress and mob cap, peeked out.

Samantha stepped forward. "Is this the Trayton house? Are you Mrs. Trayton? I'm from the College of Magicians."

The woman gaped at Samantha and her black-clad guards. "Yes, I'm Mrs. Trayton. I suppose it's about our Nora. You'd better come in. Although Trayton's too sick to speak to you."

Samantha turned to her guard. "Charles, if someone's ill, we'll need Bettie." Charles nodded and ran off.

Mrs. Trayton ignored the drawing room and led them into the large kitchen. "The maids are busy in the buttery. And work has to go on even with Trayton laid up."

A large man was sitting in an armchair, naked to the waist, his face and arms blackened by fire. His brown hair was untouched. He did not move his head, but his eyes turned to watch as Samantha approached. "Ah – ah -."

Mrs. Trayton knelt at her husband's right side. "The doctor said his injuries were not life-threatening, but there was nothing he could do except give him laudanum for the pain." She stroked his hair. "Hush, dear, it'll be all right."

Bettie came in and dropped her bag on the floor. "Oh. I hate dealing with burns. This'll be a long job. Where do you want me to start?"

Mrs. Trayton spoke first. "Can you help? Start with his mouth. He wants to tell you something."

Bettie bent over and delicately stroked the man's jaw. "His teeth are all right. And his tongue. No permanent damage. It's just – ah." She stood up.

The man worked his jaw a couple of times. "Thank God," he said. "It was all my fault. Don't blame Nora. I made her angry."

"I see. Thank you," Samantha said. "Can you get Bettie some tea? That always helps after a spot of healing."

Samantha climbed the narrow wooden stairs to Nora's bedroom. Alice followed a few steps behind. The door was shut. "Nora, my name is Samantha. I'm from the College of Magicians. I've brought a healer for your father. He's going to be all right. He wants to speak to you. Please come out."

There was no reply. Samantha glanced down at Alice, who shrugged. Had the girl done away with herself?

Samantha heard movement inside, but the door did not open. The girls' voice was hoarse. "It's all my fault. If I come out, I'll hurt somebody else. You're going to send me to the madhouse, aren't you?"

"That's what I've come here to find out. But if you behave like a madwoman I'll have to treat you like one." Samantha and Alice exchanged another look.

The door opened a crack and a girl peered out. She had brown hair and was wearing a dress printed in blue and green stripes. Her unwashed face was stained with tears. "Are you really a magician?"

Samantha wondered what sort of answer the girl was hoping for. "I'm their Chatelaine. I do their books for them. I can do a few spells too. My mother called them parlour tricks."

Samantha led the way into the kitchen, followed by Nora. She found it subtly changed. A maidservant was tending to several pots on the stove, Mr. Trayton was wearing a dressing gown over his shoulders, and Bettie was sitting in the armchair opposite, holding a teacup. Samantha realised that Mr. Trayton's nose and the skin around his eyes were now pink and smooth rather than blackened.

Mrs. Trayton, kneeling beside her husband, jumped up as Samantha walked in. "Nora!"

Nora froze as her mother embraced her, then returned the embrace.

"She says she hasn't eaten since the – accident," Samantha said. "She needs a meal."

"We can all eat together," Mrs. Trayton said.

Nora pushed her mother away. "No. I'm afraid I'll hurt somebody else. Perhaps you, mother. I mustn't stay here."

Samantha intervened. "Could you do it again? Do you know how? Were you angry when you did it?" Everyone in the room went still.

Nora looked down at the floor. "I was angry. I'm not angry now."

"Then let's have dinner," Samantha said. She turned to Bettie. "I didn't realise it'd be such a big task. Do you want me to fetch help from London?"

Bettie shook her head. "It'll take me two days. It'll take almost that long for another healer to get here. Besides, I'll enjoy a few days of countryside air. My only worry is that I can only heal one small area at a time. The poor man will end up looking like a patchwork quilt."

Samantha's coach came to a stop outside the White Hart Hotel. Samantha waited while her guards deployed and gave the all clear, then climbed out of the coach. Alice followed her, grumbling.

Samantha led the way into the hotel and was met by a waiter. "May I help the ladies?"

"I am Lady Samantha Hampden and I wish to see the town's magistrate, any of the town's magistrates."

"They're all here," the waiter said. He led the way to the smaller dining room and announced her.

Five gentlemen and three women, all in fashionable travelling clothes, were gathered around the fire. Samantha guessed that the magistrates had brought their wives with them. They all looked round as Samantha entered.

"Good evening. I was told that all of the town's magistrates were here."

The gentleman in a turquoise wool jacket took his pipe out of his mouth. "Lady Samantha? I assume you're the Magicians' Chatelaine?"

"Yes, sir. I've come on official Guild business."

"That would be the Trayton affair," a tall thin man in black said. "We were just discussing that."

"And have you reached any conclusions, sir?" Samantha asked.

"So far we have only questions. Has a crime been committed? Can a child this young be charged with a crime? Is it safe to have this child in our midst? And can we pass these questions to the Guild?"

"Well – magic was involved, certainly. I have questioned Nora and her parents. They all agree it was an accident. The parents, commendably, want Nora to remain with them. I wanted to ask whether charges had been lodged."

"They have not. But is it safe to keep the child here?" the man in turquoise said.

"Nora understands that this is not a one-off event. She's afraid that her gift could resurface at any time. I hope to train her to avoid harming herself or those around her. That could take weeks."

"And if she's unable to learn?" the man in black asked.

"But what if she's mad?" one of the ladies asked.

"We've heard that magic often sends children mad."

"Well - I have three options. One is to send her to a madhouse. But I don't think she belongs there. Second, she can be sent to the College, where she'll learn how to use magic. But that's no place for a girl. Or perhaps I can teach her just enough while I'm here to enable her to stay with her parents."

"Then we shall wish you luck, my lady," the man in turquoise said.

*

The next morning, Samantha led Nora into the field opposite her home. One of the farmhands followed at a discreet distance, carrying a spade. The sky was clear. The wheat had been cut and tied up in sheaths to dry. A few clumps of weeds, growing up between the wheat, had been left untouched by the harvesters. Nora was wearing a rough grey working dress, while Samantha was wearing a travelling dress of dark blue. Nora was reluctant and very nervous. Samantha hoped her own fears did not show.

"Now, I've told you before. You can go up to London with me. Or you can learn just enough magic to allow you to stay with your parents. But that's the most difficult."

"Why?"

"Because learning usually takes weeks or months. I can't stay that long." Samantha pointed at the nearest wheat sheath. "Can you set that on fire?"

Nora was shocked. "But that's against the law. You can be transported for that."

"But could you do it if you wanted to? Do you know how?"

"No. I was angry. Father said I was clumsy and couldn't

187

be trusted in any task and nobody would want to marry such a clumsy girl. And it's true. I am clumsy."

"So. You're angry now. Burn that sheath ... You can't do it? If a wheat-sheath is too valuable, burn those weeds instead. You're angry at me. Are you angry enough to burn it? No?"

Nora, furious, pointed a finger at the nearest patch of weeds. A ball of fire appeared at her fingertips, shot forward and set the weeds alight. The farm boy rushed forward and used his shovel to beat out the flames.

"Very good," Samantha said. "Now do it again."

"Why? Why?"

"I want you to show me that you control your gift. You can use it any time you want to, and that you can choose *not* to use it. I want you to do it until you're sick of doing it. Now, do it again. Use less power this time."

Nora walked towards another patch of weeds and raised her hand. The ball of fire was smaller this time. It sped across to the weeds and set a few stalks alight. The farm boy, less anxious, strolled forward and patted out the flames.

"Better," Samantha said. "Again."

An hour later, Samantha led the way back to the farmhouse kitchen. Nora was exhausted but pleased. "I thought you were going to make us do the whole field, miss. Charcoal is good for the ground, sure enough, but burning it is hard work."

"Perhaps we can do a bit more after lunch." Samantha ignored Nora's squeak of dismay.

Mrs. Trayton and the maid were preparing a cold lunch for the farmhands and the visitors. Mr. Trayton was sitting in his armchair. He was wearing a collarless shirt instead of a dressing-gown. The fire in the hearth was burning merrily.

Bettie looked up. "Hello, my lady. I decided to leave his face half-finished and instead repair his fingers. That's tricky work. I wanted to get it over with before I got too tired."

188

Trayton held up his hands. It looked as if he was wearing black fingerless mittens. He bared his teeth in what he meant as a cheerful grin. "Hello, lass."

"Mr. Trayton, I believe you told Nora that she was clumsy," Samantha said.

"Aye, I did," Trayton said. "But I also said that book-learning was even more important for running a farmhouse like this. And Nora's good at her lessons."

"I'm very pleased with Nora's progress," Samantha said. "Some apprentices take a week to learn that much control. This afternoon I want her to learn more delicate work."

"Delicate? How?" Mr. Trayton asked.

"Well –." Samantha held her right hand palm upwards. "Partum a luce." She produced a delicate light. She put a bit of shimmer into it.

Mr. Trayton stared. "My. That's beautiful. Will our Nora be able to do that?"

Everyone, including Nora, was staring in admiration. Samantha killed off the light. "It'll take her at least a month of daily practice."

"But will you allow my Nora to stay?" Mrs. Trayton asked.

Samantha glanced at Alice. "We won't be certain until tomorrow. But she's made good progress. And she'll have to make some promises. To me and to you."

"What sort of promises?" Nora sounded deeply suspicious.

"I'll show you those exercises. You'll have to promise to do them every day. It's not creating the flame that's important, it's turning the flame *off*."

"Even if I'm angry, you mean?"

"Yes."

Berkeley Square, 10 July

Samantha and Edward took their places at the table in the college's smaller dining room. This was decorated with wooden panelling and narrow, high windows. Tea and coffee pots, with matching cups, had been placed on the table.

Edward smiled at his guests. "When I suggested an informal meeting, I did not anticipate that so many people would attend."

Sir Charles Grey, Minister for Home Affairs, smiled back. "No-one's taking any notes, so it's still informal, surely."

Their other high-ranking guest, the Duke of Wellington, said nothing. He was very dignified, with white hair. He always turned his right profile to each speaker. Samantha remembered that he was deaf in his left ear.

The man sitting next to him was the Police Commissioner, Sir Charles Rowan. Before his appointment as Commissioner he had been a colonel in the army, and had been wounded at the battle of Waterloo.

"I had not expected the ladies to greet us, Lord Radley," he said.

"Well, I had hoped to keep things informal, sir, to keep the atmosphere light," Edward said. "If you have any specifics to discuss, let us go to Downing Street for a council of war."

"Downing Street has too many newspaper reporters hanging about," the Commissioner said.

The other two guests were Chief Inspector Bearsbridge and Inspector Arncliffe. Both looked intimidated by the exalted company they were keeping.

Sir Charles sighed. "We don't have any specifics to discuss. There's no need to chase the ladies away."

Samantha leaned forward and poured coffee for herself and Edward. This seemed absurdly domestic for such an important meeting.

Edward picked up his cup. "I had suggested a meeting with our associates in the Metropolitan Police Force to enable us to discuss the risks. If trouble breaks out, I shall be sworn in as a special constable, under the inspector's orders. I wanted to know what to expect ... Last time, I was asked to inspect a building where the plotters are gathering."

The Duke nodded. "An independent command. Suitable for a man of your social standing. Yes, I see."

Chief Inspector Bearsbridge leaned forward. "I wanted to avoid any misunderstandings, your Grace. At Bethnal Green, I asked the Guild to provide extra Talkers. The Guild was not expecting a request. The only person here was Lady Samantha, so she came instead."

The Duke stirred his tea. "I trust you have taken action to prevent a similar problem this time, inspector?"

Samantha glanced at Edward. Did the Duke have a sense of humour? "We contacted every Guild member who might be of use and told them that for that week they couldn't leave London or go to their clubs or anything. They responded by arranging a party."

The Commissioner was annoyed. "Monstrous."

"But, you see, the party is in Mayfair. So if they're needed, we only have to walk round the corner."

The Duke gave a bark of laughter.

Samantha smiled. "We told them they couldn't touch the wine before six and no spirits before ten."

"Isn't that a bit harsh?" the Duke said. "Are you expecting a night action, Charles? The last gathering was in daylight, as I recall."

The Commissioner hesitated, so Edward intervened. "That was arranged by the Chartists, your Grace. This is organised by desperate men who regard the Chartists as weaklings."

The Duke nodded. "I see, yes. A new enemy requiring a

quite different strategy."

"All of the reports suggest that the agitators are planning something, possibly in the next two or three weeks. They're getting desperate. All of their attempts to rouse the population have failed. The moderates have abandoned them. So they've decided upon a policy of outright violence. Brute force."

The Duke leaned forward. "Lord Edward, I invited myself here so that I could ask a single question. D'you think will the army be required?"

Sir Charles shook his head. "Troops would only be needed if the agitators planned a mass meeting."

Samantha whispered to Edward. "But nothing is planned."

"What's that, my lady?" the Duke asked.

She flushed. "I beg pardon, your Grace. The earlier mass meetings were planned weeks in advance. The Chartist Executive distributed thousands of posters and flysheets. Nothing like that is happening this time."

The Commissioner turned to Bearsbridge. "Chief Inspector?"

"Yes, I can vouch for that, sir," Bearsbridge said. "This is a small number of men, spreading their plans by word of mouth."

"Ah." The Duke poured himself some more tea.

"So this is likely to be solely a police matter," Sir Charles Grey said.

"Yes, Sir Charles," Edward said. "The extremists are planning simultaneous attacks, after nightfall. It's ambitious."

"Can they succeed?" Sir Charles said. Everyone was reluctant to answer.

Finally, Edward broke the silence. "Their aim is to bring down the government. They can't succeed in that. But they could cause a lot of damage and kill a lot of people. We will have to respond accordingly."

"Can't we take action to stop them, Rowan? Now, today?" the Duke asked.

The Commissioner glanced at Sir Charles. "We could arrest them. We know most of their names. But we don't have enough evidence to gain a conviction. We would have to let them go."

"And then they would start over again," Sir Charles said. "I prefer to wait."

Bearsbridge coughed. "Beg pardon, sir, but if we put them on trial, our chief witnesses are the informers. If they came out into the open and we couldn't get a conviction, our source of information would be gone."

The Duke sipped at his tea. "I don't want to see a repetition of the Paris barricades."

Edward smiled. "There's no chance of that, your Grace. The multitude are apathetic, not angry. Only a series of mistakes on our part would provoke the populace into action."

Sir Charles nodded. "Our tactics have worked so far."

Edward put down his cup. "I believe that the government in Paris deliberately provoked the workers into revolt, to give themselves an excuse to slap them down."

"These Chartists need to be taught a lesson," the Duke said.

Samantha was annoyed. "They have, your Grace. They have learned that mass meetings will not intimidate the government. So they've given up."

He frowned at her. "You sound as if you've spoken to them, madam."

"Indeed I have, sir. A few of them, anyway."

The Duke's craggy face split into a smile. "The lady at Bethnal Fields! Was that you?"

She was embarrassed. Would she never be allowed to forget that? "Yes, your Grace. They were most polite. The

Chief Inspector said one should try and get them talking, and so I did."

"The inspector should have done his own dirty work, not left it to you."

Bearsbridge leaned forward. "I would have done, your Grace, but for some reason the demonstrators preferred to talk to the lady. And she succeeded quite well."

"Perhaps they found her easier in the eye." The Duke smiled at her. "You are young for such a responsible post, my lady."

"Yes, your Grace. My aunt died suddenly and I had to take over."

"My condolences. Your mother died too, I hear. That was most suspicious." He turned to Edward. "Do you agree, Lord Radley?"

"Until two weeks ago, I would have said no. But then somebody tried to kill me with a hunting rifle. Somebody appears to hold a grudge against the Guild of Magicians."

Sir Charles was surprised. "Do you think these attacks can be blamed on these agitators, Lord Radley?"

Edward shrugged. "I would have thought the agitators would try to burn the college down, not murder our Chatelaine." He frowned. "The rioters in March almost got this far, remember."

Chapter 15 House Party

Culham Castle, Oxfordshire, late afternoon of Friday 14 July.

The train stopped at the little country station. Samantha stepped down, followed by Alice and Edward.

"I arranged for my carriage to meet us," Edward said. "Yes, there it is."

They travelled the last mile to Culham Castle in style. Lady Mary had arranged to travel down by the evening train.

Alice glanced out of the carriage window. "I was expecting a castle, Lord Radley."

Samantha shifted in her seat to share Alice's view. The house was three storeys tall, built of red brick, with tall chimneys.

"There was a castle, in the time of King Stephen, but it was abandoned as soon peace was restored. All that's left of it is the moat." Edward sounded proud of it. "The house is Jacobean, over two hundred years old. It's never been modernised because all of my predecessors put all of their money into the College. I suppose I could give it a Gothic makeover. Very fashionable."

Samantha was horrified. "No, this is far more atmospheric."

He smiled. "You think so?"

The front door opened as they approached. Several servants were waiting in the hallway to take their hats and coats. Samantha wondered whether they were curious to see the new chatelaine.

Edward led them upstairs. "My mother has her own

drawing room." This had a fine carpet, deep red in colour, and matching curtains. His mother, the dowager Countess, was sitting in an elaborate wing-chair. Edward bent to kiss her on the cheek. "Good afternoon, Mother. May I introduce Lady Samantha Hampden and her companion, Miss Alice Toledano."

Samantha paused, staring across the room at her hostess. No one had ever mentioned to her the resemblance between Edward and his mother. At the second glance, Samantha realised that the Countess had warmer eyes than her son and that her smile was kinder. The Countess's upward-sweeping eyebrows, however, were identical to those of her son.

"You are looking well, Edward. Run along, my boy. I'm sure you have a lot to do." Edward laughed and walked out.

Samantha knew that the Countess spent all her time at Culham. Samantha judged that she was sharp enough to be Chatelaine. But she was busy enough running these house-parties.

Lady Radley smiled. "Please, sit down. Perhaps you have heard that I am confined to a chair. I have heard so much about you, child. You've achieved more in four months than your aunt did in as many years."

"No, no. All I did was stand aside and let the fellows rush ahead."

"Somehow, they all rushed in a purposeful direction," Lady Radley said. "Everyone expected the role of chatelaine to be abolished. You have revitalised it ..." A maid arrived with a tea pot and cups.

"I hope you realise that this is not like the other house parties you've been to."

"This is my first, madam. Two years ago, I was too young. Last year my father was posted overseas."

"Ah, I see. Well - the usual activities at a house-party are riding and hunting. If one isn't interested in hunting, one gets up late and spends the afternoon writing letters. But at Culham Castle, all of the gentlemen are interested in magic. So we have morning seminars, followed by lectures all afternoon." The countess poured tea into three cups.

"I try to provide alternative entertainment for the ladies, but some of them want to learn about magic."

Samantha, embarrassed, glanced at Alice. Both of them wanted to study magic. She sought to change the subject. "I expected the entertainment would include, well, dancing."

"We have that too, in the evening, if you have energy enough. Do you plan to go riding tomorrow?"

"Yes, madam. My father's elder brother let us ride at his estate."

"So you have some experience? Good. But you will have to get up early. And do not be surprised if Edward is over-protective."

Edward clearly enjoyed showing the two girls around his home. Alice was eager for her first view of a real country house. The entrance hall boasted rugged beams, plastered walls, and a floor of uneven flagstones. The fireplaces were vast, more of a statement of power than a practical means of heating. The winged staircase that led up to the surrounding gallery was another statement of wealth.

Samantha was impressed. "My uncle's country house is smaller than this. But it's more modern."

"The residential parts of the house have been modernised. I wish we had a lecture hall, but we would have to demolish something to create space for it."

Edward led the way outside to show them the stables. These, like the house, were built of dark red brick. The buildings formed a large courtyard, taking up more room than the house. "There's the coach-house, the accommodation for the grooms, the tack room ..." He smiled. "A few of these horses are trained to take a side-saddle."

"I have my own saddle. It's the very latest design. I

arranged for it to be sent on ahead," Samantha said.

"You'll have to show me in the morning. Just now, we have to prepare for the guests arriving tomorrow. We'll have to plan the afternoon entertainments ... We have lectures and informal discussions. Researchers describe their findings ...

"It's one of the duties of the Earl to pay for it all. But this year I anticipate a larger than usual out-turn."

"Oh? Why?"

He smiled. "They'll come to see you, of course. They would want to meet the new chatelaine anyway, but you've achieved so much in four months."

"Oh, nonsense, sir."

"You found the healers that we've been looking for. And they were under our noses all the time. You bantered with the Chartists at Bethnal Fields ... You won't have a problem. You've spoken in public before."

*

The next morning, after an early breakfast, they reassembled in the stables. The sky was clear, so the air was cold for the time of year.

Samantha was surprised to find that Lady Mary had made the effort to get up early too. Her riding habit was elegant. The train was so long that she had to carry it draped over her arm.

She frowned at Samantha. "Your riding habit is most improper, Samantha my dear. You could almost call it skimpy. Anyone would think you couldn't afford a proper one."

Samantha felt the need to justify herself. "I would call it safer, Lady Mary. Besides, who's going to see us, here in the countryside?"

198

Edward was dressed in an elegant riding jacket and breeches. His riding boots had white tops. He frowned. "I have to say that I agree with Lady Samantha."

Samantha was surprised that Lady Mary accepted this without complaint.

Alice's habit was fashionably long, just like Lady Mary's. "What's wrong with a riding habit with a long train?"

Samantha glanced at Lady Mary, but neither wanted to explain.

Edward answered her. "Well, a long riding habit is dangerous if you fall. It could catch on the saddle, so you'd be dragged along."

Samantha nodded. "So I've chosen to defy fashion, and wear a normal–length skirt. Even if it does reveal my boot when I'm riding."

The horses were led out into the yard. Edward pointed out Samantha's horse and a stable-hand lifted her side-saddle into place. Samantha felt the need to explain.

"This is my saddle. I had it brought from home. It's the very latest development, with the second pommel on the left to keep you from moving forward. It allows a lady to gallop and jump fences. Although I've never had the opportunity to do that." She had only used it a couple of times before her mother's death.

Edward listened with interest. "So this is the latest technology. I wish it had been available ten years ago." He turned to Alice. "If you intend to take up riding, I recommend that you get a saddle like this."

Lady Mary refused to consider it. "I have no time for these new-fangled devices."

Edward had provided gentle horses for them. Lady Mary mounted first. She arranged the long train of her habit so that it covered her boot and even her stirrup. Samantha had to admit that the effect was very elegant.

Samantha and Alice mounted up. Edward grinned. "I

must say, Lady Samantha, your boot-maker is the best in London."

Lady Mary was annoyed. "You should not make things worse, Lord Edward, by calling attention to Lady Samantha's folly."

Together, they rode across the paddock to the practice field. Alice was a very cautious rider. Lady Mary was more adventurous, allowing her horse to canter, which surprised Samantha.

"I asked the stable-hands to put up a series of practice jumps," Edward said. He pointed out the low jumps, each consisting of no more than two bars.

"My horse could step over those," Samantha said.

"Have you jumped before, my lady?"

She scowled. "No, Lord Edward."

"Then you need to start slowly. You're not teaching your horse, remember. You're learning to work as a team. Try to get your timing just right."

Samantha found that he was over-protective. He stood at her stirrup and gave her advice. It was useful, but his presence was a distraction that she could have done without.

Samantha decided to take her horse over the course, one jump after another. Her horse was well trained and took the low jumps perfectly. Delighted, she turned and took the jumps in reverse order. She was dismayed when, on the last jump, the bar was knocked over.

Edward grinned at her disappointment. "It's all about timing and pacing. You're doing very well for a novice. But I suppose you'll want to do more."

"Yes, of course. I've been riding for years, Lord Edward. But this is the first time I've been able to try jumps."

Samantha and Alice watched while Lady Mary took her horse over the same practice jumps. She achieved a clear round. Samantha had to admit that Lady Mary was an accomplished horsewoman. She considered that Lady Mary's primitive side-saddle made even low jumps a dangerous exercise.

After an hour, Edward called a halt. "Your horse is getting tired. You're both doing very well ... We can raise the bar tomorrow."

"Thank you, Lord Edward. But my horse has the fidgets from these silly exercises."

"Then how about a gallop to finish off with?"

"Just the thing!" She gave her horse a hint and it broke into a canter, lengthened its stride to a gallop, and in a few moments had carried Samantha far beyond Alice. Beside her thundered Edward's black, but neither she nor Edward spoke until they reined in at the end of the field. Samantha bent forward to pat her horse's neck. "It's time to head back to the stables. Get the horses rubbed down."

They met up with Alice. She smiled at them. "You look as if you enjoyed that. This is much better than a trot round Hyde Park."

The three of them turned into the lane that led back to the stables. They heard the whistle of a steam engine in the distance. Edward glanced across the fields towards the station. "Our first guests should be arriving about now. I sent the coach to the station to meet the morning train."

They dismounted, left their horses in the care of the grooms, and walked through the house to the staircase. They found that other guests were beginning to arrive.

When Samantha reached the entrance hall, she was surprised to see Edward's cousin, the hon. Randolph Radley. He looked very elegant in his travelling clothes.

"Good morning, Mr. Radley. Are you a magic user too?"

He smiled. "No, no. I'm here as a member of the family. I grew up here."

She was uncomfortable. "I didn't know that."

He lowered his voice. "I'm four years older than

Edward, you know. He was born in 1813."

"Oh! I thought he was older." She realised that Edward was not quite twice her age after all.

"He was very sickly as a child. Perhaps that's what did it. Ill-health is most unusual among your families. It set people talking at the time. Have you noticed? Children in those families are either perfectly healthy or ..."

"Yes. Miscarriages. Wherever I go, among magic users, someone will mention it."

"When I was a child, I assumed I would inherit. But Edward survived, and when he married ..."

"He's married?" she exclaimed, before she could stop herself.

"Of course. Did nobody tell you? But she died in a riding accident. I don't know the details. I believe the horse stumbled, put its foot in a molehill or something, and she went clear over the beast's head. Apparently he blamed himself for allowing her to take risks."

This was fascinating, but she felt she had pried too much. "Excuse me, I have to change for lunch."

That afternoon, Edward led Samantha and Alice into the dining room, which doubled as the lecture hall. Samantha had changed into her best woollen grey skirt and navy blue jacket. She had bought it for functions in London, but she wanted to get the most out of it. Lady Mary had informed them that she was exhausted and needed to rest.

Samantha saw that the table had been pushed to one side and the chairs rearranged. She had expected to chat with ten people at most, but she guessed that at least twenty people had taken seats. A few gentlemen stood at the back. It seemed that all the guests wanted to hear her talk.

Half of the guests were women, wives or daughters of guild members. Most of them were as well-dressed as herself. To Samantha, this was more frightening than facing a thousand Chartist protesters on Bethnal Fields.

In a few precise words, Edward introduced her to the audience and stepped aside.

Samantha stepped up to the podium, swallowed her fear, and began. "I would like to describe an exciting new challenge for the guild. Lady Lovelace has plans to use Mr. Babbage's engine to predict the weather. She asked me to find guild members to supply the data she needs. The test phase is going well. Guild members across Britain have volunteered to provide us with regular reports. But Lady Lovelace tells me that to obtain more accurate predictions, her engine needs more contributors. Lord Palmerston has promised -."

"You've spoken to him?" an elderly woman in the front row asked. Her face was lined. Samantha guessed that she was old enough to remember Lord Palmerston at his most energetic. Another woman snickered.

"You will be pleased to hear that his manners were impeccable. He promised that the Talkers at our embassies will be encouraged to send regular reports.

"We are negotiating with the admiralty. The naval base at Port Royal in Jamaica has a resident Talker who could send useful reports." She sensed that their boredom was growing. "However, Lady Lovelace wants a hundred talkers to send in reports. She suggested that we should recruit them locally." Samantha was gratified that her remark had woken up her audience.

The lady in the front row spoke up. "Do you intend to recruit women for this task, young lady?" She was wearing an expensive mourning dress of black silk.

Another woman at the back joined in. "I hear that you have already recruited ladies."

Samantha was surprised. "But -."

"We want to know why the guild has adopted a policy of recruiting women, young lady. For Osborne House," the widow said. "It all sounds incredibly reckless."

Samantha was alarmed. She had planned a safe lecture on the weather, not a debate. "Ah - that wasn't a new policy. It was an accident."

"An accident? How could it possibly be an accident?" the old woman asked.

"Ah - her Majesty asked me to provide a female talker for Osborne House. I thought it would be impossible to find any candidates. However, Lady Mary mentioned the request to a couple of friends. I presume you are acquainted with Lady Mary?"

A slight recoil amongst the audience suggested that they were fully acquainted with Lady Mary.

"The rumour spread and ten volunteers came forward, so I was able to meet her Majesty's request. I gave the volunteers the status of apprentices to give them protection under the law."

A young matron in the front row looked unhappy. "So the College has no intention of allowing other ladies to become members of the Guild?"

Samantha was saved by Edward. "That is a decision for you to make, ladies and gentlemen. Would you accept a female apprentice as a guest here? Or would you ostracise her?" This was met with an uncomfortable silence.

A young woman at the back spoke out. "You say you treat the volunteers as apprentices?"

"Yes. That gives them a legal status -."

The old woman intervened. "If they are doing the work of guild members, then they deserve the respect of guild members." This was met with silence.

"It seems that I misjudged you ladies," Samantha said. "I had assumed that you would disapprove of ladies who wanted to practise magic."

No-one had an answer to this. The silence became uncomfortable. Samantha could see that some of the ladies disapproved strongly of any change.

Samantha was surprised that the silence was eventually broken, not by one of the women, but by a man sitting next to his wife. "There is surely nothing wrong in a lady studying magic in the company of other ladies?"

"Would the Guild let us do that?" the old woman asked. "Is that your new policy?"

Samantha, embarrassed, did not know how to answer. "Lord Edward?"

He came to her rescue. "That's for the Guild as a whole to decide. Not for anyone here today."

The old woman refused to let go. "But what is your personal opinion, young lady?"

She felt trapped. The Countess was over in the corner, listening. This was her home. "Well - the University of London allows ladies to attend its lectures. I see no objection to ladies attending a course of lectures on magic. They could book the college's lecture hall -."

"No," Edward said. "That hall is booked months in advance. If you booked it and nobody turned up, you'd be a laughing stock ... On the other hand, the ladies have the use of the breakfast room in the afternoon. It seats twenty."

The old lady turned on Edward. "What is your viewpoint, sir?"

"I think it is time that the Guild was dragged into the 19th century. I have no objection to ladies studying formally. However, every member of the Guild should be invited to comment."

"We have two more days here," Samantha said. "I suggest we draft a proposal for distribution to all guild members ... And their families."

*

205

Samantha and Alice helped each other dress for dinner. Samantha had chosen a court dress in dove-grey silk. It was, of course, off the shoulder. Her only jewellery was a jet black necklace.

"It's beautiful," Alice said.

Samantha grinned. "I told Lord Edward that I couldn't wear such an extravagant dress, because I was in mourning, but Edward told me that I was attending as Chatelaine of the College, not some obscure maiden in mourning." He had added that if he had to wear formal evening wear then she could damn well do the same.

"Alice, if I find that I'm the only woman in evening dress, Lord Edward is going to suffer for it."

Alice smiled. "I'm in evening dress too, remember. Although mine is quite modest. And I'm certain Lady Mary will be. And she'll outshine you."

"I hope she does. Come on, let's go."

Downstairs, in the dining room, she found that Randolph had changed into evening dress too. At sight of him, Alice dropped back, allowing Samantha to approach alone. "Good evening, Mr. Radley."

"Good evening, Lady Samantha. May I congratulate you on your good taste? That dress is just the right balance," Randolph said. He looked round the room. "I love this place. Not just the house, you understand, the village as well. And now Edward's ruining it. All of these 'improvements' that increase the harvest and allow the tenants to pay more rents." He scowled. "This should have been mine, you know ... But enough of me. You look splendid, my lady."

He was charming. Samantha wondered whether he had a glamour. Was that why he was so well-liked? "Thank you, sir. Have you been giving more republican speeches?"

"Certainly. My speeches emphasise that inherited office is an anachronism. It ought to be abolished. The House of Lords should be replaced by life peers, selected for their ability. I have a dislike of inherited offices. Most of the people who gain power that way are incompetent."

She smiled. "There is some truth in that, sir."

"I've heard you were at Bethnal Fields. You seem to sympathise with the aims of the demonstrators."

How had he heard that? "Are you shocked, sir? I've been accused of bandying words with uncouth persons - most improper for a lady. But my sympathy is for the complaints of the demonstrators, not their aims."

"An interesting distinction, madam," Randolph said. "You sympathised with the plight of the demonstrators. And yet you hold an inherited office."

She thought he was too intense. "I did not choose it, sir. And I cannot escape from it."

"You could resign."

"If I did that, the burden would merely be transferred to a female cousin. No, the answer would be to abolish the institution. Edward says that would need a unanimous vote by the fellows. But to get them to accept, we would have to propose some other way of selecting the financial director. I'm working to devise one."

He appeared to be surprised. "You would abolish your office - and all its benefits?"

"I want to lead a normal life, sir."

"If only Edward felt the same about his earldom."

"You can hardly abolish the House of Lords, sir."

He smiled. "True enough."

"You sound like a republican, sir."

"I merely wish that all government posts should be recruited by merit. Is that so much to ask?"

Samantha considered that Edward had all the abilities required to be elected to the post of master of the college.

To her relief, dinner was called. She found that all of the ladies had entered into the spirit of the occasion and were wearing formal evening dress. Her partner at the table was an elderly gentleman, boring but affable. Randolph was halfway down the table from her.

After dinner, the ladies withdrew from the table and left the gentlemen to their port. The old lady from that afternoon's debate asked her a polite question about Osborne House.

Edward and Randolph walked into the drawing room. Randolph exchanged a few polite words with Lady Mary, then approached her. "I hear you're learning how to defend yourself," he murmured. "Weekly practices with those guards of yours."

She tried to hide an unladylike grin. "The boys were going stale, doing the same exercises over and over. I tried to liven things up. I keep trying to think of new variations. They're most impressed."

Edward joined them "Her senior guard tells me that her guards said her ingenuity was diabolical. He seemed proud of the fact."

Randolph ignored this. "Does Lady Samantha really need protection? Do you expect any more riots, Edward? Come to think of it, what are the extremists up to? How are your investigations going?"

"I regret I can't tell you that, Randolph. The police tell me less than you seem to imagine."

"The Chartist Executive aren't planning any more rallies," Samantha said. "They aren't distributing any more broadsheets."

"That's public knowledge," Randolph said. "I hear that the police have some informers amongst the conspirators."

Edward was annoyed. "I'm afraid that I'm unable to discuss the police or their sources of information."

Chapter 16 The Fire

Print Shop, Soho, London 20 July

Samantha, left sitting her horse in the street outside the print shop, was annoyed at being ignored. She dismounted from her horse, thrust the reins into the hands of her surprised guard, and strode into the print shop. Alice hurried after her.

The printing presses were silent. The print workers had been lined up against the far wall, observed by a couple of police constables. An Inspector named Arncliffe, wearing a frock coat and silk hat, was arguing with the owner. Cobbett was tall, a big man gone to fat. Charles, her senior guard, looked on.

Neither man was convincing the other. The two men were too absorbed in their quarrel to notice her. Samantha, bored, began tapping her riding whip against the hem of her dress.

She realised that the room had gone silent. The only noise was her tapping. All the men were looking at her.

She stopped. "What's the matter, Charles?"

"Nothing, my lady," he said.

She turned to the inspector. "Well, is it sedition, Inspector Arncliffe? You asked for a Guild talker to accompany you in case you found anything interesting. Is it interesting, Inspector?"

"Cobbett here has been slandering the Prime Minister, my lady."

"But is it sedition? Here, let me see." She took the pamphlet out Cobbett's hands. "Well ... you say the new

Factory Safety Act is vital. I agree. And you say 'the Prime Minister is lazy and indolent.' That's true enough. Everyone says so. I've told him so myself."

Cobbett and Charles exchanged a one-man-to-another look. Samantha interpreted Cobbett's look as 'does this chit of a girl really talk to the PM?' and Charles' reply as 'of course, don't you read the papers?'

Samantha ignored it. "But you say here that the Prime Minister did nothing to push the Factory Safety Act through. Quite untrue, and quite unfair. He did all he could. A cabal of MPs stopped him." She looked at Arncliffe. But that's sloppy reporting, Inspector, not sedition."

"What do you mean, he did all he could? And why should any MPs stop him?" Cobbett asked.

"Why, the ones who own factories, of course. If the act goes through, they'll have to spend a fortune making their factories safer."

"But who are these men?" Cobbett demanded.

"Now you're the one being lazy and indolent, sir. The information is freely available. These men boast of how rich they are – and where it comes from. Start looking."

"Yes, my lady." He actually sounded contrite.

"Have you found any other evidence, Inspector? No? In that case ... Come on Charles, let's go home."

Downing Street, 22 July

Samantha had been invited to tea with the Prime Minister's wife. She felt as if she had been summoned to the headmistress's office to receive a reprimand.

The main topic of conversation was not the latest novel or poetry but a poster. She read the document with amusement.

"Our Baronetess, in an exclusive interview with your

210

correspondent, took him to task over a statement he had made in a previous publication. Her Ladyship made it clear that the Prime Minister was not at fault in the matter of the Factory Safety Act. I withdraw my statement and apologise to the honourable gentleman for the misunderstanding."

"Magnanimous of him," Samantha said.

"No, read the next bit," Lord Russell said.

"The Baronetess made it clear, in forthright terms, that the Prime Minister's strenuous efforts to push the bill through to a successful conclusion had been thwarted by a set of factory owners who also happen to be honourable Members of Parliament. Diligent research by your correspondent has revealed that the factories owned by these wealthy, virtuous and ethical MPs have suffered a horrendous number of fatal accidents over the last twelve months. If the Factory Safety Act had been passed, these gentlemen would risk facing legal charges for any future accidents. The MPs in question, and the number of fatalities, are listed below -."

Samantha glanced down the list, horrified.

"This is an outrage," Lord Russell said. "Sedition."

Samantha hid a smile. "I don't see why, my Lord. He merely states the truth. And he apologised handsomely."

"These MPs are embarrassed. They want this scoundrel transported. Why does he mention your name? And what does the fellow mean by an exclusive interview?"

She bit her lip. "That is annoying, yes, my Lord. I accompanied a police inspector who went to arrest him, but we couldn't find sufficient evidence. I admit, I didn't expect the impudent scoundrel to mention my name."

She read the description of grisly accidents that made up the rest of the article. "I assume all of these facts are freely available. If he made it up, we can get him for slander." The thought saddened her.

Lord Russell read through the list of factories and the

number of fatalities. He shook his head. "No, this looks plausible."

"So many? His wife was shocked.

"I'm afraid so, my dear."

The College, afternoon of 5 August

The Master of the College had finally provided Samantha with his list of the research he wanted his students to undertake during the following year. Unfortunately, he had only provided her with the number of students he would need, not the cost.

Samantha cursed his incompetence, retreated to her study, and set out the laborious task of estimating the experience required of each student, the salary he would expect, and the resulting drain on the budget. She told herself that if the Master did not like her estimate he would have to do without. It was all very laborious and she was glad when a maid knocked on the door.

"There's a Mrs. Dombey at the door, requesting an interview, my lady."

Samantha closed the account book with relief. "Show her in, Doris. And fetch us some tea, please."

Doris bobbed a curtsey and hurried away. A couple of minutes later, she returned. "This is Mrs. Dombey to see you, my lady."

Her visitor was wearing a dark green dress made from high-quality cloth and a low-crowned hat with a heavy veil. As she came in, lifted her veil to show a careworn face.

Samantha remembered her manners. "How are you, Mrs Dombey? Please, sit down. How may I help you?"

"You are most kind, Lady Samantha. I've come about the fire that destroyed my husband's factory yesterday."

Samantha wondered whether Mrs Dombey was going

to accuse a magician of starting the fire. "I heard about it, of course. A terrible accident. Eight people died, I believe."

"Nine. Another woman died last night. I am distraught at these deaths, Lady Samantha. My husband was worried about fires. He paid for as second exit to be constructed in the factory. The foreman was worried about pilfering, so he had the second exit locked, but he ensured that the key was hanging on a nail beside the door. He is most insistent that the workers could have unlocked it and escaped. Unless people panicked, of course."

"But -."

Mrs. Dombey produced a small handkerchief from the pocket of her dress. "When the fire started, half of the workers tried to use that side door. But it didn't open. Most of them went back to the main door, but eight women died. Five more were badly burned." She tugged at her handkerchief. "People are saying it was my husband's fault. They're saying that he started the fire or that he blocked the door. Some are calling it murder."

At that moment, Doris arrived with a tray bearing a pot of tea, two cups, and some biscuits. Samantha thanked the maid and poured out the tea.

"This is all very dreadful, Mrs. Dombey, but I do not understand why you came to me. I can do nothing to help. I have no authority at all. People say I meddle too much."

Mrs. Dombey looked surprised. "It's that pamphlet, about the Factory Safety Act. The author said you were most concerned about accidents in factories. So I assumed you would know the right people to carry out an investigation, to prove my husband's innocence."

Samantha wished that Edward was here to help. But he had gone off to Culham to visit his mother. She was about to say that none of her acquaintances knew anything about factory accidents when it occurred to her that she knew some very strange people. To cover her confusion, and give her time to think, she took an unladylike gulp at her tea.

"Well, I know someone who knows someone, as they say. I can ask them to help. But I can make no promises, Mrs. Dombey."

"That is all I can ask for, my lady."

Samantha exchanged small talk with her guest until she had finished her tea, then escorted her to the door. She returned to her study and sat down to write some letters.

Whitechapel, morning of 6 August

Samantha descended the carriage steps and moved aside to let Alice follow her. She looked through the wide gateway at the factory beyond. The two factory buildings were set at right angles. The powerhouse containing the steam engine formed the right-hand side of the courtyard. The high brick wall with its gateway formed the fourth side. The factory building on the left was a burnt-out shell. Samantha noted that each of the factory buildings had two doorways but no windows at ground-floor level. The power-house chimney was belching smoke.

"They're waiting for us, my Lady," Charles said.

Three men walked across the road toward her. In the lead was Dave Farringdon, accompanied by his friend Coffee Williams. Both men wore tweed jackets and neck-cloths. The third man was wearing an ill-fitting frock-coat and a top hat. Samantha recognised him as the pamphleteer, Cobbett. Dave smiled. "Good morning, my lady."

"But – why are you here? I asked you to find a locksmith for me, Mr. Williams."

He smiled. "You asked for a skilled metalworker, my lady. We decided that Mr. Williams was the best available." He grinned at her confusion.

"I wrote to the Chief Inspector, asking if he could send

214

someone -.”

A cab drew up behind the College's coach. Samantha watched in surprise as Chief Inspector Bearsbridge got out and paid off the driver. “Inspector! Why are you here?”

He took off his top hat. “I wanted to renew our acquaintance, my lady.”

“But you're too important for something like this. I – I shouldn't have asked you. I've meddled too much. I'm going to get into trouble again.”

Bearsbridge glanced at the other three men. “When I heard about this, I thought there was nothing I could do. I'm glad that somebody took the initiative, my lady.”

As they walked through the factory gate, people streamed out of the two factory doorways and headed towards the gate. Dave explained that these were workers going off-shift. Most of them ignored Samantha and her companions, but a few angry people intercepted them.

“It may have been a mistake to come here,” Samantha muttered. Was her impetuosity going to get her into as much trouble as Bethnal Fields?

“It's too late to change your mind,” Alice said.

The factory workers clustered round a tall, broad-shouldered man. “Why are the likes of you messing in the affairs of honest people?”

Bearsbridge cleared his throat. Samantha hurried to speak. “I have been asked to find whether a crime had been committed here. I was told the door was locked when the factory burned down. I would like to know whether that is true.”

“And who might you be, miss?”

“Shurrup, you,” another man said. “This is the lady from Bethnal Fields.”

There was a murmur from the crowd, although Samantha could not tell whether it was respect or mere curiosity.

"I know nothing about locks, so I've brought a worker in metals." Samantha gestured at Williams. "Do you have a similar man?"

"Yes, miss – my lady."

"Has the, ah, evidence been disturbed?"

The man shook his head. "No-one wanted to go near it, not after we got the bodies out."

"I see." Samantha led them across the cobblestone yard to the burnt-out factory.

"Your letter was very, ah, concise, my Lady," Williams said.

"The owner's wife came to visit me, Mr. Williams. She was distraught at these deaths. She had heard that her husband was being accused of complicity. She asked me to investigate."

The print-shop owner, Cobbett, was plump and moved slowly. "Why did she come to you, my lady, if I may ask?"

"That's your fault," Samantha said. "You mentioned a lady's name in your pamphlet about the Factory Safety Act."

Dave looked at the burnt-out shell of the factory building. "These factory owners kill their own factory hands with their greed."

Cobbett shook his head. "If you accused factory owners of greed and selfishness, I would agree. They're too lazy to fit escape doors. Manslaughter, perhaps. But murder – no."

Samantha felt she needed to caution the crowd again. "Please stand clear. We can only do this once. So I don't want any mistakes."

The blackened walls still stood. The bodies had been removed, but the stench lingered. "This is the doorway. But - where are the doors?"

"They collapsed, inwards," Bearsbridge said. "If you're not careful, you'll walk over them."

They gathered round.

"We pulled the doors aside to remove the bodies," the

spokesman said.

"I see it," Dave said. "Two doors, each with a standard Z frame. The planks have gone, but the beams are still there. And there's the lock."

"Nobody touch it," Samantha said. "Mr. Williams, can you inspect that lock for us?"

"I'll need some help. Those timbers are too heavy," Williams said.

"Dave?" she asked.

"Do you trust him?" Bearsbridge said.

"I do in this," she said.

Dave and Williams leant over the remains of the door. Two of the factory workers stepped forward to help. Together, they lifted the horizontal beam of the door. It proved easier than anyone expected. The lock, complete with the huge nails that had fastened it to the door, came away in Williams's hands.

"Still locked shut," he said. Dave growled.

"Was anything wrong with it?" Samantha asked. Was it rusted shut? Could something have jammed it?"

Williams, holding the lock in both hands, carefully turned it over. "The key's jammed in it. Look," he said. "The handle snapped off."

"Can I see?" the local man asked. Williams held it up for them all to see.

Cobbett bent forward for a closer look. "So the key was there, ready to hand. The owner was right about that. I'm prepared to testify to that."

Bearsbridge coughed. "Could they have panicked? Turned it too hard?"

"You always blame the people," Dave said.

"But why would it jam in the first place?" Williams asked. He turned it over. "I'd like to take it apart. Find out why it jammed. What blocked it? Was it a speck of rust, as the lady says?"

217

"May I have a look, just for a moment?" Samantha asked.

Williams held it out. She did not take it, but merely brushed it with a fingertip. She felt the tingle of magic. So a magic user had tampered with it.

"Did you feel something, my lady?" Dave asked.

"Yes. I'll be very interested in what Mr. Williams finds. But I don't think it'll be rust. Metal isn't my speciality, though."

"Magic? Did a magician start the fire?" Bearsbridge asked. "There's plenty of stories of novices setting buildings on fire."

"Usually, they're inside the building they set on fire. They kill themselves, or escape just in time." She looked round at the blackened ruin. "I can't imagine our man doing that. Starting a fire from a distance is difficult. Almost impossible to do undetected. He would have to use conventional means."

They all considered the implications of this new evidence. "Some sort of infernal device?" Cobbett asked.

"A candle stub in the wrong place would be enough," Dave said. "These machines need oil to keep them turning smoothly. That's inflammable."

Bearsbridge was frowning in concentration. "But you think it's arson? That changes things. But what was the motive?"

"Usually, I'd suspect an insurance fraud," Dave said. "But the owner let it lapse."

Samantha looked up at his tone. "My guess, and it's only a guess, is that he wanted to make people angry. People like you, Dave."

"Chartists, do you mean?" Williams asked.

"The Chartists want their rights, not a revolution," Dave said.

"True enough. Our man wants to *use* the Chartists,"

218

Bearsbridge said. He groaned. "I'm going to have to check all those other fires too."

"Hard work, inspector?" Dave asked.

"Well, that too. But after all this time, the evidence will be destroyed."

Chapter 17 The Siege, London

Mayfair, 6pm, 15 August

The party was very quiet. The rented room was large, suitable for dancing, decorated with cream wallpaper. The maroon curtains had been closed and the three chandeliers lit. The first guests to arrive, Talkers from the Guild, were subdued. Bottles and glasses had been set out on the side-table, but no alcohol was available. Anyone who asked was told that only lemonade was on offer. Opposite the door, a tall pendulum clock ticked away the minutes. Most of the married guests had brought their wives.

Samantha looked round at the guests and was dismayed. Was it going to be a failure? The guests were wearing evening dress, but in obedience to the evening's dress code they were all wearing sensible shoes, in case they were called away. The non-Talkers among the guests had followed this example.

Samantha and Alice were dressed like the others, but the Chatelaine was treated as a person apart, isolated from the gossip. "I wish that Edward was here."

"His duty keeps him away. You know that," Alice said.

"Yes." Everyone was clearly wondering whether they would get a message that things had gone wrong with the police operation.

Then the main doors opened and the female Talkers arrived en masse. They joined their colleagues from St. James's Palace, smiling and joking. Samantha guessed that they had hired a couple of cabs. Three of the ladies had brought their husbands. This arrival changed the ratio between the ladies and gentlemen and morale improved. The married ladies no longer felt isolated.

Samantha at last was able to meet the husband of the Talker living in genteel poverty. "Can you introduce me, Mrs. Broughton?"

She smiled. "Certainly. Lady Samantha, may I present Mr. Broughton?"

He bowed. "I am delighted to make your acquaintance, my lady." Broughton measured up the male talkers, clearly relieved that they were as down at heel as he was. "My wife made her own evening dress. She put a lot of effort into it. I was afraid it might be too plain, but I see that I need not have worried."

"Yes, Mr. Broughton."

He smiled. "I still can't believe that my wife will be going to Osborne House next month. Still, all of this training has been wonderfully therapeutic for my wife. She used to – fidget dreadfully."

"I am confident that she will cope, sir."

All of the guests continued to glance at the clock. They shared a thought. Would a messenger arrive from Bow Street with news that they were all needed?

The band arrived and set out their instruments.

The tall clock chimed six at last. No messengers had arrived from Bow Street. Some men gave a cheer. Charles grinned and opened a bottle of champagne. He poured out a glass and handed it to Samantha. "My lady?"

"Thank you, Charles". She took a first sip. Dinner was about to begin.

The door opened and a messenger in police uniform walked in. Everyone hushed. The man spoke in a murmur to the nearest guest. The guest pointed out Samantha.

The messenger walked across the dance floor towards her. "Lady Samantha? Miss? I have a message from Chief Inspector Bearsbridge."

"Yes, constable?"

"He says the Talker appointed to Inspector Arncliffe is drunk. It seems the night action was postponed and 'e got impatient. The Inspector asks for Lady Samantha's team to take over. The inspector, 'e says, 'e knows 'e can rely on you."

Charles was outraged. "This is unbearable. You must refuse."

Samantha and Alice exchanged a look. She was excited too. "Mr. Lloyd, you have been sworn in as a special constable. You are subject to the Chief Inspector's orders."

"But -." Mr. Smith, Charles's usual number two, had been transferred back to the Earl's team. They disliked each other, but Smith was reliable. His replacement was less experienced.

"Is my coach ready?" Samantha asked.

Southwark, 8pm, 15 August

Samantha and Inspector Arncliffe walked along the north side of Stamford Street and paused to observe the 'Angel' Public House on the opposite side. The building was four storeys high, built of red brick, darkened by layers of soot. The windows were brightly lit. Samantha could hear a woman singing, interrupted by laughter. Alice, Charles and three other guards stood at Samantha's left. They had left their coach a hundred yards away. Samantha and Alice were wearing dull raincoats over their dresses to avoid attention.

Inspector Arncliffe, wearing a frock coat and silk hat, was young for his rank. "This task should be safe enough, my lady. If my boss had thought it was going to be difficult, he would have entrusted it to a more experienced man"

"Yes, I see." Samantha was grateful that he had not objected to the company of a couple of young women.

Alice bent forward, a hand on Samantha's shoulder,

222

then straightened up. "I have a message from Lord Edward's Talker. He's made his arrests at Red Lion Square. Eleven men were arrested at the Orange Tree public house. He and his team are going on to Seven Dials. The trouble there has turned to rioting. It seems Mr. Knight has been unlucky there."

Samantha wanted to know more about Archibald's bad luck at Seven Dials, but of course Edward's Talker would not know. She turned to Arncliffe. "They've already made their arrests at the Orange Tree, but we haven't started."

"My information was that they weren't due to meet here until 8pm. I wanted to be certain. Besides, the sergeant and I looked this place over this afternoon. The Angel has a back door, so I asked for extra men to cover that. Eventually, my boss gave in ..."

"Ah. I see."

"I'm sorry to keep you away from home, my lady."

She shrugged. "The trouble with polite company is that their conversation is polite and boring. Especially if you're a single lady. Being here this evening is not boring at all."

Arncliffe looked at his pocket watch. "Eight twenty-seven." He produced a whistle, murmured an apology, and blew three short blasts.

He turned to Samantha. "Now that things have begun, my main task is to keep out of the way ... Ah, here's the sergeant." Twelve uniformed constables, led by the sergeant, walked briskly along the south side of the street.

Alice opened her pocket book and fingered one of the visiting cards inside. Samantha knew that most of the cards had two or three lines of poetry written on them. "Richard. This is Alice. At Stamford Street. Action. They're going in. Now."

"Speed and surprise are vital," Arncliffe said.

The constables and the sergeant reached the front door, then rushed inside, truncheons at the ready. Samantha heard shouts of "Police! On the floor – now."

The singing stopped abruptly. Half of the constables pounded up the stairs. "I hope it doesn't collapse," Samantha said. She heard more shouting, then the tinkle of broken glass.

"That sounds like the kitchen window. I hope the men guarding the back yard are on their toes," Arncliffe said.

Silence fell. "It can still go wrong," Arncliffe said. "One of them could produce a revolver and shoot half my men. Less bloody, but more damaging for my career, would be if they all escaped out the back door."

Charles stepped forward, between Samantha and the Public House. "What worries me is the thought that one of those scoundrels could aim a shot at a constable, miss his target, and hit Lady Samantha by mistake."

Arncliffe glanced at the grimy upper windows. "Perhaps the lady should withdraw."

Samantha turned to Arncliffe. "My place is with you, Inspector. I will withdraw only if you accompany me, sir."

Arncliffe sighed. "As you wish, my lady."

"George, with me," Charles said. His colleague stepped forward, between Samantha and Alice, shielding both women from the windows.

The policemen started leading out the customers, shouting at them to stand with their hands against the wall. Any who was tardy was pushed into place. These men, Samantha hoped, were innocent bystanders.

They heard booted feet descending the stairs. The sergeant appeared in the doorway, noticed Arncliffe, and hurried across the road. "We got 'em, sir. All thirteen of 'em, sir."

The policemen led a series of bedraggled, handcuffed men out into the street.

"Any casualties, sergeant?"

"Not anything to mention, sir. And – the prisoners

'aven't got anything where it shows."

"Well done, sergeant."

Samantha turned to Alice. "Can you report that, please?"

"Of course, my lady." Alice opened her pocketbook and fingered Richard's card. "Richard. Alice. Stamford Street action accomplished. Nine arrests. No injuries." She looked up. "Any weapons found, sergeant?" she asked.

"Er- yes, miss," the sergeant stammered. "Should I have said? Five saloon pistols. Those new-fangled revolvers. We're looking for others now."

Samantha felt obliged to intervene. "Have you found any rifles, sergeant? Lord Radley was shot at with a hunting rifle a month ago."

"No, miss. Nothing like that. We'll carry on looking, of course."

Alice nodded. "Five handguns but no larger weapons found with prisoners," she murmured.

"Where's Lord Edward? How is he getting on?" Samantha asked.

Alice mumbled something, then looked up. "He went to Seven Dials to assist Mr. Knight. He's still there, and having trouble."

"Thank you, Alice," Samantha said. "What are you doing now, Inspector?"

"I'm taking these beauties to Bow Street to be charged, my lady."

"Then I would like to accompany you. I need to make my own report to Lord Radley."

Seven Dials, 9pm

Edward stood behind the line of policemen in Mercer Street. He felt that everything had gone wrong with this part of the operation. It was probably unfair to blame Archibald for the mistakes made by a police inspector - or the consequences of simple bad luck. The attempt to reach the house where the conspirators had assembled had been clumsy, and had antagonised the local populace. The residents had started throwing stones, the police had retreated and the disturbance had turned into a full-scale riot.

The inspector had wanted to call in the army. Chief Inspector Bearsbridge had asked Edward if the Guild could solve the problem discreetly.

Hotheads in the rabble were shouting insults and occasionally throwing stones. Now he had to earn the Chief Inspector's trust. The streets of Seven Dials were narrow, with high buildings on each side. Twelve police constables, standing shoulder to shoulder, were sufficient to block it. Edward judged that the mob facing them was inspired by a desire for mayhem, not hatred.

"Let's begin, then," he said. The magicians standing behind the constables threw a series of thunder-flashes – intense light, intense noise, but no heat – that forced most of the mob to recoil.

Edward suspected that the police sergeant at his side was a Methodist. Magic did not form part of his world-view, so he tried to ignore it. "We can cope well enough without you gentlemen, sir." He continued in an undertone, "We don't need your grenades or guns ... It's all fakery, isn't it?"

Edward chose to ignore him, but Mr. Smith was outraged for his sake. "Show some respect for the Earl."

Edward was angry for a different reason. "Of course we don't use grenades, sergeant. I don't want blood on the streets – do you? Most of these men regard a riot as an entertainment. If we frighten them enough, they'll piss themselves and go home. Then we can arrest the leaders."

Most of the rioters fled to the end of the street, but half a dozen stalwarts stood their ground. Setting the ringleader's jacket on fire, with the added illusion of bright flames, forced his colleagues to step back. Two Peelers armed with truncheons rushed forward to arrest the ringleader. Edward had ensured that the sergeant had a bucket of water ready.

The Peelers forced their way up the street to the crossroads. Edward left a contingent of Peelers to hold the other streets and turned right. Before they had advanced twenty yards, gunshots from a window on the right side of the street forced them to stop. At the sound of gunshots, the rioters scattered in panic. One problem solved, Edward thought. The Peelers were forced to take cover in doorways. The dwellings on each side of the road were narrow, one room wide and four high.

Edward realised that this was a stand-off. It could develop into a siege and last a week. He turned to his Talker, James. "Mr. Knight's Talker is still with Bearsbridge, isn't he? Tell him we've got the leaders cornered. We're going to need reinforcements. Bearsbridge may want to take over." The police had no strategy for this. He remembered that Bearsbridge trusted him to clear up the mess that Archibald had created.

Edward turned to make sure that his own men had taken cover.

James started swearing. "My lord, Archibald - Mr. Knight - told the Duke's Talker that the leaders had been trapped. So the Duke's asking whether we want his help." Edward and the sergeant exchanged a look.

"Not the redcoats," the sergeant said.

Edward nodded. "I agree. James, tell the Duke he can't do anything in the dark. Tell him we'll try to solve this ourselves. If we haven't cleared it up by dawn ..." He knew that Bearsbridge trusted him to clear up the mess without calling in the army.

The sergeant's eyes were wide in panic. "We've gotta do something, my lord, sir. Before the Duke - not in Lunnun. "I was at Waterloo, you know. Drummer boy. My first battle — and my last. I don't want that here. Not the Duke. Tell the inspector. Bearsbridge."

"Very well, sergeant. They've only got handguns. Not very accurate," Edward said. He turned to the sergeant. "I want a couple of volunteers, sergeant. Daredevils."

"That would be Brown, sir. They call 'im the Bruiser. And, mebbe, Llewellyn." He called two men forward.

Edward called his guards. "Give me covering fire. Follow me as soon as I reach the doorway." He turned to his volunteers. "Right, follow me. Keep close."

At his word, a magician set off a thunder-flash outside the upper storey window. Edward knew that if he ran he would probably trip; if he sidled along the wall he would take too long. So he created a shield and walked down the right side of the street. He kept close to the wall, his shield up. Any gunman leaning out of the window could have spotted him, but none did.

Most of the Peelers did not believe in magic. They regarded his self-confidence as aristocratic arrogance. Fortunately, Llewellyn trusted him just enough to follow him and Brown followed his companion.

The gunmen took a couple of shots at the policemen further down the road until another thunder-flash encouraged them to stay out of sight. Edward reached the doorway of their house, which gave him a bit of cover.

He sensed that the door was fastened with bolts as well as locks, so he could not use magic to unfasten the lock. He would have to abandon subtlety

"Avert your eyes, you two." Brown did so, expecting a

228

flare, but Llewellyn watched in fascination as Edward blew the door off its hinges. He pushed and the door toppled inwards. He could see stairs to the left and a doorway to the right. The two Peelers followed him in. "Clear those rooms."

They rushed forward, shouting "Everyone! On the floor ..."

Llewellyn came back out. "The room's empty, sir. This is sinister. These tenements are usually packed, ten mattresses to a room."

"This is their arsenal, like," Brown said. "Weapons store. Saloon pistols."

"You're probably right," Edward said.

A man came hurrying down the stairs. He was carrying a handgun so Edward felt no reluctance in using magic to knock him off his feet. The gunman slid to the bottom of the stairs, groaning. Brown jumped forward. He slapped his handcuffs on the prone man. "You're nicked."

Edward saw another man at the top of the stairs. The man had a gun so Edward, acting on general principles, knocked him down too.

He heard more shooting upstairs and then three more magicians joined him. They were all from his personal team. Smith, the plebeian boy, was in the lead. "We're unharmed, sir."

"Good." Edward wanted to take the stairs himself but he had taken too many risks already. He turned to Smith. "You. Form a shield, take the stairs. I know it's difficult, but you're the best we've got." He turned to the next man. "You, follow him. Knock down anyone who tries to stop you. Llewellyn, take third place and arrest that fellow at the top of the stairs."

Smith nodded and pounded up the stairs. He began shouting, in the best police manner. "Everyone - on the floor -." Then, in an entirely different tone, "This floor's clear, my lord."

The sergeant and a squad of Peelers arrived at the front door. "The inspector didn't want you doing all the work yourself, sir."

"Glad to see you." Edward turned to his other two guards. "Go up the stairs, go past Smith, find out if the next floor is empty too." He turned to the sergeant. "Can you ..."

The sergeant nodded. He called off six names and the men hurried up the stairs.

They heard the sound of glass being smashed. The sergeant hissed. "They're trying to escape. Upper storey window. They'll break their necks."

"Don't count on it, sergeant. Take some men, check out the back yard."

"Yessir."

Before they could say anything, he heard Smith shouting down. "My lord! They say they want to surrender!"

"Stay where you are, Mr. Smith. Don't take their word for it." Negotiating would minimise the bloodshed. He had no authority to negotiate. But he would have to do it anyway.

Duchess of Kent tavern, 9.30pm

The tavern, named after the Queen's mother, was a grand institution on Charring Cross Road, its brick façade decorated with horizontal strips of white stone. Its interior boasted etched glass windows and a mosaic floor. This evening it had the air of a command post or field hospital.

Samantha jumped down from the cab and explained her business to the sergeant at the door. He nodded. "Guild business? The Earl isn't here, miss, but the Chief Inspector's upstairs."

"Thank you." Inside, she noticed an array of mirrors with etched decoration, marble columns, and varnished wooden wine racks. All of the seats were occupied. Exhausted constables slouched against the wall or sat on the mosaic floor. One of the rooms had been taken over as a dressing station.

Upstairs she found more mirrors and, above them, a ceramic frieze with gilt overlay. The seats were leather. She met Chief Inspector Bearsbridge and Archibald Knight. A sergeant was making a report to Bearsbridge.

A sketch-map of the district had been put up on an easel. Bearsbridge was marking the map as the sergeant talked.

Mr. Knight was relaxed, in a tweed jacket, but his Talker and Bearsbridge were still wearing their coats. Bearsbridge smiled. "Good evening, my lady. A pleasure to see you again. The rioters have been broken. When they saw that their leaders had abandoned them, they gave up and dispersed." He glanced at Alice. "Would you and your companion like a drink? A glass of wine?"

Samantha ignored this. "But where's Edward – the Earl?"

Mr. Knight's Talker looked pained. "Lord Edward and his Talker are on their way back here, my lady. He said he wanted to search the place for rifles. He won't be long."

"In that case, thank you, a glass of wine, Inspector." But if Edward was on his way back, where was he now?

*

The rioters were dispersing at last. The gunmen had been arrested and the police were advancing eastward, clearing the streets. Edward felt that his job was done. The police could complete their search of the building without his help. He and his team headed back to the command post.

"It's lucky that the rioters were abandoned by their

231

leaders, sir," Mr. Smith said. The boy had not lost his East End accent, despite four years at the College.

"Yes ... But we're going the wrong way. This is taking us north-west." Edward turned left, down a narrow alleyway, that took him towards Charing Cross Road. Smith stepped back, taking his place as rear-guard. These buildings were warehouses and tenements, with high brick walls and high, narrow windows. This place was a warren.

"The leaders knew they would be arrested if they stood their ground. But where did those runaways go?" His destination was just round the corner. He was safe. He could relax.

He heard footsteps behind him, but ignored them. His team had no need to fear individuals. Then he felt a 'compulsion' teasing at his mind. "Kill them all. You hate them. Kill them now". The command was a weak effort and he brushed it off.

He turned to check his companions. His junior guard, Smith, used his magic to strike down his companion, Roger. The boy turned to the next guard, Richard, and crushed him too. The last remaining guard merely gaped at him.

Edward finally woke to the danger and summoned his own magic. 'Strike!' Smith fell, his ribs crushed. Only Edward, the last guard and his Talker were left standing.

Edward turned to his Talker. "Go get help, James. Don't waste time making contact! Run and get help."

A man walked along the alleyway towards them. He was wearing a long shabby raincoat, left unbuttoned to show the fine suit beneath. Edward was shocked to recognise his cousin, the hon. Randolph Radley.

"So you're a magic user. You have been all along."

Randolph ignored this. "Got you at last. I'm the rightful earl. Culham is mine, you know. It's always been mine."

"Yes," Edward said. He wanted Randolph to get closer.

"The aristocracy in this country is a farce. Cuckolds deceived by drabs. Your guild is a farce." He turned to the last guard. "Your master does not need your help any more. He trusts me. Go home, Run."

Edward shrugged off the compulsion, but his guard turned and walked away.

Edward was horrified. "Stop, stop!" But the guard, mesmerised by the compulsion, ignored him. Edward turned back to Randolph. "You may become an earl, but you'll never have a place in the Guild. Your powers are puny."

Randolph laughed. "I don't want a place in your bourgeois guild. I don't need any powers." He reached inside his coat and produced a revolver. Before Edward could put his guard up, Randolph fired two shots. The first one hit; the revolver recoiled and the second went wide; but the pain was all-consuming and Edward fell.

*

Samantha, chatting to Chief Inspector Bearsbridge, sensed something was wrong. "I felt a compulsion. Charles, come on. Follow me." She ran down the stairs and out into the street. She knew that if she tried to run any faster she would trip on the hem of her skirts. In this backstreet there was no street lighting. She created a ball of light and sent it skimming up the lane in front of her.

Charles overtook her. Up ahead, someone was shouting. But, just before Charles reached the corner, he ran into Edward's Talker coming the other way. Both men fell.

"Idiots!" Samantha ran past Charles and round the corner. She sensed that Edward was still alive. She saw a man in a long coat, kicking something on the ground.

He was shouting. "I'm the Earl now. Do you hear me?"

She recognised Randolph Radley and realised that the bundle on the ground must be Edward. Anger pulsed through her. She knew she had to distract Radley. "Stop, stop!"

Radley took a step back and turned to face her. At least she had forced him to stop kicking Edward. She concentrated. "Scutum meum partum." She got her shield up.

He did not attempt to use magic. Instead held up a revolver and fired. The force behind the blow rocked her on her feet but she managed to deflect the shot. She could hear her friends approaching. She needed more time. She stepped closer, so her shield could cover Edward, and sneered at Radley. "Go on, try it."

"Bitch. I should have done this, six months ago." He suppressed his anger and took careful aim at her sternum.

Her action suddenly seemed less clever. "Scutum meum partum." She re-established her shield and prayed.

He fired and hit her dead centre. Her shield absorbed the blow. She was unharmed but the force of the blow caught her off balance. She stepped back, tripped, and fell over. The cobblestones were hard.

She realised that Radley still had his revolver. She sat up and tried to maintain her shield. "Scutum meum partum."

Alice ran up. She halted, panting for breath.

Radley turned to face her. He lifted the revolver. Alice gestured and sent a fireball at Radley, hitting him squarely. It was weak, doing nothing more than singe his jacket.

He screamed, dropped the revolver, and beat at the smouldering garment with his hands. He screamed again at the pain in his hands.

Samantha could hear others running up. Radley turned and ran up the dark alley, back towards Seven Dials.

Charles was the first to arrive. He turned towards the alley.

"No," Samantha called. "Make a light first. Or you'll fall

over again." They heard Radley's footsteps slow down and then speed up again as he turned a corner.

"Too late. Seven Dials. Six possible paths." Charles turned towards her. "Are you all right? My lady?"

"Yes. The worst injury is to my pride. Help me up. But how's Edward?"

Charles lent a hand and she struggled to her feet. She turned to look at Edward.

Bearsbridge pushed past Charles and knelt at Edward's side. He pulled a huge handkerchief out of his pocket and used it to staunch the wound. "I think he's still got the bullet in him. Lost a lot of blood. He'll need a surgeon."

She sighed. "The healers are going to hate him. They've plugged him up once already."

*

The 'Duchess of Kent' tavern was less cheerful now. Most of the policemen had been sent home. Most of the oil lamps had been put out. Bearsbridge slouched in a leather armchair in the corner. Edward had been laid out on a table, face up. Doctor Jones checked his bandages one more time. One of the Healers and the Lascar peered over his shoulder.

"He's lost a lot of blood. His heart has to beat twice as fast to keep up. And if I operate, he'll lose more."

Samantha was shocked. Edward was slowly bleeding to death.

"So he needs more blood. Is transfusion an option?" Bearsbridge asked.

Jones sighed. "We've been over this before. Transfusion is a risky process. I believe that blood comes in different types. Giving someone the wrong type is as bad as poisoning him."

"And there's no way of telling them apart?" Samantha was morbidly curious.

"None."

"But he's dying, doctor! We have nothing to lose by trying."

A cab drove up. Jones straightened up at the sound. A constable escorted the passenger into the saloon bar. "Doctor Ringer, sir."

"Good evening, Doctor." Jones said. "This is my patient. The Earl has a bullet in him. I need to get it out. But he's already lost a lot of blood."

Ringer was wearing an elegant frock coat. He stared down at Edward. "Is he really a peer of the realm?"

Bearsbridge was annoyed. "Certainly, sir. He has been assisting the police in maintaining order. He was shot by an agitator."

"Good lord. I had assumed an unsavoury brawl. Some sort of scandal."

Jones ignored this. "If I operate, he'll lose more blood. That loss could tip him over the edge. I was hoping that you could give him a saline solution. That would give him enough fluid in his veins to make an operation viable."

Ringer was unhappy. "I've used a saline drip on cholera victims. I have achieved some success. But it's never been attempted during a surgical operation."

"Why not?" Bearsbridge said.

Ringer shrugged. "This situation is very rare. If he had lost any more blood he would be beyond help; if he had loss less, he would not need my help."

"We have nothing to lose." Jones echoed Samantha.

"You say the man's a peer of the realm. Are you mad? I refuse to take part without the permission of his next of kin."

Samantha took Edward's hand. "Edward's next of kin is his mother. But she lives just outside Oxford. She couldn't reply until the morning. There's me. I'm his cousin."

236

Ringer was not impressed. "I would prefer the permission of the Earl's male next of kin."

"His cousin was the man who shot him." Samantha spoke more sharply than she intended.

"Don't be absurd, woman."

Bearsbridge spoke from his armchair. "I have arranged a warrant for Mr. Radley's arrest. We have reason to believe that he is responsible for several deaths, besides the attack on Lord Edward."

"And what might your name be, sir?" Ringer asked.

Bearsbridge was annoyed. "Chief Inspector Bearsbridge, sir. At your service."

"Oh." Doctor Ringer went silent. Samantha assumed he was taken aback by Bearsbridge's statement.

Jones stared at Ringer, angry at his excessive caution. But there was nothing he could do.

"Does Doctor Ringer need the permission of the next of kin, if you carry out the operation, Doctor Jones?" Samantha asked.

"Good point," Jones said. "You can give him the saline solution now, Doctor Ringer. It is non-intrusive. At worst, it will be a waste of our time. Then I can operate to remove the bullet. We could ask the Earl's mother to give her permission, but I don't want to wait. We can keep the Earl alive that long, but I think he would be too weak to survive an operation."

Ringer considered this. He checked Edward's pulse. "Fast, but strong ... Very well, Doctor Jones. I shall prepare my equipment. The patient must be kept still. In fact, it might be best if he did not recover consciousness."

Samantha observed the administration of the saline drip with fascination. Ringer checked Edward's pulse again, nodded in satisfaction, and said he would be back in the morning. That quiet nod reassured Samantha more than any speech could have done.

Jones pulled on a white paper apron. He smiled at Samantha. "Do you want to hold his hand or something? He might wake up when I'm half way through. I want you on hand if he does."

"Very well, Doctor."

Samantha took Edward's hand. "Everything's going to be all right." She was disconcerted when Edward's grip tightened.

Ready?" Jones asked. The Lascar, Salman, held Edward down. Jones cut, probed, cut again, and withdrew the bullet. "Got it. Is the wound clean?" he asked. He looked up at Samantha. "Sometimes, the bullet carries a bit of cloth into the wound with it. Then it begins to fester. Somehow, your girls can tell."

"No, it's clean, Doctor," the Healer said. She pushed the musculature together and Jones applied a few stitches. The Healer stepped forward and began the healing process. After a couple of minutes, she turned away and washed her hands.

Doctor Jones applied a fresh bandage. "After your girl has got her strength back, she can give another boost to the healing process."

"I see," Samantha said.

"You might as well go home now. There's nothing more you can do. You won't do any good here."

"Yes. Alice's mother would kill me if I let her spend the night here."

Alice smiled. "For once, I'm going to play the lady of leisure and stay in bed until noon."

Jones checked Edward's bandage. "I assume you'll write to Lord Edward's mother in the morning?"

Samantha glanced at Alice. "She already knows. She'll send a courier on the first train in the morning."

Jones looked startled. "Did you send a message? As

easy as that?"

Samantha shook her head. "It isn't easy at all. Alice here sent a message to someone at the College, who sent another message to someone in the Countess's household. I haven't Talked to anyone today. Except -."

Realisation dawned. She had spoken to Edward, without any preparation.

Epilogue

Osborne House

Samantha and Alice had brought their overnight bags, a change of day wear, and their evening dresses. Their dirigible had reached the Isle of Wight just after noon. Samantha and Alice had been escorted to the 'household wing', where the staff asked them to share a room. Samantha was annoyed. The room was a bit small for two girls to change into court dresses.

Samantha made the final adjustments to Alice's dress. "There's no need to be frightened."

Alice tried to smile. "You're frightened too."

"You stood up to a murderer. Chased him away."

"This is different."

"Yes." Samantha stepped back and checked her friend's appearance. "You'll do. Come on."

One of the Queen's ladies-in-waiting was standing in the corridor outside. She gave both girls an appraising look. Apparently she was satisfied by what she saw. "If you will come this way, please ..."

She led the way downstairs and along the grand corridor. At the end she turned right into a windowless corridor.

"We're going to the formal receiving room?" Samantha asked faintly.

The lady in waiting smiled at her. "Yes. Come on." She pushed open the door.

Samantha's first impression was of extravagant decoration. The huge mirror over the fireplace, the paintings,

240

the embroidered carpet, the maroon curtains. And, of course, the windows were open. Only then did she take in the two people, her Majesty and Prince Albert, sitting in their elaborate chairs. Several ladies-in-waiting and queries stood in a semicircle behind them.

"You look well, Lady Samantha," the Queen said in her light voice. "We trust that Lord Edward is in good health."

Samantha stepped forward and bobbed a curtsey. "Lord Edward is convalescing, your Majesty. He is healthy enough to return to his duties."

"You must ensure that he does not exert himself," the Queen said.

"Yes, madam, I shall try." She swallowed. "May I present to you Miss Alice Toledano. I commend her to you for her bravery. She saved my life."

Alice, prompted, sank into a deep curtsey. After a moment, the queen held out her hand. "You may rise, my dear. We are delighted to meet you at last."

"Thank you, your Majesty."

The Queen smiled: "I do not approve of young girls staying unwed. You're old enough to be married. Is there anyone?"

Alice blushed but said nothing. Samantha thought of Charles. "Yes, I think so, madam. The thing about the college is all those young men, recently qualified, earning a salary for the first time."

The Queen smiled at Alice. "Now, my dear, tell me the true story about Bethnal Fields."

About the author

He studied the history of science at Britain's Open University, which was one of the pioneers of distance learning. He lives an hour's travel from London.

For his employer, he writes technical guidance and publicity material, published on the internet, but most readers will not be interested in those.

He uses research for these novels as an excuse to make regular visits to the City of London.

His hobbies have included sailing yachts and flying sailplanes. Writing is his oldest hobby. He is a member of the British Science Fiction Association.

E-mail address:
sailknot2001-2@yahoo.co.uk

Facebook address: james.odell.9022662@facebook.com

Lightning Source UK Ltd.
Milton Keynes UK
UKOW04f1357270616

277170UK00010B/259/P